"'Arry?" said somebody the hill.

Arry flinched. Someone was badly hurt; somebody sounded as if he had fallen out of the tree and broken his back. She began to skid down the hill, calling, "Who is it?"

"It's Oonan," said the voice, rather indignantly. How could anybody in that much pain be indignant?

"What did you do to yourself?" she said, arriving at the bottom of the hill.

"Nothing." His voice had pain in it and did not have pain in it. He was in her province but not in it.

"I'm not hurt, Arry; I lost two sheep," said Oonan. "Wolves is what it looked like."

"Con can do a spell for—"

"But it wasn't wolves. I found wolves' prints. And they killed like wolves; but they didn't eat. Wolves don't do that."

## Other Books by Pamela Dean

The Secret Country
The Hidden Land
The Whim of the Dragon
Tam Lin

# Pamela Dean,
## P.J.F.

# The
# Dubious
# Hills

A TOM DOHERTY ASSOCIATES BOOK
NEW YORK

This is a work of fiction. All the characters and events portrayed in this book are fictitious, and any resemblance to real people or events is purely coincidental.

THE DUBIOUS HILLS

Grateful acknowledgement is made for permission to quote the following:

An excerpt from *Possession: A Romance* by A.S. Byatt is reprinted by permission of Random House, Inc. Copyright © 1990 by A.S. Byatt.

Lines from "The Alchemist in the City" and "The Habit of Perfection" by Gerard Manley Hopkins, from *The Poems of Gerard Manley Hopkins*, edited by W.H. Gardner and N.H. MacKenzie (4th edition, 1967), reprinted by permission of The Oxford University Press.

Lines from "Shared World" by John M. Ford, from *Timesteps* (Rune Press, 1993), reprinted by permission of the author. Copyright © 1993 by John M. Ford.

Lines from "Procession Day/Remembrance Night: Processional/Recessional" by John M. Ford, from *Liavek: Festival Week*, edited by Will Shetterly and Emma Bull (Ace, 1990), reprinted by permission of the author. Copyright © 1990 by John M. Ford.

Edited by Terri Windling
Cover art by Dave Henderson

A Tor Book
Published by Tom Doherty Associates, Inc.
175 Fifth Avenue
New York, NY 10010

Tor® is a registered trademark of Tom Doherty Associates, Inc.

ISBN: 0-812-52362-8

First edition: April 1994
First mass market edition: March 1995

Printed in the United States of America

0  9  8  7  6  5  4  3  2  1

# THE
# DUBIOUS
# HILLS

ARRY OPENED THE door to call the cats. It was a cold night, but with a green spring cold, not the dry baked cold of autumn or the damp and penetrating cold of winter. The moon was full; it crowded out the stars in its half of the sky and put a thin blue skim-milk light over the mud of the yard, the slate stepping stones, the cover of the well, the lilac bushes with their new leaves—and there was the white cat crouched under the pine tree, from which during the day the squirrels teased her.

Arry stepped outside, leaving the door open. The black cat shot around the corner of the house and through the doorway. The white cat yawned.

"Come in, Woollycat, you doubtful beast," said Arry.

Woollycat got up and walked around to the other side of the tree. Arry's mother had always said Arry was too tender of those cats, which were supposed to spend their nights outside working, catching rats and mice and the little sleek voles that ate the tender shoots of the new oats. Arry preferred to have the cats sleep on her feet, and she knew that cats loved to be warm. She stepped into the mud and squelched her way over to the tree.

"Arry?" said somebody out of the dark at the bottom of the hill.

Arry flinched. Somebody was badly hurt; somebody sounded as if he had fallen out of the tree and broken his back. She began to skid down the hill, calling, "Who is it?"

"It's Oonan," said the voice, rather indignantly. How could anybody in that much pain be indignant? And oh, wonderful, it would be Oonan. Oonan was their Akoumi, the one whose province was broken things, and the fixing thereof; you could hardly expect him to repair himself—could you?

"What did you do to yourself?" she said, arriving at the bottom of the hill.

"Nothing." His voice had pain in it and did not have pain in it. He was in her province but not in it. Arry was silent, and Oonan added, "I didn't think you'd still be awake."

"I was cutting Con's hair. Can you walk up the hill, or should I get a light?"

"I'm not hurt, Arry; I just needed to clear my head, and I knew I'd have to come by in the morning, so my feet led me here."

"Come and have some tea, then." Arry began slogging back up the hill, trying a little harder this time to keep to the stepping stones. Oonan came behind her.

"Why would you have to come by in the morning?"

"Why did you cut your sister's hair?"

"If Con were a sheep," said Arry, "she would sleep in a gorse bush. It was dreadful."

"It was pretty. It reminded me of your mother's."

"Mother combed hers."

"Con's looked smooth enough to me."

"She'd comb it on top and let it go all to knots underneath. She said she was counting them. She said she was having a race with Zia."

"So Zia's won?"

"Zia always wins," said Arry, a little grimly.

"Who says so?"

"Zia," admitted Arry, and they both laughed. Oonan's laugh showed that his throat and ribs were right. His step showed his legs and feet were right. Arry wondered if he had been hit in the head.

As they went through the door into the house, the white cat whipped between their feet, thudded across the wooden floor, and scrambled up the ladder into the attic. At least, thought Arry, she wouldn't have to go out again looking for her later. She shut the door, and in the light of the lamps she had lit to cut Con's hair she looked at Oonan.

He was tall and thin, twenty years old last month, with a long nose and hair the color of maple leaves in the fall but the texture of a bird's nest. He had not hurt his head. He was not in ordinary pain at all; but then why did he feel like that?

"I lost two sheep," said Oonan to the ceiling.

He looked at Arry. He had such large eyes that he always looked surprised, but they were almost without color. "Wolves is what it looked like."

"Con can do a spell for—"

"But it wasn't wolves. I found wolves' prints; Derry

came up with me and said so. And they killed like wolves; but they didn't eat. Wolves don't do that, Derry said. Derry didn't know what to think.''

"Do you want me to come and look at them?" Arry asked hesitantly. Pain was her province; Death might come out of it, but she did not know Death.

He tilted his head at her and let his breath out. "No," he said. "If it happens again, perhaps."

Arry held her hand against the side of the teapot; she decided lukewarm tea was good enough, and poured him a bowl.

"Sit down by the fire," she said. "You're cold. Where's your jacket?"

Oonan sat, and took the bowl from her. "I don't remember," he said; he sounded surprised. "Wait—I took it off, when I got up there. I'd been running, and then there was the blood."

He took a swallow of tea.

"Why were you running? Did you hear the wolves howling?"

"No, they were entirely silent. To my ears, anyway. I had a dream that woke me up."

He drank more tea and settled back in the chair Arry's mother had made, just before she went looking for Arry's father. It was a good chair of its sort, but it creaked.

"What sort of dream?" said Arry.

"The sort that wakes you."

Don't let me help, then, thought Arry, irately; then she remembered that he was not Con, not a child: he knew what he knew, and perhaps talking about his nightmares would not help him in the least.

"At the end of the dream, all the sheep had gone,"

said Oonan. "So I thought, what harm would it do to go and look at them? Do you understand about those times when you can't be certain you banked the fire, and even though you think you did, you must go and look? I felt like that. So I went up to the meadow."

"Were they gone?"

"No, they were all there. I counted them. But they were uneasy."

"Because you'd sneaked up on them in the night?"

"No. They recognize me. It was cold, I thought it might be that; but they didn't act cold. The meadow felt as if it were at the bottom of a well, and the moonlight was worse than darkness."

He shivered; but he was not cold. The fire was flushing all one side of his body. He shivered again. Arry got up and put on her jacket, and gave Oonan a blanket. He wrapped it around his legs without saying anything.

Arry hugged herself under the red wool jacket and stared at him. He was whole and sound, yet in considerable pain. If he was afraid, it did not feel like fear—and anyway, Oonan wasn't afraid of anything. He was the one who helped people have their babies, even though having a baby was a thing that hurt, and therefore was Arry's province. Having a baby was rarely Oonan's province, because it was rarely a thing that need fixing. But it frightened her, and it did not frighten him.

What had happened up there in the meadow? The meadow was only a triangular flat space where the mountain, in a fit of absentmindedness, went out for a bit instead of down. On one side of it the rest of the mountain stood up like the tallest wall in the world; on all the others was the blue air, with the round hills everybody toiled up and down all day as small as stream pebbles at the bottom. Arry's mother had liked it: she said it was the only place in three days' walk where you could see what might be sneaking up on you.

It was an alarming place in the dark—only it would not have been dark when Oonan went up there, but full of blue moonlight and strange shadows. More alarming, according to what he said. Rocks that looked like sheep, sheep that looked like bushes, and then moved; the few small trees like hands, flexing their fingers in the spring wind. Moonlight and shadow on the grass like a net to catch your feet; smooth ground roughened by shadows, rough ground made smooth by light.

"Which way did the wolves come from?" she asked him.

"The prints showed they came down off the mountain and went on down along the river. I didn't hear them at all. The sheep and I were there, and then the wolves—if they were wolves—were there. They didn't make a sound. I smelled the blood before I heard a thing, and then what I heard was the sheep, crying." He put his bowl down on the flagged floor with a rattle. "They didn't take any lambs," he said.

"Oonan, are you sure they didn't get you too?"

"Can't you tell?"

"You sound different than you feel."

"Grownups do that."

Arry did not say another word while Oonan finished his tea, folded the blanket and gave it back to her, thanked her and told her good night, and went away down the hill.

ARRY HAD BEEN dreaming about her mother, and when the sparrows squabbling in the eaves woke her, she thought for a moment that she was still nine and all was right with the world. But then she saw that her pillow was blue, not green as it had been then; and she remembered.

According to Halver, today was the first day of May in the four-hundredth year since doubt descended. According to Wim, it was the second hour after dawn. But since dawn in its wandering way moved about, back and forth over the same small span of hours like a child looking for a dropped button, some of the leisured scholars at Heathwill Library (according to Mally they were leisured, according to Halver they were scholars, according to Sune there was indeed a structure called Heathwill Library) had named all the hours of the day from their own heads without regard to the shifting of the sun. By that naming, it was eight of the sand (according to Wim), sand being the way (said Sune) that the scholars (who were scholars, said Halver), numbered out the hours—

"Oh," groaned Arry into her pillow, "I say, I do hate mornings. They make my head hurt." She sat up, disentangling herself from her long (Wim), black (Wim), all-too (Arry) curly (Wim, who should not—said Mally— have known it) hair (Halver).

"Shut up," said Arry, panting slightly. "Just shut up. I wish I were nine again. I wish I were five. I am certain of nothing save the holiness of the heart's affections and the truth of imagination. Bah!"

She got out of bed, and by performing her morning routine without thinking about it, managed to get herself washed, combed, dressed, and into the main room of the house. Her sister (said Halver), named Con (said Frances, their mother), who was five (Wim), knelt mumbling on the hearth. "I'm forgetting," she said, without turning, when Arry came in.

"You'll remember again later," said Arry, invoking their teacher Halver and her own experience. "Try once more. Or we'll have to get Niss in here to start the fire, and she'll laugh at you."

"Oh," said Con, scowling ferociously all over her round face, "for a Muse of fire, that would ascend the brightest heaven of invention."

The neat structure of wood that Arry had built the night before took on flame like a garment.

"There, you see," said Arry. She looked at Con's cropped head, and she remembered the other thing she must have in her mind today. Oonan had come and told her he had lost two sheep to the wolves—or rather, to things that left wolf-prints but did not act like wolves.

Their brother Beldi, who was nine, came in from the kitchen, staggering a little with his full bucket of water. He filled the iron kettle with half the water, hung that over the fire, and put the bucket in its corner, where Con, after three false tries and a flood of tearful proclamation that she would never grow up if this was what it felt like, made the spell over the water that would keep dust and flatness and the invisible growers out of it.

When the water was hot Arry made them oatmeal, with milk from Niss's cow and honey from Vand's hives. She felt a little odd about the honey; it was a gift, not an exchange. She had told Niss several times when the cow was hurt, so Oonan could fix it; but the pains of bees, if any, were beyond her; and the sting of the bees no longer hurt Vand in the least. Maybe Con or Beldi would know something that could help Vand, when they were older.

After they had eaten she set the younger ones to washing the dishes, and went back to her own room to read over once more what their teacher, Gnosi Halver, had said yesterday. She was not very far into it when Con came shrieking through the door, dragging a huge-eyed Beldi with her. His chin was covered with blood.

"Does that hurt him?" wailed Con.

"What did you do?"

"I hit him."

"I've told you and told you not to hit." Arry crouched down to Beldi's level and looked at his mouth. His lip was well and truly split. His round brown eyes blinked at her; but unlike most children who thought they might be hurt, he was quiet. Probably he thought Con was making enough noise for both of them. Arry put a firm hand on Con's shorn dark head and shook it a little. Con stopped yelling but looked ready to begin again. "Why did you hit him?" said Arry.

"I wanted to see what happened."

"I've told you and told you what happens."

"I forgot."

"That's not the sort of thing you forget."

Con stared at her.

"Mally says," said Arry. "Now show me the hand you did it with."

Con proffered it, still gulping. She had split the skin over two knuckles.

"It did hurt," said Arry. "It hurt so much it hurt you too. Now you both must go to Oonan and we'll all be late for school."

"What do you want Oonan for?" said Con, looking with fascination at Beldi. "It's not dripping much."

"I want Oonan because it needs must be sewn up like the burst elbow of a shirt," said Arry, in their mother's accents. "Now put your hurt fingers in your mouth, thus, and come with me."

"Gnosi says it's dirty to put your fingers in your mouth."

"That depends on where they've been," said Arry, hauling the heavy door of the house shut and shaking her head at the two cats who arrived, just too late.

"Beldi's mouth," said Con.

"Well, you think it over. Let's go."

They went, followed by two hopeful cats, down the hill their house sat on, and along a rocky, muddy path, much rutted with spring rains, between their hill and Niss's; and then around the side of Niss's hill and up and down and up and down again and up once more to Oonan's door.

The door was open. The cats bounded through it, making enthusiastic noises. Arry followed with her brother and sister and found Oonan sitting on a pile of cushions staring at his fire. There was a cup of milk on the brick floor beside him. Both cats made for it, and bumped heads. Oonan tipped the milk onto the floor, and they began lapping busily. Oonan looked up. His face was sadder than usual; maybe he wasn't really awake yet. He liked to stay up half the night, but most people who hurt themselves, he said, did it in the morning. Arry disbelieved him, but there was no use, said Mally, in telling him so.

"Good," Oonan said, when he caught sight of Beldi. "Something I can fix." Arry remembered his lost sheep. Of course he looked sad. It was she who wasn't awake yet; and no wonder, after wrestling with Con's hair for half the night and listening to Oonan sound hurt when he wasn't for the other half.

Oonan got up and took the wooden box that held his tools from its corner. Then he sat Beldi down on the floor in the light from the southern window. "What happened?"

"I hit him," said Con.

"Did you? Well, you'd better keep him happy while I sew this up, then. If he gets bored and fidgets at the wrong moment, it won't be fixed as well as it should be."

Con looked helplessly at Arry, who was stricken with inspiration. "You may sing to him," she said. "You may sing 'I Had a Dove.' "

"I hate it!"

"So does Beldi's lip hate being split like a ripe plum.

You sing. And next time you think about how you hated it, before you hit somebody.''

Con, glowering, flung herself on her stomach on the floor between Beldi and Oonan and began bellowing into her brother's face. "I had a dove and the sweet dove died.'' Beldi beamed at her, as well as he could with his bleeding lip.

Oonan got up stiffly, moved around Con, sat down on Beldi's other side, and resumed getting his tools out of the box. The needle looked big enough to sew shoes with. The thread was as black as a sheep's nose. He wiped them both with the potato liquor Jony made, out of the green glass bottle that came from Wormsreign. He threaded the needle, knotted the thread, and took Beldi's chin in his hand. Con sang even louder, whether through duty or perversity Arry would not have wanted to say.

She put her hands behind her back, squeezed them tight together, and watched the needle punch its first slippery red hole. The black thread followed it like a poisonous worm. Arry tucked her own lower lip under the upper one. This was not a situation in which informing the patient he was hurt would be useful. She just had to bear it. Beldi was perfectly happy. Con was well into the song's second verse. She had better have the wit to start over again if she had to. Two stitches, three, four. Oonan made another knot and nipped off the thread.

Beldi looked up at Arry and burst out laughing. "You look just like a rabbit!" he said. Con abandoned the tira-liras with which she had been filling out the end of the song, and laughed too. Arry untucked her lip.

"Don't go laughing like that all day, or you'll undo all my good work," said Oonan. He got up, still stiffly.

His muscles hurt him; he must have been climbing too many hills.

"What about Con's fingers?" said Arry.

Oonan walked over to Con and squinted at her hand. "Wash it," he said. "And don't go making mud pies until all this red—see, here—is hard and dark. Halver says that's called a scab. It sits on top of the hurt tissue and keeps it safe until it's healed."

Con went into Oonan's kitchen to wash her fingers. Arry poured the rest of Oonan's milk on the floor for the cats. Beldi said, "Was there a thing earlier that you couldn't fix?"

Oonan nodded, standing before his cold fireplace like an untidy tree. "I lost two sheep," he said.

"Maybe they'll come home again," said Beldi. "Gnosi says—"

"No, not lost that way. They're dead."

"What do sheep look like when they're dead?" said Beldi.

"Broken," said Oonan.

"Like my wagon?" said Con, returning. She shook water from her hands onto the cats, who leapt indignantly away and then circled, waiting to get back to the milk.

"No," said Oonan, thinking about it. "More like the tree the lightning struck last fall—remember?"

"I can't remember anything," said Con, gloomily.

"I can," said Beldi, unwisely.

Arry wondered if such a discussion was the reason Con had hit him in the first place. There might be no pain in the Dubious Hills, except in her, the Physici, but certain instincts to hurt remained. The History of Doubt denied this, but the History of Doubt was wrong.

Arry knew this, though she would much rather not have. She knew that Oonan, too, often wished that he did not know what he knew. Pain and Death were among the things the Shapers had wanted to do away with. They had managed to preserve pleasure, but they had not managed immortality: they had created only ignorance of death, except in the Akoumi; and in a kind of slant-wise fashion they had left knowledge of death in the Physici too. Ignorance is Bliss, they had said, and Halver said the same. Arry did not say that, but had not thought yet of what to say instead.

Beldi added, "Derry says wolves don't always come back." Arry wondered if there were also some instinct to heal in all of them, not just in her. Beldi was looking at Oonan as if he wanted to sew up some part of Oonan not visible.

"When will *I* get to say something?" said Con.

"When you're ten."

Con glowered.

"Halver says."

"I really hate this, Arry," said Con crossly. "Why can't we keep our magic until we get our knowledge?"

"Halver says, so we can play for a little between our first responsibility and our last."

Con seemed to consider this for a moment and then shrug it off as foolish. She said, "Can't Oonan fix it?"

Oonan looked amused. "No, my puppy, I can't fix it, because it is not broken. It is what happens."

"But I hate it!"

Oonan said again, "It's what happens." He looked rather helpless.

"Con," said Arry, "you and Beldi run along to

school. You'll *really* hate what Gnosi Halver says to you if you're late."

"What about you?" said Beldi.

"Tell him I am conferring with Oonan and I'll be there as soon as I can."

"Wish I were fourteen," said Beldi.

"No you don't. Go on, now."

They departed, leaving the door open. A damp, green-smelling breeze came in from outside. Oonan sat down, with a tremendous thump for such a thin person, in a tall carved chair, and waved at the other one. Arry's mother had made those chairs, and her father had bought white cloth from the traders of Wormsreign and dyed it red and sewn and stuffed the cushions. The cushions were a little faded, and furry each on its right front corner where Oonan's and everybody else's cats scratched them. The chairs had darkened a little from their first pale pine-color, but were otherwise just the same.

Arry sat down on the floor, almost in the damp spot left by the puddle of milk. "Did you lose more sheep, Oonan?"

"Just the two," said Oonan. "Wim says we can afford so many, or even three times so many. But I hate it." His slight smile commiserated Con and mocked himself all at once.

"Is Con really unbroken?"

"Entirely."

"But why does she hurt?"

"What?" said Oonan, with extreme sharpness. "Did she say her hand hurt?"

"No, I don't mean that. But doesn't it seem to you

that her hating what is happening must be a hurt also?''

"If you say so, Arry, then it is so.''

"But a hurt is a breaking, and if you say Con is not broken and I say she does hurt, then what?''

Oonan leaned his bright head back against the red cushion of the chair and closed his eyes. "I'm older than you are," he said, "but pain has precedence. Might we ask Gnosi?''

"I'll talk to him after school," said Arry.

"Good," said Oonan, without opening his eyes.

"Your head hurts," said Arry. "Take some almond-water." Willow-bark tea would be better, but Oonan wouldn't drink it.

"I will," said Oonan. Still without moving, he added, "I'm going to watch with the sheep tonight.''

"Do you want me to come?''

"Can you bear it?''

"Can you?''

Oonan sat up with a jerk and glared at her. "This isn't a spelling game.''

"I didn't mean it that way.''

"I suppose you didn't. Mally says people who perceive pain always talk oddly. I should have remembered. Meet me here at twilight, then.''

Arry got up, shook out a foot that had fallen asleep, and went out.

The sky was the faint color of Oonan's eyes. The new green of the Dubious Hills was as flat as one of Beldi's paintings. The grazing sheep were as still as stones. Mally said it was a late spring. It was certainly cold yet, and the leaves on the thornbushes and the small trees beside the stream were as little as the ears of a squirrel.

Arry stood still on Oonan's worn slate doorstep. Nobody had had to tell her that the sky was the color of Oonan's eyes, that the grass in this odd light looked like Beldi's paint or that the sheep looked like the rocks that were everywhere on the hillsides. She had thought of it; but she didn't know it as she knew that Oonan's head and Beldi's lip and Con's skinned fingers meant pain. She had thought of these things; nobody had told her; were they true?

Her own head hurt. That was true. Arry rubbed the back of her neck and walked briskly down Oonan's hill.

Gnosi Halver's house was by itself, halfway (Wim said) along the road to the next fort of reason, which (Halver and Sune said) was called Waterpale. The people there did not raise sheep (Mally said), but fished and quarried stone and, either because of their proximity to the Hidden Land or a gap in their knowledge, used money instead of barter. Arry had two of their copper coins that her mother Frances had brought back. Each of them had square letters on one side, the same square letters, though nobody could read them. On the other side one coin had a running fox and the other an oak leaf.

Arry stepped into a deep puddle, started, and looked around her. She had passed Gnosi's house without seeing it and was therefore more than halfway to Waterpale. Return would be as tedious as go o'er, her mother used to say, before Con was born, when she would take Arry and Beldi berrying and Arry would whine at her for both of them that they were tired. She looked behind her. She was standing between two steep hills, which explained the puddle, and the muddy road stretched wearily up to the misty sky.

Her feet were cold, though the water had not yet

seeped through the seams of her boots. Arry stepped out of it slowly, on the home side of the puddle. She thought of a whole fort smelling of the dried fish Frances had brought back from Waterpale with the coins; of an entire town dusted in the powder of worked stone; of a river wider than all Oonan's fields, with on its other side the wide grassy plains and strange-spoken folk of the Hidden Land.

They said, travel not in the Hidden Land. The two coins were in a box in Arry's room. She was late for school. The hill on Waterpale's side of the puddle was just as high as the hill on the side of home. Arry turned and squelched up the home hill.

From its crest she could see Halver's little stone house. It was really too small for school; but Halver's mother had been the master of herbs, which required more space outside than in; and the old Gnosi's daughter was Mally, who did not *know* what a teacher must, so that was that.

Arry started downhill again, and Halver's blue door burst open and let out a flood of small children. She had missed the entire memory time and was about to miss the middle lessons, where she belonged. She went on squelching, down and up again, and stopped in Halver's muddy yard to speak to Con, who was scowling at the crowd of fascinated children around Beldi.

"I'm the one who did it," said Con.

"But you shouldn't have. He suffered it; he should get the attention."

"I don't guess you'd hit me," said Con, with hope but no expectation, the way she always asked for a fourth oatmeal cake at midsummer.

"Don't tempt me," said Arry.

Con stared at her. "Do you want to? Why, if it's so awful?"

"Because I know," said Arry, between her teeth, "and you don't."

"But Gnosi says people who know about pain never want to cause it."

"I'd be sorry, after," said Arry.

"What's sorry?"

"I'd hate having done it."

"If I hate the way nobody talks to me and they all look at Beldi, does that mean I hate hitting him?"

"Having hit him. I think so."

"Don't you know?"

"I'm only fourteen!" snapped Arry.

"Well, there isn't anybody else to ask!"

"No, there certainly isn't."

"When I know something," said Con, "I won't just think so."

"Wait and see," said Arry, and went into Halver's house.

He was sitting on a stool her mother had made, surrounded by the eight members of Arry's class, who were sitting and lying on a carpet of Mally's that Mally had botched the pattern of. Halver, like Oonan, had not slept well and had a headache. The gray teacher's wig he wore hurt his ears and made the headache worse. None of this showed in his voice at all. He was telling the class about the geometry of the sphere.

Arry got her school book from the shelf beside the door, crept quietly across the bare stone to the carpet, and sat down carefully beside Niss's daughter Elec. Elec wrote the best notes of geometry, said Halver, though for history you might as well assume she had never been in class at all. Halver noticed Arry's arrival. His head hurt more as he did, probably from the way he looked out of the corner of his eye. But his voice didn't show that, either. He went on talking; and when he needed a figure drawn, he got up, strode to the open door, and hollered for Con.

"Gnosi?" said Arry. "She's almost six, Wim says."

"And?"

"She's forgetting."

"Well, let's see what happens," said Halver.

Con came breathlessly in the door and glared at Halver. "I can't remember anything," she said.

"You haven't forgotten how to talk, have you?"

"I can't remember anything important."

"Well, if you can't remember, I can't believe what you say; you'll have to show me. Mora here needs to see this flat thing made round." He handed her the board he had been drawing on.

"Can it be purple?" said Con.

Halver rubbed his aching forehead with two fingers, and Arry prepared to intervene. But Halver said only, "If you like."

Con screwed her round face up ferociously and said in grim tones, "All sorts of things and weather Must be taken in together To make up a year And a Sphere."

In the middle of the air, right over Elec's head, a faint violet ball as big as the rising harvest moon took on form, deepened to a violent purple, faded, deepened again, and with a bewildering silence disappeared.

"I told you," said Con.

Halver patted her shoulder; Arry hunched up her own back as if she had been bitten by a spider. Con's face was expressionless, and Halver would never, never hurt anybody—but in Con, that was pain. "Five years of freedom for you, then," said Halver. "You've earned them. No more work until you're ten. Send Lina to me, Con, and then please yourself."

Con ran out the door. She was not going to fetch Lina, whom in any case she scorned for a coward because Lina knew what burned and would not ever light a fire or a lantern. Arry went after Con, but Con was gone already when she got outside. Arry found Lina in a mud puddle, and sent her in. She ought to go in herself: her geometry was better than Elec's, Halver said, but far from good enough. Con would go home and sit on the potatoes in the root cellar. If Arry went after her, what would there be to do? Almond-water and black thread would not help this pain.

Arry slunk back into school a second time, and tried to attend to Lina's bright red bubbles.

At lunch time, Arry told Halver to take some willow-bark tea, and went home. Con was indeed sitting in the root cellar, and had progressed to carving horrible shapes out of the potatoes with their father's vegetable knife, brought with considerable trouble from the Kingdom of Dust.

She had not, for a wonder, cut herself. Arry delivered a lecture on the dangers of knives. Then she dragged Con, and her works of art, up the ladder to the kitchen, and made her cook them. The two of them gulped the hot mess, liberally decorated with cheese, and trudged back to school in silence. If Con wanted to talk, she would talk; if she didn't, no earthly force would move her. Mally said so. Arry wanted desperately to tell Con to talk, as she had told Oonan and Halver to take their almond-water and willow-bark tea. But that would make things worse. She considered forbidding Con to talk: they had once gotten Beldi to eat turnips by telling him not to dare do any such thing. But Con, as Mally had said often enough, was made of sterner stuff. She did what she had decided; that was all.

Halver would know what to do. That was what he was for.

Arry endured a miserable afternoon of history, poetry, and logic. Then she sent Beldi and Con home with instructions to make dinner, any dinner, so long as it had no potatoes in it; and waited while Halver dealt with three transgressing students and two who wanted to ask him long involved questions. The willow-bark tea had made his head hurt less, but he was not in a very happy state when he finally beckoned her up to his stool and said, "And what can I tell you?"

"I have a difference with Oonan," said Arry, formally.

Halver closed his eyes with his thumb and forefinger, ended by pinching the bridge of his nose, and then dug the heel of his hand into his forehead. None of this helped his headache in the least. "What is it?" he said.

Arry told him.

Halver looked at her with his brown eyes just like Beldi's, very large; he had forgotten his headache for a moment, she was pleased to see, but in its place was a pain something like Con's. Then he rubbed his hand over his forehead again, and when he got to the edge of the gray wig, he pulled it entirely off his head and dropped it onto the floor. He had yellow hair. Arry had been told this already, because Halver seldom put the wig on with any great care, and Wim said it was yellow, after which one could see for oneself if one looked. But

Halver had never taken the wig off before—Mally said so. Teachers usually did, when they were not teaching, Mally said—but Halver did not. And it was not because of the headache that he had done it now.

"Pain has precedence," said Halver.

"That's what Oonan said."

"What else is there to say?"

"But I don't know what to do about it."

"If you don't know, Arry, nobody does."

"I'm only fourteen. Is there something I could read?"

Halver put the wig back on, which seemed even stranger than his taking it off. "I'll look," he said, "and I'll ask Sune, and I'll tell you tomorrow."

"Thank you, Gnosi."

"Thank you, Physici," said Halver, as he ought. His head hurt again.

"How much willow-bark tea did you take?"

"Half a bowl."

"Well, have some more. You won't sleep well if you don't."

Halver laughed. Arry jumped. That was not a thing he did much of either, Mally said. She stared at him as sternly as she could; after a moment he said, "I will, of course."

"Good night," said Arry, and went home hurriedly.

**3**

THE FIRE HAD gone out, so Con and Beldi had made cold oatmeal-and-onion balls for dinner. They had forgotten the peppers and herbs that made this dish edible, but Arry ate it anyway. She felt that to save her life she could not have done anything to upset Con. She was also beginning to feel guilty about Beldi, but if he was unhappy, she did not know it.

Not upsetting Con was a great deal of trouble. It meant settling her and Beldi with Frances's chess set, which Arry did not like to bring out, and then slipping out the back way and trudging muddily through the dark to Niss's house to beg a pot of coals for the fire. It was going to be like being bitten by fleas, this not having a magician in the house any more, one tiny itch after another until suddenly you were covered with welts and scratching like mad and snapping at your family.

If their parents had been alive, of course, there would have been a two-year-old around by now, a little clumsy and overpowerful, but very happy to oblige, even while saying, "Won't!" Arry thought of having one herself; but being pregnant with no magician in the house would be miserable. Besides, there were no fathers she fancied; and she supposed he might have to move in, too, and Beldi, for all his forbearance, might very well hate that. And so would Con, of course. If only we never grew older, she thought, bearing the little earthenware pot carefully up the last hill to home, we would get on very well.

She had left the door open a crack; now she eased it over the wooden floor just to the place where it would stick, and slid through the opening, holding her breath. In the dark kitchen, she stood and listened.

"Diagonals!" said Beldi. "The bishop moves on a diagonal, Halver says so."

"What's a bishop?" said Con.

"A mythological beast of the Hidden Land," said Beldi, austerely. "Halver says."

"It looks like a magician with a stomachache."

Arry grinned and moved softly across the kitchen to the door of the main room. It was dark, too, except for the rectangle of lamplight from Arry's own room, where she had installed her brother and sister with the chess set. She would have to cross the light to get to the main fireplace. She stood clutching the pot; she could feel its warmth through the thick wool wrapping Niss had lent her with it. It was not likely to burn her hand any time soon, but it ought to be dealt with.

She thought of the cold kitchen hearth, unused for three years. Con had said "Won't" and meant it, marched into the main room, and made a fire in there. The kitchen had become the place where you put things you didn't have a place for. The bark and sticks and log laid ready that day three years past were still there, dusty and cobwebbed but certainly dry.

Arry took the pot across the room, stumbling over a pile of Con's outgrown clothes that nobody had gotten around to making rugs of, and then bumping Beldi's wagon, which he would neither use nor give up. She had come back in here a week after Con's rebellion and shut the damper. It would probably make an unknowable noise. Arry pulled cautiously on the chain. It felt very stiff, but slowly the damper gave to pressure, with only a faint groan that Con might, if she heard it, attribute to the wind.

She knelt on the tiled hearth (tiles from Worms-reign, brought by her grandfather, said Wim), and lifting the kitchen tongs from the hook they had hung on for three years, took a red coal from the pot and started the fire. Niss had given her a lecture, derived from Lina, on how to make it sustain itself all night; she hoped she had paid enough attention. While it was still burning brightly she hung the kettle over it. Then she lit a candle or two, to keep her from falling over Con's rocking swan or the pillows the cats had thrown up on, and sat down on a stool while the water heated.

It had just begun to rumble when Arry realized that if she gave Con and Beldi tea, Con would ask where the fire had come from. She had hoped to use the tea to make them sleepy, so she could join Oonan in his watch before whatever was going to happen began. There was no point in making Beldi sleepy if that meant he couldn't keep an eye on Con should she get exercised and go on a rampage.

Arry took one of the candles and the packet of

sleepy tea, went into the other room, put the sleepy tea back in its cupboard, and got out the strong black tea from the Outer Isles. They could both stay awake, then, and make sure the house didn't burn down.

"What are you doing?" called Beldi.

"Making some tea. I'll bring it."

When she came in with the tray, they had, as usual, ceased actually playing chess and were engaged in enacting the story of the Dragon King and the Little Girl's Brown Cat. Con, once she had looked up, never took her eyes off the tray; but she did not say a word.

"I have to go help Oonan with his sheep tonight," said Arry.

"I'm not going to bed," said Con.

"No, I understand that you aren't; that's what the tea's for."

Con scowled; Beldi gave Arry a pleading look that she could only counter with a shrug. She said, "There's a fire in the kitchen."

"Who the doubt put it there?" shrieked Con.

"I did," said Arry coolly. "Don't swear. Do you want to be cold and wet as well as unhappy? Don't you think that cold hurts too? And screaming makes my ears hurt, and Beldi's. Act your age."

And that was going too far. Con, however, did not protest; but she did open her soft brown eyes very wide and fix Arry with a look that hurt the heart as fire hurts the skin. Something would have to be done about Con. It was all very well to say that pain had precedence; Arry was beginning to think that all that really meant was, "You deal with it, Arry."

"I'll be back very late," she said to Beldi. "Con needn't go to bed until she wants to."

She turned quickly away from whatever look Beldi might be going to give her, and went out into the damp night.

Oonan was cloaked and booted and waiting for her. He fussed at her for coming out in only her shirt and skirt, as if he knew what cold was, and gave her an old sheepskin jacket. "I'd give us both a suit of armor if I had it," he said, shooing his cats inside and shutting the door. Arry realized he had been thinking about whether the wolves would bite her, and not about cold at all.

They climbed Oonan's hill to the hill above it, where the sheep grazed. It was overcast again and very dark. Arry had forgotten a lantern, as she had forgotten her coat. But Oonan ought to have remembered. He was out here often, for lambing, or if a sheep were sick for some other reason, or just if they had seemed restless to him.

"Can you see in the dark?" she said.

"My feet know the way," said Oonan.

Arry was as much startled as if he had said, the other night, that Niss knew what hurt. "How?" she said.

"They remember," said Oonan, rather hurriedly.

Arry, chewing over the difference between knowledge and remembrance for the first time—that she could remember, she thought, and almost giggled—did not answer him. The path got steeper and rockier; the wind began to strengthen. They came finally to the meadow halfway up the hill where most of the sheep, Oonan said, gathered for the night; and where last night had come the things that Oonan said Derry said were not wolves.

There was a stone hut with a fireplace, for the lambing. They went in. Oonan always put the fire out, he said, for fear of burning the meadow. Arry stood in the sheep-smelling dark and listened to him find flint and tinder, without fumbling. He got a spark at the first try, and the dry grass at the bottom of his ready-built fire caught so fast Arry wondered if he had oiled it.

"Where are the dead sheep?" she asked.

"I gave them to Rista and asked him to salt the meat and wait to give it out until we'd found out what killed it."

"I don't suppose I'd have been able to tell much if they were dead already."

"I thought of that," said Oonan, "but there's time enough for that if it happens again."

"What hour did the wolves come?"

"Last night of all, when yon same star—"

"One. Why are we here so early?"

"Because they might come earlier this time."

"What are you going to do?"

"I got a spell from Niss."

"But who's going to cast it?"

"I am," said Oonan.

Arry peered at him with considerable alarm. In the firelight she could not see much. Then he grinned at her. "Niss says that if I say certain words before I begin the spell, it will reach out and take her power—which she's stored up, I gather, as if it were raspberries dried, and the words the water you soak them in—and so work the rest of the words as if she herself said them."

"What does the spell make the wolves do?"

"What I tell them," said Oonan.

"How can they understand?"

"If they're wolves, as dogs do. If they are something else, as children do."

"Have you got a knife, Oonan?"

Oonan laid his hand on his belt, where his knife always hung, as far as Arry could remember, and looked impatient. Arry decided to keep quiet, and found herself asking, "How will you know when they're here?"

"Niss thinks they're broken," said Oonan.

"What if they're just wolves?"

"Then the other spells here will keep them from us."

Arry heard in his voice a tone she often used to Con. She kept quiet. After a moment she sat down on the floor. Oonan went on standing. The fire crackled. Arry thought about Con, and in particular about Con's refusal to make a fire in the kitchen after their parents left. She mulled it over for some time, and knew finally that Con had been hurt then, as hurt as she was now over the loss of her magic. Con had been hurt for three years, and Arry had only just noticed.

She thought about Beldi. He had not refused to do anything after their parents left; nor had he insisted on doing anything. He had been just the same, except that now he made their clothes, with some help from Mally, and he watched Con when Arry couldn't. But of himself he did nothing. Arry could think of nothing he used to do that he had stopped. But she felt an obscure unease about him just the same, as if she would know what was wrong with him if she could just be quiet enough.

Oonan was quiet, leaning in the door of the hut with his back to her. Outside was quiet too; inside only the fire talked to itself. Arry thought about Con, and Beldi, and Con again. Their mother was the one who was supposed to know these things. Halver was supposed to know some of them. And he had said there was no fixing them.

"I hear something," said Oonan, and darted out the door.

Arry got up, stiff from sitting on the cold floor, and looked out the doorway. It still seemed very dark, but because Oonan was moving she could see him striding towards the far end of the meadow, where there was a pile of rock fallen from the hill above. The sheep often gathered there, though Oonan tried to prevent them, since Inno said that where rock had fallen once it usually fell again. You could not tell that to sheep, apparently, or expect them to know it.

Oonan's voice broke out of the darkness. "Property was thus appalled," he cried, "That the self was not the same; Single nature's double name Neither two nor one was called." There was a moment in which Arry heard a sheep make a querulous noise, and then Oonan bellowed as if he were trying to be heard over a howling blizzard. "Hence loathed Melancholy Of Cerberus and blackest midnight born, In Stygian cave forlorn 'Mongst horrid shapes, and shrieks, and sights unholy, Find out some uncouth cell, Where brooding Darkness spreads his jealous wings, And the night-raven sings; There under ebon shades, and low-browed rocks, As ragged as thy locks, In dark Cimmerian desert ever dwell."

Arry stood stock-still, staring. She did not know what half the words of the spell meant, but she knew that this was the worst curse she had ever heard in her life. A single howl rose out of the meadow, and something large and dark came towards the hut with a peculiar lurching gait. It was not running as fast as she would have run, had those words been directed at her; and it was not running down the hill. It was coming to the hut. Arry slid back into the room and snatched a burning stick from the fire.

The irregular footfalls had ceased. Something dark and bristling was standing in the doorway. It was as tall as Beldi. Arry came slowly forward. She knew what the stick would do if she thrust or slapped with it. "Go away," she said, but her voice cracked.

The shape in the doorway made no sound. Arry brought the burning stick closer to it, and saw gray and cream fur, and green eyes where the reflection of the flame stood like a window into blinding sunlight, and tall pointed ears. And she saw something else. "Your paw hurts," she said.

The animal blinked once, the way Halver did when you startled him. Arry knelt on the rough floor. Oonan and Halver said wolves would hurt you; but she knew that something else had hurt this one already. Teaching fought with knowledge, and lost. She held out her hand.

The wolf made a whining growl and stayed where it was, the hurt paw held a little off the floor. Arry knew what it wanted; the glowing stick hurt it more dimly but just as truly as whatever was wrong with the paw. She got up and put the smoldering end of the stick back into the fire, and when she looked back the wolf had come into the hut.

In here it looked enormous. She was afraid, not that it would slash or bite her, as Derry said wolves did, but that if it moved carelessly it would crush her against the wall and fill her slowly full of splinters. Arry swallowed hard. She must be imagining; and her mother had said they had had nobody to do that for thirty years, since

Arry's grandmother died. Her father had said it was not an enviable occupation.

The wolf whined, briefly, like a dog reminding you that you had just been reaching for the bowl of scraps. Arry sat down on the floor and held out her hand again. The wolf came unevenly forward and stood holding the paw up. Arry took it. It was as big as her face, smoothly furred on top, like a dog's, and very hot and tight about the pads. She felt gently at the hottest spot, and frowned. There was something stuck in there, but what she could not recognize. She wished Oonan were here, instead of guarding the sheep from something that didn't want them anyway.

She moved her finger around the edges of the stuck thing. It was as big around as the tip of her littlest finger, but must be narrower at its other end, or it would never have gotten lodged in there. Arry wished she had obeyed her mother and not bitten her fingernails. The thumbnail on the other hand was still long. She shifted hands, got a delicate grip on the stuck thing, and pulled gently. Her own stomach knotted up and the hair crawled on her head, but the wolf made no motion. Arry pulled harder, and in a small gush of hot blood and the throbbing pain you got when a spider bite swelled up, the thing came out.

Arry leaned on her free hand, breathing hard. The wolf backed two paces, lay down, and began licking the foot. That hurt too, but more cleanly. Arry opened her bloody palm and held it to the light of the fire. The thing in it looked like a thorn, but a thorn from no tree she knew. The gorse prickles, painful though they might be, were tiny compared to this.

Something scraped outside the door of the hut. The

wolf jumped straight over Arry and was gone out the window while she was still thinking about being afraid. Oonan ducked in through the low doorway. "I lost them," he said. His voice altered. "Do I smell blood?"

"It's the wolf's," said Arry. "He had a thorn in his paw."

"He had a *what.*"

Arry realized that this was not a question. Oonan flung himself down on the floor beside her and peered at the thorn in her hand. "That's a nasty one," he said. "I don't think I've seen it before. We must show it to Jony, perhaps." His voice was still rather flat. Arry could not recognize the tone; he wasn't in pain, exactly. He sounded almost as if he were trying not to laugh.

"How many of them did you tame?" he said.

"Just the one."

"I saw three. They move too light for wolves; are you sure?"

"Well, it was dark. You said it was a wolf."

"I did?"

"Well—"

"Never mind."

"What happens now?"

"I'll go sleep and you'll watch. When the moon touches the top of that birch, you'll go to sleep and I'll watch."

"And if they come back?"

"Wake me up."

"Huh," said Arry. "Mother always said waking you was like bringing a rock to life."

There was silence of a peculiar sort that Arry did not recognize. The fire popped; the wind sighed; a sheep mumbled. Oonan said, "Then you must say, 'not marble nor the gilded monuments of princes shall outlive this powerful rhyme,' and I will wake up.''

''Who says?''

''Niss!'' snapped Oonan, and stamped away into a corner of the hut, where there was a wooden bed with a couple of wool blankets on it instead of a mattress.

''Fine,'' said Arry, and sat down on the hearth. He was angry; why, she had no idea. She stared at the small hollows of orange and red in the yellow mass of the fire, and thought of the day her mother left.

Her father Bec had gone a month before, and Frances had known that he would come back on a certain day; but he hadn't. None of the three children was old enough to know anything. Remembering, Arry knew now that her mother had been frightened. But Halver had not taught them about fear then; and she herself had not known, as she just this moment began to, that fear is a form of pain.

Arry shoved irritably at a stray stick. She was beginning to feel that *everything* was a form of pain. Fear, anger, memory. She worked these theories out in detail, and felt herself smiling. Did that mean that thought could turn pain to pleasure? It seemed unlikely. What form of thought could turn Con's hurt inside-out?

Arry sat up straight, shivering. Memory was pain, that was certain. She remembered her parents talking about Oonan, and her mother saying, in the outlandish accent Arry loved better than anybody's, ''Therein the patient must minister to himself.'' But the patient couldn't; that was what she and Oonan were for; the patient didn't know anything, that was the whole problem with being a patient. Those who knew what hurt could make it stop.

"Ha," said Arry. That was what they had told her; that was what she had thought. But it wasn't what she knew; not after today. And it seemed that they had known what she knew now, and not told her.

Unless they were telling her now. Like the milkweed or the dandelion, did they send their knowledge floating through your heart, to take root when it would, far away from them and the flower that made it?

The seed knew how to grow by itself; Jony said so. Arry thought that perhaps she herself did not know how to do this. She lay on her back on the hard dusty floor, and through the window the wolf had leaped out of, she considered the close bright stars. Her mother had said Oonan snored; but he didn't.

4

THE WOLVES DID not come back that night, and
Oonan sent Arry home in the misty dawn. Con and
Beldi had not burned the house down. Con had gone to
bed in her clothes; Beldi had put on his nightgown.
They had forgotten to feed the cats, who were sensibly
asleep on the hearth when Arry crept in, but immediately leapt up, yelling their doubtful heads off. She gave
them last night's milk, which looked unpleasantly thick
but smelt sweet enough. They glared at her and lapped
it anyway.

She must find some way to keep the milk cool. She
must find some way to do a hundred other things Con
had done for three years. Beldi had done them before
that. Frances had told her that Arry herself had done
them first of all, but Arry remembered nothing of it. She
wondered, if she did remember, if she could still do
them. Were sour milk and a cold hearth hurts? Hunger
and cold were, certainly; but the cure for them was food

and warmth: magic did not enter into it. But if she could remember—It was no use asking Con, because Halver and Mally and Frances and Niss all said every child did these things differently. Beldi had never ceased to be horrified at Con's method of calling the cats.

Arry's fire had gone out. She drank cold tea from Con and Beldi's pot and stared at the chess board, which of course they had not put away. If Con had stayed with the red pieces, she had learned fast and been about to win when they stopped. Beldi might have been letting her, of course. He had done it before. He had used to let Arry win at skipping rocks, until she found out and stopped playing with him.

She wondered now if that had hurt. Probably; everything did, it seemed.

No. Everything did not hurt. She knew that. Arry dropped her cup, which bounced on the hearth rug and rolled clanging into a corner. Arry let it go. Seeming and knowing made hideous faces at one another across the breadth of her mind.

"Arry?" said Con's voice, clouded with sleep, and Con came padding barefoot across the floor, in her wrinkled red smock and trousers. She picked up the fallen cup, came slowly back across the room, and held it out to Arry as if it were something precious. Arry supposed it was. Halver had made it.

"Do you want your breakfast?" she said.

"You don't have to hurry," Con informed her, "because I'm already dressed. Why don't people always sleep in their clothes?"

She sounded alarmingly pleased. Arry got up. "You think about the clothes you wore the day Wim made the mud slide. You wouldn't want to sleep in those."

"Why not?"

"Grel says it's dirty. And the mud would dry up and fall off in little rocks and hurt you."

"Huh," said Con, trailing after her across the room.

Arry rummaged among their stores and discovered that Beldi had forgotten to get more oatmeal from Wim, and that if she had meant to make them bean porridge for breakfast, she ought to have set the beans to soak the night before.

"Fried potatoes and onions," she said to Con, hopefully.

"That's a very good idea," Con said. "The smell will wake Beldi up."

"When did you two go to bed?"

"*Very* late," said Con, also hopefully, though Arry could not make out what she hoped. Unless it was to be scolded, which made no sense, because, by the new laws Arry was discovering, scolding hurt. She sliced an onion, thinking about that. Did it hurt invariably?

"Can we put in the mustard seed?" said Con.

"A little of the black, if you like. Why don't you mix it up with the butter and put it in the iron pot?"

Con did these things with a willingness that made Arry deeply suspicious. Unless Con had just decided that helping in mundane ways rather than magical ones was better than not helping at all.

"Can you go over to Niss's and get me some fire?" she said, as if she were asking Con if it were raining. She did not dare look at her.

There was an ominous silence, during which Arry decided not to peel the potatoes and chopped them up briskly.

"If I can go barefoot."

"You'll hurt yourself."

"Will not."

"Will you look very carefully for rocks and not step on them?"

"Yes," said Con, scornfully.

"Go, then."

Con went. Arry shoved aside a pile of cut onion about the size of an egg, for flavoring the butter and mustard seed, and set about reducing the rest of the on-ions and potatoes to a coarse mush. Most people fried them in large pieces, but Bec had always done them this way for Frances, and everybody was used to it now. And if Con was any example, being deprived of what you were used to certainly hurt.

But if you were used to a lame leg, or the sore throat Arry had had all one winter? Arry went on chopping.

"Seeds're popping," said Con, appearing suddenly at her knee. She had brought the fire and the wood in, laid the wood, started it burning, and melted the butter, and Arry had never seen her.

"Let me look at your feet," said Arry.

Con sat down on the floor and thrust her legs out in front of her. Her feet were dirty, but not cut or bruised.

Arry got up, carried her piece of wood over to the fire and scraped the large onion pieces into the butter. They made a fury of bubbles and sent a fine smell up. It was odd that chopping an onion into little pieces and tossing it into hot fat didn't hurt it in the least. Even pulling it up out of the ground, though it made Arry wince, did not hurt the onion. Not that Arry knew. She shoved her mush of onion and potato into the pot. Con, without being asked, had gotten the wooden spoon and at once began stirring.

Arry stood there with the board dangling from one hand, dripping starchy oniony juice on the floor, and wondered if she should ask Jony if it hurt onions to be pulled up. Or roses to have blight. Or grass to be gnawed by sheep or oats to be cut at harvest time.

"Doubt," she said fiercely.

Con looked over the pot at her, shocked.

"Never mind," said Arry; and she yawned.

"Are you coming to school today?" asked Con.

Arry began to shake her head, and then remembered that she had missed part of school yesterday, and that Halver had promised to find out about Con for her. She nodded.

"Because Tany says he knows when *he* hurts, but other people don't hurt."

"Tany's only four. He doesn't know anything." Arry felt cold just the same. Tany was Niss's youngest, and those children all knew things before their time. Everybody said so.

"Why's he *say* it, then?" demanded Con.

"We'll ask Halver," said Arry. "Go see if Beldi's awake."

Beldi was not awake and did not want to be awake. Con suggested dumping the cats on his head; Arry decided that it was Beldi's turn to miss school, and put the cats outside lest Con be tempted past bearing.

They ate their potatoes and onions. Arry wondered when there would be eggs to put in with the morning meal. Nobody knew about hens just at the moment, though the ones that lived at Niss's and at Mally's seemed to be going on as usual. Sune had read about hens, and the book she used seemed less doubtful than some of her other books. Arry could ask her, anyway;

then both of them would at least share what the book said, though Arry could not be said to know it. She felt sorry for Sune, doomed to believe what she read whether it was true or not.

Arry poked around in the pantry and the root cellar while Con was finding her socks and boots, which, along with the rest of Con's clothes, had a habit of scattering like spilt lentils whenever Con took them off. Beldi would have to eat potatoes and cheese. Arry went outside and dug in the leaves and old hay that covered the garden. Cold May or not, the new onions were green as emeralds. Arry stood there in the sharp wind, smiling, and pulled up four of the thinnest ones. Beldi loved spring onions. He and Mally and Frances all said so.

Con met her at the back door, wearing one red and one brown sock. Her boots matched because this was the only pair she had. "Aren't you ready?" she said.

"I want to leave Beldi the stuff for his nuncheon, or he'll feel deserted. Have you got your coat? It's cold."

"I want to get to school early and talk to Tany."

"And I'll talk to Halver," said Arry. "Where's your coat?"

They set off finally with Con wrapped in an old blanket of Beldi's. The wind was fierce. The trees shivered in their new leaves. Old and new grass together were whipped flat to the ground. The sky was brilliant blue and full of minute clouds; it looked as if the wind had broken them and would not let them join again into the big clouds that brought rain. Arry didn't mind. It had rained enough for the year, Grel had said so.

All Con's friends were playing in the mud outside Halver's house. Poor Halver was probably trying to drink his tea in peace. He might not even have had time, yet, to delve in his knowledge, his experience, and at a pinch in his books, to find the answer to Arry's question about Con. Arry was glad it was Halver and not she who had to decide all this. Oonan and Zia and Mally had a long-standing argument over whether the Gnosi, the Physici, or the Akoumi had the most difficult task. Arry would have been welcomed into the discussion, since difficulty and pain had a common boundary; but she couldn't see the use of it.

Con ran ahead of Arry and plumped down in the mud between Tany and Zia. They both had very dark skin and very red hair, Wim their father having come from the Outer Isles and Mally's mother Irene, their grandmother, from Fence's Country. Every fall when they gathered the walnuts Con would try to stain herself all over to look like Zia. It never worked.

Arry left her there in the mud and went on up the slope to Halver's house. The door was ajar; she put her head inside. Halver was indeed sitting on the floor with a mug of tea. He was talking to Sune, who was showing him a large and raggedy book with red edges and a drawing of a plant on each page. She was flipping the pages rapidly, with a shocking disregard for their fragility, but whatever she was looking for wasn't there. No— Sune thought it was, but Halver didn't. Sune's back hurt a little, because of the baby.

Arry thought it might be better to go away, but as she moved back in the doorway, Halver caught sight of her.

"Come in, Physici," he said.

Sune looked up and smiled. She had a round face and short yellow hair. "I've ruffled him up," she said. She unfolded her long legs and used Halver's shoulder to help her stand up. Her feet immediately began to hurt too. "You smooth him down." She started to bend, found it impossible, and gestured to Halver, who handed her the book. Sune closed it and walked at Arry. Arry stepped aside in a hurry, banging the door back against the rock Halver kept there to prevent the door's making a hole in his wall. Sune went out, balancing carefully.

"Have some tea," said Halver, as dolefully as if he were Con reporting some new loss of memory.

There was something the matter with him. His head hurt—no. His back, his eyes, his tongue, his knee he had hurt on the mountain when Arry was two—no. What, then?

Halver smiled at her. "Sit down, do, have some tea."

Arry sat, and he poured more tea into the mug Sune had left. "I don't know about Sune," he said, still dolefully.

"Of course you don't," said Arry, in considerable surprise. "Mally does. Ask her."

"Mmmm," said Halver, as he did when the little ones worked their arithmetic incorrectly.

Arry was nettled. She looked at him again, seeing with the part that knew. His hand hurt him: it was swollen between the thumb and the first finger.

"What did you do to yourself?"

"Sliver," said Halver, much more cheerfully. "It's what Sune was talking about. She wanted me to try drawing it out with herbs."

"Wouldn't it come out? Oonan—"

"It didn't need Oonan at all," said Halver. "She's had this in her mind for months, but nobody has obliged by getting a sliver."

"She should talk to Oonan—or to me."

"Ah, well."

"Do you want me to take it out?"

"It's not in," said Halver.

"Then why was Sune—"

"In case any was left."

"But—"

"Never mind," said Halver, rather tiredly. Was there something hurting him besides the sliver that wasn't in? Arry couldn't tell, which nettled her even more.

She said, "What about Con?"

Halver looked so empty of thought that she knew at once he had forgotten her question. After a moment he said, in not quite his accustomed tones, "You'd best ask Mally, I think. She knows Con."

Nobody knows Con, thought Arry. She contemplated that thought. It was as if somebody had said—though nobody would—that water was dry.

"I will, then," she said.

She went outside into the sunshine, and pushed through the crowd of children, and took the path for Mally's house.

MALLY'S HOUSE WAS midway down a hill, dug half into the slope, its windows facing south and west. Tiln had painted the shutters flat red on the outside, but on their inside surfaces he had painted what the view through each window would look like in the middle of the best summer the Dubious Hills had ever seen. It made Mally's house a crowded place in the winter, especially during February.

Even from the next hill, even scrambling through the mud, Arry could see that the shutters were all open. She could make out the fragmented views of what, in summer, would lie behind her: rolling hills and rocks all covered with flowers and vines and scattered with clean sheep, and a hot dark-blue sky with the sun glaring halfway down like a child refusing to go to bed. She looked over her shoulder. The new green grass looked back at her, bare and precise, and the shadows of the land lay all the other way. She was looking at the western sky, and the sun was still in the east.

Arry went on down the hill, splashed through the little stream at the bottom, and climbed on up to Mally's house. The path had flagstones, but the winter had moved some of them about, and there was a lot of mud. Arry's father would have had something to say about the state of her boots.

The door of Mally's house was open, too, and on it was painted the neat flagged path with thyme blooming in its crevices and sundrops glowing just like their name on either side. Arry looked over her shoulder again; she couldn't help it. In the cracks of the path last year's thyme sifted in gray crumbles. Where the sundrops would bloom, crocuses had come up and budded but not yet opened. Arry felt oppressed.

From the house came the sound of Mally singing. "In May get a weed-hook, a crotch and a glove, and weed out such weeds, as the corn do not love."

This was a spell that did not work on children. As a spell, in fact, it did not seem to work on anybody. It was more in the nature of a reminder, perhaps.

Arry put her head inside the doorway. Mally was sitting on the floor, on one of her own red rugs, sorting the dried peas for planting. Her short white hair stood out around her head like the puff of a dandelion. On the hearth the black sheepdog moved his tail briefly.

"Good morning," said Arry.

"A lot of use you are," said Mally. She was talking to the dog; she always said that when people came in. Your telling her what use Blackie was was not what she had in mind. "Come in," added Mally. "More mud won't make any difference at all."

Arry came in, surreptitiously scraping her boots on

the threshold, and sat down on the red rug next to Mally's.

"Mind Tiln's brushes," said Mally. Her own brown leggings were smeared with orange and purple.

Arry moved her skirt. Tiln might paint a landscape so well you would try to walk into it, but he was only twelve, and he left things lying about like anybody else.

"Is Con giving you trouble?" said Mally.

"Yes, she is."

"It stands to reason," said Mally.

"Because she's almost six?"

"Because she's Con. She loved doing magic. It made her the biggest one in your household, even if she was the smallest in body. She felt as if magic were what she knew. Think about losing what you know; then you'll know how she feels."

"What about all the other children who lose their magic?"

"They want to grow up," said Mally. "You have to lose your magic to grow up."

"But Con doesn't want to grow up?"

"Do you?"

"Don't you know?" said Arry.

"You know when Tiln's tooth hurts; he doesn't. Don't you tell him?"

"But you're asking."

"Yes, I am," said Mally.

This was Mally's knowledge, so Arry thought about it. "I think," she said after a moment, "that I already am grown up. I run the house, I know what I know, and I keep making questions that nobody can answer."

"Before you were grown up," said Mally, with a peculiar expression on her face, "did you want to be?"

"I didn't think about it."

"Never?"

"Well—I wanted to find out what I was going to know; but I didn't want to know it right away. I just wondered sometimes."

"And I wonder," said Mally, "if Con's going to be a wizard."

Arry looked at her hard.

"I wonder if she'll be getting her magic back again. Wim's cousin was like that: she never gave anybody a moment's peace between losing her child-magic and getting her knowledge." Mally added reflectively, "She was slow, too. She didn't get her knowledge until she was sixteen. Everybody thought she wouldn't have any."

It might be a long ten years, thought Arry. "Does anybody ever really not have any?"

"Not here," said Mally.

"Here where?"

"In the Dubious Hills."

"What made them think she wouldn't have any, then?"

"All the farmers," said Mally, rather angrily. "If it hasn't come by now, it won't come, they kept saying. You'd think they of all people would know better. Jony says half the time when you plant chive seeds they come up two or three years later in the wrong place."

"Maybe oats are different."

"Maybe."

"What happened to Wim's cousin?"

"She was so angry at them all that she went away to Heathwill Library."

"In the Hidden Land?" Arry was always interested in the country her mother had come from.

"North of there. Fence's Country. Sune showed me the map."

"Sune was trying to show Halver something in a book, but he didn't believe it."

"He may know better," said Mally, without any apparent thought; then she dropped the last pea onto her right-hand square of clean cloth and looked at Arry. "What was she trying to tell him?"

"I'm not sure. Something about herbs. I didn't notice; I wanted to ask him about Con."

"You haven't really asked me, yet."

You wouldn't let me, thought Arry. She said, "I think there's something besides the magic. I think our parents' going away hurt her. Could that happen?"

"If you don't know—"

"It's not like a broken leg!" cried Arry. "It's to do with people and what they're like."

"Pain is your province," said Mally. "But," she added, forestalling Arry's getting up and flinging out of the house, "there are some stories that may help you." She got up heavily and went into the other room.

Blackie stood up from the hearth and put his muddy nose into Arry's ear. She rubbed the coarse fur around his neck and wondered why he wasn't out with Wim. He didn't hurt anywhere. Mally came back with three books, one covered in red leather, one in green, and one a collection of scrolls in a cedar box.

"Is anything wrong with the dog?" said Arry.

"Oonan told Wim to keep him home today," said Mally.

She didn't sit down again, so Arry got up and took the books. "*All* the stories in all three?" she said.

"You like to read."

"I've been missing school."

"That," remarked Mally, "is why you should reconsider this notion that you're grown up."

"Grown up isn't the same as educated," said Arry, irritably. She thought a moment. "Is it?"

"No," said Mally. "But it helps."

It was clear that Arry had not asked the right question, but Mally said nothing more. She took hold of the loose skin around the dog's neck, meaning she expected Arry to go now. Blackie wouldn't go out the open door of his own accord, but Mally said he was fond of following visitors out and looking innocent about it.

"Thank you," said Arry, from the doorway. "I'll return them as soon as I can."

"Nobody else needs them," said Mally.

Arry went home, made a pot of peppermint tea, and sat down in the chair nearest the window. She started with the scrolls first; they would be the oldest, and this made her nervous. She wanted them read and back in their box and the box hidden before Con got home.

She read three stories, by the end of which the teapot was empty, the white cat was on her lap, the black cat was under the chair, and her mind was muddled.

The stories all began, "Once upon a time," and none of them said where any of their events happened. One was about a little boy and girl whose mother died, after which their father married a woman who hated them and finally sent them off into the woods to be lost and starve, only they came upon a house made of honeycake, in which there lived a witch who tried to fatten them up and cook them, only they tricked her and put her into the oven instead. The story didn't say if they had eaten her.

The second one was about a girl whose mother had died, after which her father married a woman with two daughters, all of whom were ugly and cruel and made the girl do all the work of the house, only a fairy came and helped her go to a dance, where the prince of some country fell in love with her, traced her through a shoe she left behind, and after refusing to take either of her stepsisters, carried her off and married her. Nobody in this story, it seemed, had anybody to tell them what hurt, or the stepmother and stepsisters would never have cut off bits of their feet so the girl's shoe would fit them.

The third story was about a girl whose beautiful mother died and whose stepmother gave her a poisoned apple.

Arry put the book down. "Who *says* so?" she said.

Mally? No, Mally had only given her the books. Sune might not even have read them, and in any case Sune hadn't said anything to Arry about any of this, ever. Who *would* say such things? This wasn't knowledge: it must be history. Stories, Mally had said; stories that would help. Arry had asked her, might it hurt Con that their parents were gone; and Mally had handed her these un-catalogued and incomprehensible narrations.

It had hurt all these children that their mothers died, because the new mothers were cruel to them. And what were their fathers doing, thought Arry irritably. She sat up straight, and the white cat complained and jumped to the floor. Was she the new mother? Was *she* cruel?

Arry got up, quickly. Con and Beldi would say she was, if there was nothing for them to eat when they came back from school, which they would do very soon, even if they played in every mud puddle between Halver's house and here. She had been reading for a long time. Having put the scrolls carefully away and hidden the box in her bed, she made more tea and rummaged about, thinking of honeycake. Then she went down into the cellar and got out some of the dried apples.

When Con and Beldi came in, she watched them narrowly. They were both muddy and windblown, especially Beldi. She ought to cut his hair. Con shrieked happily at the apples and splashed four slices into her cup of tea so they could swell up. Beldi asked if there were any bread, and settled for oatcake. If anybody was hurting at the moment, thought Arry, it wasn't Con. Beldi looked as if his head might hurt, but it didn't.

"When are you coming to school again?" said Con with her mouth full. "Zia says—"

"I don't know," said Arry. She might as well ask them. "Am I cruel?"

"Very," said Con, promptly. "You never make us any pudding."

"Who says that's—"

"She made some six days ago," said Beldi, spitting out an apple seed.

"Didn't have enough raisins," said Con.

Arry tried again. "Who says that's—"

"That's not cruel," said Beldi.

"What is, then?"

"Making you do all the work would be," said Arry, without thinking.

Con's whole face clouded over. "I *did* do it when I wasn't *old!*"

Not cruel, thought Arry, just stupid. And what was

the difference, when pain was the outcome either way? She thought about telling Con that Mally said she might be a wizard when she grew up. No. "What did you learn about today?" she said.

"I hate learning," said Con. "I like knowing."

"Be glad you don't live in the Hidden Land," said Arry, rather desperately. "They have to learn everything. They don't know anything."

"Who says so?"

"Sune."

"Oh, well."

"Con."

"But it just means she read it."

"Somebody has to," said Beldi.

Arry added, "Mother used to say just the same. You remember."

Nobody said anything more. Beldi scooped the last of the apples out of the bowl Arry had put them in. He had made it last year and seemed to feel that this gave him rights in anything it contained. "I was thinking," he said.

"What about?" said Arry, faintly. Mally had never said Beldi didn't think, but he had certainly never mentioned doing it before.

"Did you wonder about what you were going to know before you knew it?"

"Yes."

"Were you right?"

"Not really. I wanted to be like Oonan, just before I found out. Before that I thought of lots of things."

"So you were almost right?"

"Well—"

"I've just been thinking, maybe I'll be like Sune."

"What do we need two for?" demanded Con.

"You be quiet," said Beldi.

She was, probably from sheer astonishment. Arry said, "Would you like that?"

"I like to read."

"You can do that anyway."

"Yes, but it's very muddling."

"It certainly is," said Arry, feelingly.

"I'd like to be sure of what I read."

"Even when you're wrong?"

"Well—"

"I'm never going to be wrong," said Con, slurping the last of her tea and sliding out of her chair. "Where are the cats," she yelled, and ran back outside.

Beldi followed her with the last of the oatcake. Arry put her head in her hands and thought Con was probably right. Then she laughed, but not very heartily.

CON WANTED TO cut off the heel of her right foot so she could fit it into a shoe of honeycake and thus always be right about everything. Arry knew the only way to dissuade her was to make Oonan explain what going about without a heel was like; but if she left to get Oonan, Con would go ahead and cut. Beldi was there, eating a marzipan doorstop shaped like a hedgehog. He wanted the knife to cut pieces of marzipan off, but wouldn't promise not to give it back to Con when he was finished. Arry's mother came in from the kitchen with a basket of kittens and said, "Take the knife with you, Arry."

Arry picked it up, and Con threw back her head and howled like a wolf. Arry waited for her mother to make Con shut up, but her mother only turned around and went into the kitchen again. The whole back of her was not a person at all, but a huge cookie made of the honeycake dough rolled flat. Arry started to throw the knife at her, and dropped it.

It made an appalling clatter that mixed with Con's howling. All the kittens started to mew shrilly. Beldi put the marzipan doorstop over his head. Arry bent for the knife, and opened her eyes on the darkness of her room. The clattering and howling were still going on. So was the mewing. Arry put her hand on Woollycat, who was sitting on her pillow. Woollycat stopped fussing, which only meant that Arry could hear Sheepnose under the bed, making the noises that meant there was a large dog taking liberties with the cats' property.

The other sounds were outside the room. Arry climbed out of the bed and dragged her father's walking-stick from under it. Then she opened the door of her room. In the center room the banked fire was a muted red spot; the moon shone through the windows, except where two white-shirted figures with tousled heads blocked the light by craning out the back window. Arry sprang across the room and stared over their heads. The trees were still; the moonlight followed the paving stones down the black hill and up the next one. A few puddles glinted faintly. The cold wind blew Beldi's hair into Arry's face.

"What's happening?" said Arry.

Neither one of them so much as started.

"Isn't it wolves?" said Con.

"What's the *clattering*?"

"Milk pans, maybe?" said Beldi.

*"Doubt!"* said Arry, and ran for the door. The day before Oonan lost his sheep, she had scalded three of the four pans she owned, put them outside to sun, and forgotten them utterly. They came from Druogonos and, according to Bec, had cost the earth. She wrenched the bar aside, flung a furious "Stay here!"

over her shoulder, and pelted around the side of the house. The door banged behind her: good, they had some sense; more than she did. Sliding in the cold mud, she plunged to a stop beside the flat rock where she had left the pans.

They were gone. Looking over the far side of the rock at her was a wolf. The wolf tilted its head at her. Very slowly, it lifted its lips away from its teeth. It made no sound, but all the hair stood up on Arry's neck and arms. Arry took a slow step backwards. The wolf's lip crinkled more, and Arry bumped into somebody small but solid. She swallowed a hysterical exclamation and breathed, *"Con. Get back in the house this minute."*

"Beldi gets to—"

*"Both of you. Slowly. Quietly. Now."*

The pressure of Con against her legs vanished. Arry kept her eyes on the wolf. It was looking at her. The rustle and pad of Con and Beldi's bare feet on the rocks and dry leaves and pine needles did not even make it twitch its ears. Maybe they were too small for dinner; it seemed unlikely. Nor did the wolf look at her as the cats would look at a bird or a vole. There was consideration in it, a consideration like Oonan's, looking at Beldi's lip.

It was a very large wolf. Its ears were bigger than her hand. Oonan would know, if he were here, what the teeth it still showed her could do; and she knew, all by herself, what they would feel like. She showed it her own flat, blunt teeth, half sheep's, half dog's, essentially unlike those of any animal she had seen.

Its tilted head straightened and it uncurled its lip. Then the wolf stood up and trotted down the hill, tail waving. Arry thought of the milk pans; then she backed and finally ran. The door opened before she got there. She skidded inside, and Con slammed the door and Beldi shot the bolt.

"Did you get the milk pans?" said Con.

Arry sat down on the cold floor and began to laugh. After a moment Beldi started giggling. Con was unimpressed. "It's what you went out for, isn't it? Didn't they cost the earth?"

"Indubitably," said Arry, still laughing.

"What's funny?" said Con.

"Nothing, really," said Arry. "It was stupid of me to go outside for the milk pans when there was a wolf out there."

"You mean it might hurt you?"

"Yes."

"And she cost even more than the earth," said Beldi.

Arry stared at him. He shrugged.

*"Did* you?" said Con, fascinated.

"So did you," said Arry. "So did every one of us."

"Who says?"

"I just know."

Even in the moonlight she could see Con struggling with this and deciding not to press it. Con said, "But how does Beldi know?"

"I told him."

"When?"

"By laughing."

"But it wasn't funny."

"That's why," said Beldi.

It was clear that Con didn't understand this, either. Arry wasn't sure she did herself.

"Con," she said. "The next time I tell you to go into the house, go into the house. Don't argue."

Con scowled. Arry, looking at her, thought for the first time in all the months they had been without their parents: I can't manage this; I don't know what to do.

"Let's go back to bed," she said, and went over to close and shutter the windows.

They went without saying anything else, and Arry went back to her own bed. But she stared at the dark for a long time, and wondered if Oonan too had been visited. When she slept, it was to dream of snarling sheep with dogs' teeth and glass hooves.

She sent Con and Beldi off to school in the morning and walked over to Oonan's house to ask him. It was a cold gray day with a wind like the slap of a wet cloth. Oonan's house was entirely surrounded by sheep. They were quiet for sheep crowded like that. Oonan's two dogs, Mud and Water, and Mally's dog Blackie, and Jony's puppy Mouse, were keeping them from spreading out all over the hill. Arry pushed through them, paused to let the puppy sniff her ankle, and put her head into the open doorway. Oonan was lying on the cold hearth with his head propped on his hands.

Arry sprang through the door, and the thump of her muddy boots brought Halver's gray dog, Wind, in from the other room. It was not until the dog barked at her that Oonan turned his head. He had blue circles under his pale blue eyes and you could have counted his freckles, if you had nothing better to worry about. He gazed at her vaguely for a moment; then his whole face sharpened, and he sat up, looking like himself.

"What's the matter?"

"Nothing," said Arry. "I mean—I thought something was the matter with you."

"Are you sleeping?" said Oonan.

"Are you?"

Oonan drew his knees up and wrapped his arms around them. "Sit down," he said, very patiently, "and tell me why you came to see me."

"I wanted to know if you'd had any more wolves."

"You may well ask," said Oonan. "We brought the sheep down in the afternoon, and Wim stayed with them, and I went back up to the meadow."

"And?" said Arry, though she thought she knew.

"I had wolves, yes," said Oonan. "Two of them. Not the sheep. They came to see me."

"What did they do?"

"You tell me," said Oonan.

Arry sat down on a stool. "They looked at you," she said. "As if they were thinking what was wrong with you. And they went away."

"Is that all?"

"First they showed you their teeth."

"How many visited you?"

"Just one. The big one."

"The same?"

"I think."

"Well, did it limp?"

"Oh. I don't—I think I would have seen, but maybe not."

"Mine didn't. They weren't very large, as wolves are said to go." He rubbed his eyes. "There was something wrong with them. Was yours in pain?"

"No."

"I didn't think mine were either. Something other was wrong."

"That's what I think about Con," said Arry.

"It's not what I know about her."

They looked at each other for a long time. The wind blew the smell of muddy sheep in through the open door, and the cold green smell of spring, and a thread of woodsmoke from some more responsible person's fire.

"Who should we ask?" said Arry.

"We'd have to ask Mally. This is outside the bounds of anything she's said to me." Oonan rolled back and stared into his fireplace.

"I was just to see Mally yesterday. She gave me some stories."

Oonan looked at her again, but said nothing.

"I couldn't tell if they were knowledge or history."

"Ask Sune."

"I didn't think," said Arry.

"I'll come with you. I want to ask her what the books say about wolves."

SUNE LIVED IN a small house halfway down the hill from Halver's. Usually she was up at the school most of the day; but this morning they found her at home, spinning. Her back hurt, her feet hurt, and her stomach was uneasy. As they put their heads around the door, the baby gave an enormous kick. The spindle sprang out of Sune's hand and wrapped its yarn around the rocker of her chair.

"I'm going to call this one Knot," said Sune, a little grimly. She ran the offending yarn through her hands, shrugged, and let it fall. "What is it? Is the baby coming?"

Arry began to laugh. What else should Sune think, with both the Physici and the Akoumi come to see her unexpectedly?

"No," she said, after looking at Oonan in case he knew something she didn't. "Mally gave me some stories, and I don't know what they are."

She handed the cedar box to Sune, who said, "There's tea in the kitchen," opened the box, and began to read.

Oonan went into the house's other room and came back with three mugs on a tray. Sune had the only chair, and all the cushions, so Arry sat on the hearth rug. Sune moved her lips when she read, and frowned heavily— not from the baby, who had quieted down again. She took the mug Oonan handed her and held it without drinking. Arry drank hers. Peppermint. Good for the uneasy stomach. She wished Sune would drink some.

Outside a robin sang in the willows down by Sune's stream, and occasional bursts of laughter came out of the school. Finally Sune looked up. "Why did Mally give you these?" she said. She rolled them neatly as she spoke, and put them back into their box.

"I was asking her about Con," said Arry. "And if having one's parents leave could be hurtful."

"Ah," said Sune. She had no lap to lay the box in, and dropped it on top of her wool.

"I can't tell if it's knowledge or history."

"There's something else," said Sune. "These are that."

"What's it called?"

"I don't know. But I know it when I see it."

"What else *is* there?"

"Maybes," said Sune, incomprehensibly. "Might-havebeens."

Arry looked at Oonan, who was in fact already looking at her. Sune was the strange one, Mally had always said so. Was she hurt or broken or simply herself, that was the question.

"I thought," said Arry, "that you knew what you read?"

"I know about what I read, too," said Sune, rather wearily. It wasn't the baby. Maybe she had told Mally this already.

"But not what it's all called?"

"No. Nobody knows why I don't know that, not even Mally."

"Why would she give me these books, then?"

"Ask Mally."

"I mean, what's in them that would tell me what might hurt Con?"

"I can't think," said Sune. "You're supposed to know what hurts Con already."

Arry took a deep breath. "If there are other kinds of hurt, I might not know it yet. Could these stories help me know?"

"I don't see how," said Sune. "But I'll read them again if you like."

"What do they tell you?"

Sune considered. The baby kicked her again. She was crowded in there, though not dangerously. "What does a chair tell you?" said Sune. "Or wait, no, not a chair." She thought some more. "Think of the prettiest thing you can," she said.

"Sunset," said Arry, cautiously. They had no Kallosi at present, nobody who knew what was beautiful. But Mally had talked to the the old one a lot; Frances said the old one had been Mally's sister. Frances said she herself had been friends with a Kallosi in the Hidden Land.

"Sorry," said Sune; she felt, in fact, rather happier

than she had before. "Something a person has made, the prettiest one of those you can think of."

Arry thought of Tiln's paintings; of the vest her father had made for her when she was five, with triangles of blue and green cloth in the shape of the sun and a mountain; of the kaleidoscope Oonan had, that came from Druogonos with the milk pans. She even thought about the milk pans. "Jony's garden," she said finally. "Not now, but in July."

Sune smiled. "Why?" she said.

She was acting just like Mally—though Mally wouldn't say so. But this was the field of Sune's knowledge, so Arry thought as well as she could.

"When you come into the garden," she said, "you see the marigolds, all bright and crowded. And then the daisies, white and crowded. And then you go around the side of the hill and there's the crabapple tree with the spurge and the borage under it. The colors are different and they look airier."

She paused for breath. This was hard. You had to remember what name and color you'd been told the flowers were, and then say what you had seen. "Then you go around the next part of the circle and see the long straight path with enormous white lilies and the arch at the end of it with red roses all over it. And through the arch you can see the water, and the purple loosestrife. And if you go all the way through the arch and cross the water on the stones, then you go along another path with red lilies and through another arch that has white roses, and there's a birch tree with yellow lilies under it and then more marigolds, and then you're out again on the grass." She breathed and looked at Sune.

"Why is that pretty?" said Sune.

"I'm not sure it is," said Arry.

"Yes, of course you're not. If it were, though, why might it be?"

"It's the same and different at the same time."

"Why is it prettier than the high meadow in spring?"

"Because it's ordered."

"Ah," said Sune.

Arry looked at Oonan. He shrugged.

"So are the stories," said Sune. "More than history, and more than knowledge, the stories are ordered. Also—" The baby kicked her again, and she caught her breath. "This one doesn't want to me think," she said. "Also—you can make a bigger order out of stories of the same type. Mally gave you stories about children whose parents left. With them you can make a pattern."

"I don't know how to do that."

"Mustn't Mally know you can do it?"

"Oh," said Arry.

"Must she?" said Oonan.

"Oh, not necessarily, I suppose," said Sune, irritably. Once again, the source of her irritation was not the baby, not her stomach or her feet or her back. It seemed to be Oonan.

Arry got up. Oonan said, "Sune, in the intervals of being pummelled, might you see what the books say about wolves? In especial their more strange behaviors with regard to approaching people and with regard to things they choose not to eat?"

"Did you lose some sheep?" said Sune.

"Two," said Oonan.

"The lambs?"

"No, they left the lambs."

"I'll look as soon as I finish this spinning. If young Knot's to have a blanket to receive her, I must be busy."

"We'll leave you to it," said Oonan.

"If you need other clothes," said Arry, "you could have some of Con's." Since there won't be any more babies in this family any time soon, she added silently.

Sune smiled. "I'll come and look at them tomorrow after school, shall I? I can bring your stories back then, too."

"Yes, do," said Arry, and they thanked Sune for the tea and went outside. The wind pounced on them hard. It had blown some of the clouds away and stretched the rest across the sky like rags on a loom to make a rug. A blue and white and gray rug like that would be pretty, thought Arry. But how do I know that? Do I know it?

"What now?" said Oonan.

"I expect I should go to school."

"Or to sleep."

"School's easier."

"Go, then. I'll talk to you after Sune's told me about the wolves."

"Or if you think of anything about Con."

"Well, yes," said Oonan.

He turned and went back down the hill, past Sune's little stone house and into the willows, his jacket flapping in the wind and his red hair blown straight backward. Arry looked after him until the wind made her eyes tear. Then she turned around and stood with the wind at her back, looking up at Halver's house. She could go see Mally and ask if Mally thought she was good at making patterns.

Or she could try making some and see how far she

got. She hadn't read all the stories yet, either. But what of the ones she had?

"It was the mothers that left," she said, to the mud and the rough pink speckled rocks and the tentative green around them. "And the fathers found new mothers and they were all cruel." But her father had gone first, and her mother after him; nobody had gone and brought Arry home, she had been home already, she was one of the children. She shivered inside her jacket, the jacket her father had made. Was the cruel mother coming? But who should choose her?

She thought she could guess what Mally would say about her talent at making patterns. Mally said school could teach you most things. She walked up the hill through the mud and went into the school.

Tiln and Jony and Beldi were in a corner with the maps. Beldi must have mastered the second form of memory, to have been allowed to study with those two. He must be growing up. He looked small beside the older children, stocky and short like his father. Tiln and Jony were tall for their ages, and thin. Tiln's hair was as white as Mally's, and he had Mally's round face. Jony had her father Jonat's long thin one, with large eyes and nose. They both had Jonat's greeny-dark skin. Jony had his dark hair, too.

Arry stood in the doorway, wondering if she should catch Halver's eye. He was in the corner opposite Beldi's, with Con and Zia and Tany, writing something on the big slate. His pencil squeaked. Arry decided to talk to him later, and went on over to her companions. Beldi saw her first, and flashed her a delighted grin. Jony noticed that, and looked up, and moved aside so Arry could share her cushion. Tiln, his head bent over the map, never noticed. He did speak, after a few moments.

"Who drew this map?"

"How should we know?" said Jony.

"Why?" said Beldi.

"It's ugly."

Jony looked at Arry. There was a moment of perfect stillness. "How do you know?" Jony said to her half-brother.

Tiln said impatiently, "It's obvious. Look here." With a long grubby finger he traced the line the mountains of Fence's Country made southward into the Hidden Land, west to Druogonos, east to the Kingdom of Dust. "That's a bad shape," he said.

"Is it wrong?" said Jony, a little cautiously. "Are the mountains otherwise in truth?"

"How should I know? Ask Frances."

Frances had not known geography, Mally said; but she had, she said herself, been all over those mountains with people who did know it, as far as Outsiders could be said to know anything. Somebody in this corner of the room hurt. Arry looked at Beldi. He was eyeing the map, obedient and dutiful as always. But his eyes squinched a little, like somebody's with a headache. It was not his head that ached.

Arry felt as if hours had gone by, but when Jony spoke she was answering Tiln, as one did seem often to answer one's brother, a little scornfully. "We can't, oh doubter; she's gone."

"Mally says swearing means you aren't thinking."

"Frances is gone just the same," said Jony. Her head came up; Arry saw her searching for the authority to back up what she had said. Jony looked at Arry, who shrugged at her; at Beldi, who was staring steadfastly at the map. "Mally and Halver said so," said Jony.

"What are we supposed to be studying here?" said Arry.

"Halver supposes us to be memorizing the map," said Jony. "Tiln got us off track, worrying about how the mountains look."

"You aren't sheep," said Tiln, moving his dirty finger along a river with "Owlswater" written along it. "I'm not a sheepdog."

"Mally says you are utterly without the ability to comprehend metaphor."

"What's metaphor?" said Arry.

Jony blushed a little. "She said I should ask Sune or Halver, but I forgot."

"It's saying something's like something else when it isn't really," said Tiln, impatiently.

I think I do that all the time, thought Arry. She said, "Have you looked at the map enough? Shall you draw it while I watch to see if you're right?"

"Yes, or Halver will say something about all this talking." Jony took out their slate and went to work. She could draw all the lines perfectly, mountains, rivers, lakes, the desert of sand and the desert of dust and the desert of salt water. She could name them all, too. But she had not learned where the lines went between all the little countries. Arry pointed this out, and Jony said crossly, "It makes no sense anyway."

"Where do the wolves come from?" asked Beldi. He had been quiet so long that all three of them jumped.

Jony shouldered Tiln aside a little and looked at the original map. "Derry says here," she said, laying her clean dark hand on the western edge of the Dubious

Hills. "Halver says they come from Fence's Country and also Wormsreign. Sune says they used to be in Druogonos, too, but Belaparthalion drove them out."

"Who?" said Tiln, looking up.

"Sune says he was a dragon."

"What about the Hidden Land?" said Beldi.

"Sune says they used to have wolves a long time ago but Belaparthalion drove them out of there as well," said Jony.

"Can you draw the map?" Arry asked Beldi.

Jony handed him the pencil and wiped her own correct and nameless offering from the slate.

By the time Halver was ready for them they could all draw the map and name everything on it, and Tiln had insisted on drawing a new map with the mountains in a more beautiful configuration. Halver walked over to their corner and caught sight of it just as Jony, to Tiln's protests, wiped half of it away.

"What's the matter?" said Halver.

"Tiln," said Jony, with a long-suffering air, "says the mountains aren't right."

"Which, these?" said Halver, touching with his own slate pencil the mountains at the Hidden Land's southern border. "He's probably right, though I don't know how he might know. It's difficult to get any geography in those lands right. The Wormsreign spells down there are thick as sorrel. How did you see that, Tiln?"

"Not those mountains," said Tiln. "Ours. They're ugly."

His tone made Halver look at him, and at Jony and at Arry. Beldi was wiping the rest of the map off the slate, and he kept on doing it as if nothing had been said.

"Are they?" said Halver.

"*Look* at them," said Tiln, impatiently. "Anybody can see it."

"No, I don't think so," said Halver. "Talk to Mally when you get home, and ask her to talk to me."

This time it was Tiln who became perfectly still. Arry looked at him. He was twelve. He hadn't started growing notably, his voice wasn't changing. Arry said, "Mally says knowledge comes with growing up. But he hasn't yet."

"Mally may say it," said Halver, almost absently, "but—" he stopped. Arry thought it was the four shocked stares that had awakened him. Nobody talked about Mally that way, any more than they would talk about Oonan or Arry or Derry or Halver himself, or anybody who had come into knowledge.

Halver looked around the circle of his students, and rubbed at the place on his hand where the sliver had been. It didn't hurt, but it was itching. Not really enough to make him behave so oddly. Arry concentrated on him. He had not slept, either. Perhaps that was it.

"Ask Mally when you go home," said Halver. "In the meantime, draw me these ugly mountains."

"I can't," said Tiln. "Truly, I can't. It makes my head hurt."

Halver looked at Arry. "Try a bit," said Arry. Tiln wrinkled up his forehead and did so. Arry nodded at Halver. "It does make his head hurt—Tiln! How do you know that?"

Tiln looked helpless. "Should I go home now?" he said.

"Yes," said Halver. "Jony can show you what else we do today."

Tiln stood up slowly. His face was more green than dark. He was as tall as Halver. "I'll see you at supper," he said to his sister, and went out of the schoolhouse, shutting the door quietly.

"Will we have a party?" said Beldi hopefully.

"If Mally says so," said Halver. "Now, tell me what I've said about the Owlswater."

While Jony did this, Arry looked attentive and remembered the day she came into knowledge. Her birthday, Wim said, was in August, and it had been her birthday. She was helping her mother put up the beans; there had been, Mally and Jony and Wim all agreed, an enormous crop that year. They were working in a wooden shed Frances and Beldi had made, with a roof for shade but open sides. Con had chosen that day to learn to walk, and being Con had toddled straight outside and put both hands in the fire they were cooking the beans over. It had hurt more than anything Arry had felt since, though probably less than having a baby. She had hated it. She screamed and grabbed Con, who of course had screamed too, deprived of her interesting play.

The celebration, which had had to wait until the bean crop was dealt with, had been awful too. Everybody treated her as if she were grown up, which was very nice, but it was all punctuated with the sensations of children burning their lips on their tea and Jony falling out of the pine tree and Con pulling the cat's tail and Zia hitting everybody she could reach, which she had been doing all year: Mally said that since Zia had survived that year she would probably live forever. Arry sometimes felt that anybody else who had survived Zia's bad year ought to live forever too.

The knowledge of pain had narrowed and sharpened over time, until people could fall out of trees a few hills away without Arry's starting up from her chair. But at the beginning it had been most horrible.

Did the ugly mountains make Tiln feel that way? Did every less-than-lovely thing he saw sting like the burn of hot tea? She should have attended to him more. He hadn't screamed, certainly.

But thinking of people who ought to be attended to—Halver was extremely uncomfortable, between his itching hand and his headache. Arry wondered if the sliver had had a sickness in it. She would have to stay and talk to him about it.

He was rather short with her when she did. "It isn't the sliver," he said. "Oonan looked at the wound and said all the wood was out and it would close up cleanly."

"Well, it's something," said Arry. "Maybe you should close school for a day or two, or let Sune read to us, perhaps."

Halver looked impatient, and then thoughtful. "Maybe I ought," he said. "Just until half-moon." He rubbed at his hand. "We'll let everyone come to school tomorrow as usual, and I'll tell them then, and give them a few lessons to do. And while school is closed they can help plant the beans." He beamed at her.

Arry felt uneasy, but she smiled back.

ONCE HOME, ARRY fed Con and Beldi early and set them to throwing pinecones for the cats, while she settled down with the rest of Mally's stories. The book covered in red leather had seven of them in it. The first one was called "The Cruel Sister." In it the older of two sisters drowned the younger so she could marry the younger's swain. The body of the drowned girl was found by two minstrels, who made a harp of her breastbone and took it to the wedding, where it accused her sister, who was then hanged. Arry could hardly bear to read it. What in the world was Mally thinking of?

She made herself some of the strong green tea from Wormsreign and started cautiously on the second story. It was devoid of hurtful things, merely detailing a young boy's meeting with a soldier on the road and their exchange of riddles. She looked at the third story. It was a song, but not one she had ever heard. In it a mother asked her son why his sword dripped with blood, and after telling her he had killed his hawk, his hound, and his horse without being believed, he told her he had killed his brother. She asked him what he would do now, and he told her; and when she asked what of his goods he would leave to his mother dear, he said, "The curse of hell to burn you with, mother, such counsels you did give to me."

Arry dropped the book. The cats both came running to see what it was, followed by Con and Beldi. Beldi picked the book up, smoothed the pages, and handed it to her.

"What's that?" said Con. "Will you read it to us?"

"No," said Arry.

"Why?"

"It'll hurt you."

"I bet it won't," said Con, climbing onto the arm of the chair.

Arry sighed and opened her mouth. Then she caught sight of Beldi. He was hanging back a little, his eyes still on the book he had handed back to her so carefully. He looked wistful.

Arry said, "Well, the one about the riddles is probably safe. Bring up another chair, Beldi."

Beldi did so solemnly, but some small tangle at the edge of Arry's mind smoothed itself out and vanished. She was still squinting after it when Con pulled her hair.

"Don't do that, it hurts," said Arry, opened the book, and began to read.

Con guessed all the riddles before Arry could read them. She did not word the answers as the book did, but Arry felt faintly alarmed nevertheless. Beldi looked chagrined.

"Read us another one," said Con.

She was now sitting on Arry's lap, and dislodging her would involve a great deal of work and more noise. Besides, it might be cruel. Arry paged past the awful song to the fourth story. Unlike the stories in the scrolls, none of these had a name. It began harmlessly enough—no swords dripping with blood, no vanishing parents, no older sisters—and if it were frightening, maybe that would show Con that Arry knew what she was doing. She began to read.

"In the dark long-ago, before all countries and all wizards, before books and castles and candles and water-jugs, the first people in the world were cold."

The story was about a dragon, never named, who was always too hot because of her armoring scales. She came to live with the cold people and after a time took pity on them. She flew far through the bright black spaces around the world until she found a star so small nobody could see it, and this she swallowed, and brought back to them, and showed them all the things they could do with fire.

Arry had begun to relax by this time: there seemed no hurt here. She read on through the triumphant cooking of food and forging of metal and baking of clay, until the dragon went back out to the bright black spaces, because it was too hot now where the people were. There the dragon met the great powers of the outside, who asked her what she had done with the star. When she told them, they were angry. And they took the dragon and put her in the hottest place they could find, and chained her to a rock, and sent an eagle every day to eat out her liver.

Arry stopped.

"Is that all?" said Con.

Arry squinted at her. She looked unalarmed; in fact interested.

"Did it hurt the dragon?" said Beldi.

"I'm sure it did," said Arry.

"Why were they angry?"

"I don't know, it doesn't say."

"Is that *all*?" said Con.

"How could it eat her liver more than once?" said Beldi. "Do dragons have lots of livers?"

"It says it grew back so the eagle could eat it again."

"Oh."

"Is that—"

"Not quite," said Arry, resigning herself. " 'And this is the fate of teachers, the best of which do their job featly just the same.' "

"That's all," said Con, contentedly, and she wormed her way down from Arry's lap and hurled a pinecone across the room.

The cats had long since fallen asleep on the hearth. Woollycat opened one eye, stretched, and subsided again. Con went over to poke their bellies and generally stir them up before they were ready, and Beldi said, "Is that really the fate of teachers? Will an eagle come and eat out Gnosi Halver's liver?"

"I don't think so," said Arry. "I'll ask Mally, shall I, and Sune; they know about these stories."

Beldi looked at her with no expression, nodded, and went away into the room he shared with Con. To the sounds of Con harrying the cats around the room, Arry began to read the fifth story. It was about a strange far-away place where it was never night except once in ten thousand years, and the bizarre ways in which people behaved when they were in darkness for the first time.

She was in darkness herself now: the last light of sunset was almost gone. The cats were back on the hearth in a heap.

"Con, Beldi," she called, "did you work your lessons?"

"You said no school tomorrow," said Con from their room.

"That's not the same as no lessons."

"But we can stay up far into the night and work them, then."

"Only if we light the lamp."

There was a stifled pause. Then Con said, "There was a time when meadow, grove, and stream, the earth, and every common sight, to me did seem appareled in celestial light."

The banked fire flared up like a hundred sunflowers. The lamp at Arry's elbow, two others awaiting cleaning in the corner, the long-unused one by her father's chair, burst into brightness. Arry jumped out of her chair and ran into the kitchen. Three more lamps, containing neither oil nor wick, burned like the sun in August. Arry moved pillows away from them and made certain there was nothing on the floor near them that might burn. Then she turned to go deal with Con, and found Con at her elbow, looking smug.

"Con, what did you do?"

"It's a spell," said Con. "Niss gave it to Mally, and Mally gave it to me. Mally said sometimes stronger spells work until you're seven or eight. She said some people don't ever lose their magic at all."

"Did she say you were one of them?"

In the brilliant light, Con's face took on a look that Arry instantly pegged as untrustworthy, though character was not her province and she did not remember seeing it on Con before. Con said, "I am one of them."

Arry bit her lip until the urge to reiterate her question had passed. "Do we have to have all of them burning?" she said, as temperately as she could manage. "It seems a bit of a waste." She was sorry as soon as she had said it, but Con's face did not fall.

Con said, staring hard at the three flaring lamps, "Turn whereso'er I may by night or day, the things that I could see I now can see no more."

The lamps went out. Arry turned fast, feeling frightened; but the glow from everything burning in the other room was still there. She went back to it, and Con went with her. After a while, Arry remembered to thank her.

Con and Beldi did stay up far into the night working their lessons. Arry sat in the chair and pretended to read more stories. She had had enough for the time being; she felt like an overrisen loaf, and expected to collapse into a flat puddle of sour thoughts at any moment. Just before she roused herself to hustle Con and Beldi off to bed, she did page through the green-covered book and find one very short story that looked as if it might not bite one's mind. It was called "King Conrad and the Forty-Nine Advisors," and was a tale of the Hidden Land. Arry read it with considerable satisfaction. Then she packed Con and Beldi off to bed (where they were willing to go by then, although they put up a protest to retain their dignity), and fell blankly into bed herself.

She woke suddenly to a cold gray light punctuated with the howling of wolves. Arry got up in a hurry, entangled in her quilt, and made sure Con and Beldi were still sleeping. Then she stood for a moment until she thought she had located the howls, and pressed her nose to the glass of her bedroom window.

She jumped back before she could govern herself. The largest wolf was right outside the window. When it saw her, it stopped howling. Once again, it stared at her with a disapproving, bitter scrutiny that no wolf's face was made to express. Arry stepped forward again. Was it hurt?

The wolf held up one front paw. She could see nothing amiss with it in the moonlight, but it might well have festered; or perhaps she had not gotten quite all the thorn out; or the thorn had carried dirt or irritant sap into the wound. Any of those was quite possible. She knew nothing, but with the glass and the walls of the house and this being a wolf and not a fellow person, she might not know unless she were closer, as she had been on the night she took out the thorn.

She would have to go out, and go out in such a way that the wolf would stand no chance of getting in.

She put on an assortment of warm clothes over her nightgown, and went into the main room to get her boots from beside the fire. She picked up the poker, and put it down again. It had not hurt her before; why should it hurt her now? Because it's a wolf, Derry would say, and that is its nature.

She put on her boots and went to the door. It opened inward, unfortunately. The wolf howled again, from the back of the house. Well, then. Arry moved the bolt back, opened the door a very little, slid herself through the smallest opening, and shut the door. It was cold out. The moonlight made it colder. A little wind searched out the vents in her strange assortment of garments. With a slither of fur and the click of claws, the wolf came around the side of the house and stood still, looking at her.

Then the wolf came towards her, not quickly. Arry clenched her hands in the pockets of her jacket and stayed where she was. The animal padded right up to her and pushed her shoulder with its nose. Arry heard herself squeak, a foolish sound.

"What?" she said.

The wolf pushed again. Arry turned her back on it, which made her stomach hurt though her stomach was not injured in the least, and took a few steps. It slid past her and trotted ahead, just like a huge dog, except that it did not wag its tail or even look over its shoulder to see if she were following.

She followed. They came to the top of a hill; the wolf stopped and sat down. Arry, who was out of breath, stopped too. All the houses she could see were dark. The moonlight made them like toys to hang on your winter tree, little and shining. She wished it would do the same to the wolf, but the wolf was too close, and breathing. She thought about its paw again. It was a little sore, perhaps.

"Let me look at your paw," she said, frightening herself even as she made the words.

The wolf, unperturbed, held up one paw without looking at her. Arry squatted down and took it. Yes, this was the one, healing well but still tender.

"Maybe you shouldn't walk on that," she said.

The wolf turned its head and stared her in the eyes. Its breath dampened her cheek. Its eyes were green, were red, were silver in the moon. It exhaled suddenly in a sound that was not exactly a growl. Arry sat down just as suddenly, in startlement; and the wolf made a

sound that was nothing like a bark, a kind of strangled
wheezing, like somebody trying to laugh with no breath
left.

The path was damp. Arry put her hand on a cold
rock and got up again. The wolf gave another wheeze or
two, and getting up itself it went trotting down the path,
tail waving. Arry went after it. She hoped Con and Beldi
wouldn't wake up and go padding around in the dark
looking for her.

Up hill and down and up in the chilly spring night,
where the mist lay on the new grass and the trees rustled
their new leaves. The wolf was going to Halver's house.
Was Halver hurt, had the sliver in his hand festered, had
the wolf hurt him—and come for help? Arry snorted
under her breath; the wolf never looked back.

The door to the schoolroom was open. Firelight and
lamplight slid out and made a strange green and gold
square in the dim moonlit dark.

"Halver?" called Arry; it seemed wrong to let a large
wolf walk over his threshold without giving some sort of
warning.

The wolf looked over its shoulder at her and then
trotted briskly into the house. Arry followed, taking the
time to kick off her boots and leave them on the rug by
the door. The wolf was leaving muddy footprints all
over.

The lamp was in the schoolroom, the fire in Halver's
room beyond. Arry had seldom been there. She put her
head around the edge of the door. The bed was empty,
flat and smooth. The window was open. The clothes
Halver had been wearing earlier were folded and
stacked on the clothes-chest.

The wolf was sitting in Halver's red chair; Arry's

mother had made that one, as she had made many of the chairs people seemed to like best.

"You're getting that all muddy," said Arry. Her voice cracked. "Where's Halver?"

The wolf lifted one front paw and licked at it, delicately. It itched. Oonan would know if the thorn were all out, if the wound would heal cleanly.

People broke in much the same ways, said Oonan; but no two people hurt in the same way, each of them felt different from all the others.

"Halver," said Arry.

The wolf came down from the chair and licked her hand.

ARRY SAT ON the floor with the mud Halver had tracked in soaking through her nightgown, and Halver laid his large hairy gray point-eared head on her knee, and they waited. She asked him several times what they were waiting for, but he only growled a little. She was puzzled because, aside from the paw, he was in much less pain than he had been earlier today, when he was not a wolf. Headache, irritation, sleeplessness, none of those troubled him in the least. Arry tried to notice the other forms of hurt, the ones she was just discovering; but with Halver in this form she could notice nothing. She thought a great deal about wolves. Her mother had told her that the Hidden Land had fought several great battles with shapeshifters (nobody in Arry's village knew about shapeshifters), but none of those had been wolves.

Her left leg fell asleep. When she twitched it, Halver growled again.

"My leg's asleep," said Arry.

Halver got up, walked around behind her to her other side, and settled back in with his head on her right knee. The bar of moonlight moved across the room. The fire burned low. Arry dozed and woke and thought she stayed awake until a shrill outburst of birdsong made her open her eyes. The sun had come up. Arry was considering what might be the effect of announcing that she was cold, when Halver shot to his feet and ran through the doorway into the schoolroom. When she stood up stiffly, he growled. Arry stood shaking the cramps out of her knees and listening for what he had heard. The sun could slip only a sliver of light into this shuttered room, and the fire gave no useful light.

Arry was assaulted by a sensation less like pain than like an enormous dislocation, like the huge twitch one sometimes gave just before falling asleep, having half-dreamed that one had stepped too near the edge of a cliff and slipped. In the schoolroom, something rustled, and somebody two-legged strode across the floor and stopped in the doorway.

"Let's have some light, shall we?" said Halver.

He walked on past Arry, bent to the embers of the fire, and stood up with a lighted lantern in his hand. He had put on a black gown; Arry and Oonan each had one like it, for greeting strangers, when there were any. He was barefoot. His yellow hair curled over his forehead and around his sweaty neck. His head hurt, his back hurt, his hand hurt. He was feverish.

He smiled at her. The light flashed on his teeth and put a red spark in each eye. A man who had been a wolf was far more a cause for unease than the wolf he had been.

Arry swallowed. "Have you been to see Oonan?"

"No," said Halver. "I wanted to see you first. Which hurts the more, the wolf or the man?"

"The man," said Arry, "at the moment. But—"

"I knew that," said Halver, tranquilly.

He smiled again, and Arry wished for the wolf back, even the wolf of two nights ago, rattling the milk pans, growling. She said, "I think you should see Oonan."

"I shall, in time," said Halver. "In the meantime I bind you to secrecy by the certainty of knowledge and the strictures of doubt."

"You do?" said Arry. He could do it; he was the Gnosi. But he was sick; need she heed him? "What is the occasion?" she said cautiously. Mally said Halver was touchy about his prerogatives, as anybody saddled with everybody's children for hours every day might well be. It made him speak sharply sometimes.

He did not speak sharply now. "The occasion," he said, as if he were explaining geometry to Zia, "is the breaking of history. I so bind you; do you submit, or lodge protest?"

Arry thought fast, keeping her eyes on Halver's expression of mild inquiry and her heart on his various pains. She would have liked very much to know if he had the power to change back into a wolf should she displease him. Even more she would have liked to know what had precedence here. He was her teacher; Mally had said she was yet uneducated; by what he knew and she did not, he had the right to bind her to secrecy. He had taught her so himself.

She took a deep breath. "Until my knowledge outrunneth yours," she said, "I do so submit."

She had used the least of the three possible promises, and Halver looked displeased. All he said was, "Sit down now, and listen."

"You always said we learned better after a good night's sleep," said Arry.

"There are too few nights left," said Halver.

Arry sat down, on a chair this time. Halver sat down too, on the floor, which felt wrong. Arry was not used to looking down at him. She did so anyway, as austerely as she could manage. Halver, no more moved by this than he had ever been by anybody's tantrums, scratched his hand briefly and smiled yet again.

"Did Frances tell you about shapeshifters?" he said.

"A little," said Arry.

"I am not one of them," said Halver. "They are distinguished by a multiplicity of shapes and by the operations of will upon their changes. Also they are born so, from parents the same as they. The condition I have comes upon one like a sickness, passed from the already infected to the still healthy; and is governed by the changes of the moon."

"How is the sickness passed?" said Arry, wishing for Oonan.

"It is not a sickness," said Halver, very sharply indeed. "It is merely passed like one."

"Like which one?" said Arry, becoming irate herself. "This is my province, Gnosi."

"Where's the pain in it?" demanded Halver.

"In your voice," said Arry. "In every moment you are a man and not a wolf. *How is this passed?*"

"Physici," said Halver, much more coolly, "you ascribe the pain to the wrong causes. But I shall answer your question, because it is my place to teach you."

Arry looked at him, as steadily as she could manage,

and bit gently on her tongue to keep herself from saying what she wanted to say.

"It is passed by biting," said Halver.

"Where? Let me see. Where is the pain in it, indeed."

"Or by choice."

"What?"

"I had thought I might teach about the moon," said Halver. "We have no one who knows about it, since Frances left; but I had Sune read what Frances wrote, and what others wrote, and on the first night it was full I stayed up to look at it. And the wolves came, two of them. They looked at me, as I looked at you on the path. What did you think, then?"

"Nothing," said Arry, and then, "That you might not be a wolf exactly; but I had thought that already, because of what Oonan said, and what he said Derry said, and the other things you'd done."

"What I thought," said Halver, "was a spell I had not heard, a spell that Niss, when I asked her, did not know." He shut his eyes, and said, "Feet in the jungle that leave no mark, eyes that can see in the dark, the dark, tongue, give tongue to it, hark—"

Arry felt the spell, as she had rarely felt any: when Oonan cursed the wolves in the meadow, she had understood the intent if not the words; when Con summoned the fire, the words had been plain to her. But this was like wind, like rain on your head, like mud sucking you down. She stood up, fast, took three quick steps backwards, and tripped on an end of her shawl that had come unwound. She caught herself on Halver's table; and it was the shock of almost falling that woke her up, as the same sensation will wake people from the edge of sleep.

"What are you doing?" she said. "That's not choice."

"Oh, yes, it is," said Halver. "You chose to stand up. The rest follows."

"Who would choose to sit still?"

"I did," said Halver. "For the knowledge I would have of it."

"How did you know you would have knowledge?"

"I am a teacher."

"Well, I'm not."

"There might be knowledge suited to you as well, in running under the moon."

He did not, Arry noticed, say, "might have been." He did not think that her having chosen to stand up meant there was no knowledge for her in this change.

"I think I need to go home now," she said.

"I'll walk with you," said Halver.

What's out there worse than you? thought Arry, and glanced swiftly at Halver, as if he might have heard her. The thought had come with the solidity of knowledge, and yet it was a question. Her head hurt. If she had such thoughts of Halver, he must be hurting her. She yanked up the trailing end of shawl. "Thank you," she said, and led the way outside.

It was even colder, and beginning to be misty. The moon was down. The wind had dropped, but the early sunlight dripped onto her shivering head like milk that had been down the well for a week. I'm sickening for something, thought Arry; it's the ague.

Halver delivered her to her front door, bowed, and

walked away into the morning. Arry slipped inside, bolted the door, and jumped like a pinched melon seed at the touch of a cat's cold nose on the calf of her leg. She had to sit down on the floor while both of them sniffed her over thoroughly, with special attention to the folds of nightgown and skirt and shawl on which Halver had laid his wolf head.

While she sat, she thought, and came to the dismal conclusion that, since she could not tell anybody what had happened to Halver, or ask any questions that might lead them to find it out, she must do a great deal of discovery herself. Trying to find out what ailed Con was tangled and time-consuming enough; this would be far worse. Unless, she thought. Unless. Unless the pain this state caused Halver was of the same sort as the pain she thought she knew in Con. Then her knowledge would truly outrun Halver's, she would be free to tell Oonan all about it, and she might in the end know what to do about Con.

That was a pleasant story, but it did not feel at all right. Arry sighed heavily, dislodged the long-somnolent cats from her lap, and went to have a look at her brother and sister. Beldi was in bed where he belonged, and had not even kicked his quilts off. Con was not in bed, nor in the main room, where she occasionally crawled under the table to sleep; she was in a corner of the washing-room, in one of the beds Arry had made for the cats before it became evident that if you made a bed for a cat, the cat would never sleep in it—even in the warmest room in the house. Arry covered Con with Con's own towel, which, because Con had not washed as she should, was quite dry. Then she went to bed herself.

Falling asleep was difficult. Over and over she half-dreamed she slipped going down a muddy hill, fell out of bed, fell out of the pine tree, missed the slate step at Sune's front door; and came wide awake at once each time she began to fall. When she did sleep, she dreamed about wolves. They sat in the kitchen and looked at her; they tripped her up when she went outside; they lay before the fire at night and showed her their red jeweled eyes. When one of them—not Halver—bit her on the wrist, she woke up, and discovered that Con was poking her arm and saying plaintively, "Who put this towel on me, Arry?" over and over.

"Towel-sprites, no doubt," said Arry, sitting up.

"Halver says swearing means—"

"I've heard him. Go get dressed, Con, and wash your face and hands, or the towel-sprites will cover you with water next time."

"You don't know about towel-sprites."

"Neither do you."

"I will, though," said Con, cheerfully, and ran out of the room.

Arry put her head in her hands, pushing away the dim chorus of who said what about children, the future, morning, sunlight, dreams, cats, cotton, wood, going barefoot, eating breakfast.

"There's no food," said Beldi from the doorway.

"Certainly there is," said Arry, without moving her hands.

"If Con can make fire, why can't she make potatoes?"

"Ask her," said Arry, and then yelled, "No, don't!" at the empty doorway.

She got out of bed. "Maybe I'd rather be bitten by a wolf after all," she snarled at the sunlight.

CON REFUSED TO eat breakfast, saying she was going outside to make not just potatoes, but potato pancakes and the strawberries and cream to go with them, and to eat everything all by herself. Arry and Beldi sat on the floor by the fire, roasting potatoes in the embers and burning their fingers. The cats had gone outside with Con, possibly to find mice, more likely in search of somebody with milk to spare.

Con had not gone far: Arry could feel her seething out there, in a way very unsettling to good digestion.

Beldi said, "Are you going round to get more food today?"

It was certainly past time to do it. But the people from whom Arry would be getting the food would not, except for Derry, be the ones she needed to ask questions of. She said carefully, "I was going to ask you and Con to do it."

"Con won't do anything," said Beldi.

"I thought of asking Mally to take her," said Arry.

"If I can go by myself I'll get the food," said Beldi at once.

"Will you watch her while I go ask Mally?"

"If you hurry."

Arry scraped the last bit of her potato out of its blackened skin with her bottom teeth, and decided against having another. Better to go before Beldi changed his mind or Con wandered off too far and did something indescribable. Besides, if she left a potato or two, Con might eat them once Arry was safely gone.

"Con ought to eat something," she said to Beldi, opening the door.

Beldi gave her an eloquent look, as if she had told him that the sun should shine on a rainy day. Very nice, no doubt, but not easy of accomplishment. They went outside. The morning was half over, but still rather chilly. The sun had burned the mists away. It lay kindly on the small new leaves of the ash trees and on all the beginning grass. In the brown needles and rocks under the pine tree all the crocuses had bloomed. They were so late this year Derry had said perhaps mice had eaten them.

"Tiln should see *that*," said Arry.

Beldi looked at her.

"If he knows what's beautiful."

"I thought he knew what was ugly."

"Mustn't it be both?"

"Well, you know what hurts, but do you know what feels good?"

"I know what stops the hurting."

"Yes, but—"

"I see what you mean. I'll ask Mally, maybe."

"There's Con," said Beldi.

She was sitting with her back to them, on the rock where Arry had left the milk pans, singing a song with no words.

"I'll be as quick as I can," Arry said to Beldi, and ran down the hill, away from both of them and the house and all.

The mud of the paths was drier. In the meadows between the hills, the old dead grass was undercut with new green, and starred with minute blue and white and bright yellow. High up in the dazzling air a lark was singing. It was the first one Arry had heard this year. Somebody had called it, perhaps. There was a song for it. Hark, hark, the lark at heaven's gate sings, and Phoebus 'gins arise, his steeds to water at those springs on chaliced flowers that lies, eyes that can see in the dark, the dark.

Arry stopped running and sat down on a rock. Her shadow was plain before her, tangled hair, fringed scarf, shaking hand; but she felt as if there were some large shape between her and the sun. Her heart hurt her. Her stomach jerked, as if she had missed a step and almost fallen.

"Oh, no," she said, with what breath she had. "No wolves."

She looked over her shoulder, and the mild meadow smiled back at her. Her mother had once taught her a charm against the nightmare, which she said worked for as long as a child had need of it, even if the child's other magic had waned already. She said shakily, "You spotted snakes with double tongue, thorny hedgehogs, be not seen; Newts and blindworms do no wrong." She was getting her breath back. "Never harm," she sang, "nor spell, nor charm, come our lovely lady nigh. So good night, sing lullaby." Which was funny enough in the bright morning that she laughed, and got up, and went on. But she kept an eye on her shadow, in case she should see another following it. She could not decide whether to see Halver as soon as she had delivered Con, or to avoid him as long as she could, while she gathered more stories.

Mally's door was shut. Arry beat on it with the knocker. She could hear the dog barking inside, but nothing else for a long time. If Tiln had his knowledge, perhaps they had stayed up late drinking to it. She banged again. It was not early by anybody's standards but Oonan's.

"They're putting the beans in," said a shrill voice behind her.

Arry gripped the knocker hard, and managed not to jump visibly. She turned around. It was Mora, Mally and Jonat's youngest; she was Con's age, but they did not often play together. They would do it today, if Arry had anything to say about it.

"Are you all by yourself?" she said.

Mora wrinkled her nose. Even so young, it looked like Jonat's formidable beak. "Blackie's here," she said.

"But he's in the house and you're outside."

Mora looked guilty. "I was *going* in," she said.

Arry gave up any notion of leaving two children with the dog instead of one. Suggesting that Halver let school out for a few days had not been so fine a thing as she had thought.

"You go in, then," she said, "and I'll find Mally. I was hoping Con could come play with you today."

"She likes Zia," said Mora, with finality. "I'm not

brown enough for her.'' She was in fact greeny-brown like Jony, and her hair was much the same shade as her skin.

"I didn't know Con demanded brownness in her friends,'' said Arry, rather haphazardly.

"Mally knows, though,'' said Mora.

There was no arguing with that. "Well, I'll go talk to her, then,'' said Arry. She stood waiting, and after a moment Mora opened the door, went into the house, and shut the door again.

Arry set off down the hill for the bean fields. It was getting warmer. As she came down the hill into the plowed field, the heat hit her in the face as if she had leaned very close to a fire. She passed Lina sitting on a rock, eyes closed, face fierce. She was chanting, "Sumer is icumen in, lude sing cuckoo.''

That spell was so old the language had changed since somebody wrote it down. Arry went by her softly, and stood at the bottom of the slope looking at the figures scattered over the tumbled dirt. Most of them were small; but there was Mally. Arry walked along the path until she was at the end of Mally's furrow. It was hugely and impossibly hot. The sun and sky could not have made it so hot down here. Arry waved, and after a moment called. Mally unstooped herself and came briskly along the furrow to Arry. Her face was damp and shiny and red. Her white hair looked like a hundred seeding dandelions after a rainstorm. She seemed extremely pleased.

"Why is it so hot?'' said Arry.

"Beans need warm soil, but we really couldn't wait any longer to plant them if we want three crops. Lina may be overdoing it a bit. Have you come to help?''

"I can't today. I'm seeking knowledge. I wondered if Con could come play with Mora, but Mora says Con thinks Mora's not brown enough. And two of them with only the dog might mean mischief."

"Send her here," said Mally. "We'll see if she can make the beans fly through the air and bury themselves in the proper places."

"I will, then," said Arry, a little faintly. "Thank you. I wanted to ask," she added, as Mally showed signs of going back to work, "if she told me aright, that you've given her very powerful spells and think she may not lose her magic at all, and grow up to be a wizard."

"I told you I thought she might be a wizard," said Mally. "There's no knowing until the time comes. I do think she may never lose her magic."

"Doesn't that always mean a wizard?"

"No," said Mally. "Your mother never lost hers either."

"She wasn't even born here."

"It's the water," said Mally. "The earth, the air, something. Born doesn't matter."

"Mally, do wizards, or people who are going to be, hurt differently than others?"

"How should I know?" said Mally, gently enough.

"Isn't that a part of what they're like, a part of their character? Wouldn't you know?"

"You'd think so, wouldn't you?" said Mally.

Arry looked at her. Not being Mally herself, Arry did not know what Mally was like. But she had experience; and her experience told her that it was unlikely, after such an exchange, that Mally would answer the question, no matter how long she was looked at.

"I'll send Con along," said Arry, and turned back up the hill.

Lina had stopped chanting, and when Arry drew level with her, she opened her eyes and said, "Is it hot enough for you?"

"Yes," said Arry. "But I'm not a bean."

"Beans like it hot," said Lina. "Beans hate it cold."

"So I understand," said Arry, and went her way.

Having dispatched Beldi, scowling, with Con, protesting, she sat down on her own front doorstep and thought about the order of her visits. She thought Sune had agreed to come by for those old clothes of Con's, but she could not remember. She could take the clothes to Sune, find out what stories Sune knew about wolves and what Sune thought of the stories Mally had lent her; then, when she had nothing to carry, she could go the long hilly way to Derry's house and ask about wolves. Vand or Derry would give her honey and oats and possibly some aged cheese if it were ready, and milk if there was any and Sune hadn't had it all. Oonan lived close to home: she could take him in last of all, and if she were lucky he would give her some tea.

It would have been much easier just to go to school.

Sune was sitting in her rocking chair and spinning, as she had been before; but she had moved the rocker outside into the sunlight. On her bent head the short, smooth yellow hair glowed like the flame of a well-tended lamp. When she heard Arry coming, she looked up. Her face was a little puffy, and she felt generally puffy as well; nothing hurt at the moment, though, and the baby was quiet.

"Oh, thank you," said Sune, looking at Arry's basket of clothes. "Just put them inside the door."

"They're not as tidy as I remembered them," said Arry, coming back out and sitting down in the grass by Sune's chair. "Con was very vigorous with them."

"Knot won't mind," said Sune. "Maybe by the time she's old enough to notice I'll have made her something new."

"Have you thought of her whole name?" said Arry.

"Well, I've been thinking what Knot would be short for, but it's heavy going. Nottingham, Nostradamus, that's all I can think of. We might make a joke of it, I suppose. The Unicornish for knot is kathamma. That might be pretty."

Arry wondered if they would be able to ask Tiln. She had not asked Mally about him, nor seen him in the field. She said, "My mother said our grandmother was called Kath."

"That would be from Katherine," said Sune, nodding. "That's a common Hiddenlander name." She smiled. "If I wanted a double joke, I could call her Katherine."

The baby kicked her.

"Or maybe not," said Sune. Then she smiled in a startled way, and Arry laughed, because what Sune had just said was a joke, too, but she had not meant it so. Sune put down her spindle and looked at Arry. "You wanted me to think on those stories, didn't you, and read more of them?"

Arry nodded.

Sune said, "Some of them are history and some are mighthavebeens. But for the moment we'll put them all together and call them stories. If we do, we see that they aren't of a kind. Some of them are about parents leaving, and what happens to their children; but only some. That's what you asked Mally about, isn't it?''

Arry nodded again.

''So she wants you to think not just about parents leaving, but what kind of occasion that is. All I can see now is that all these stories are about change, change of every kind, and what people do when it happens. Some of them make it happen. And—I wonder if Mally meant this—many of them are about the kind of cruelty the Eight Shapers wanted to make impossible. It never happens here; none of us could do those things.''

''Thank you,'' said Arry, faintly.

''Think about it,'' said Sune.

''I will. I also wanted to ask, have you any stories about wolves?''

''I had most of them from Derry, who knows better than I,'' said Sune, ''except for one book from Fence's Country about the Lukanthropoi.''

''The what?''

''Wolf-people,'' said Sune.

Arry felt cold. ''What are they?''

''A strange sort of shapeshifter,'' said Sune. ''They turn to wolves at the full of the moon, and they change whether they will or no. Prospero thinks it a curse of the Unicorns on oathbreakers; Chalcedony writes that it is one of the failed spells from the Wars of the Sorcerers' Schools; but their accounts jar so it's hard to know anything. I don't like reading them close together, but that is how one must.''

''Do you think,'' said Arry, she could not tell why, ''that the stories might be mighthavebeens and not history?''

''I've thought of it,'' said Sune, ''but—'' She frowned.

"I have never found anybody who understood this," she said. "Some things I read I know are true; some things I know are not; but many may be either, and then there's only feeling, like one thread in a carpet. My feeling says there is history here. But sometimes a thing might *feel* true to me, not because it is, but because the writer believes it is."

Arry stood up. "I have to go about and collect food. Do you need anything?"

"No," said Sune, placidly. "The clothes were all. I'm well provided otherwise."

Arry went off thoughtfully. Sune was not obliged to say who Knot's father was, but Mally said Sune was the first mother since Mally's own great-grandmother who had chosen not to say. Sune had no brother or sister to object if a father moved in with her; but perhaps she liked her solitude. How strange it sounded, not even to read a thing and know it, truly or falsely; how strange to have a thing neither known nor denied, in the very field and center of your knowledge. Perhaps it was hard to live with anybody else's certainties. She would have to ask Mally, in case this might hurt one day.

Vand and Derry lived in a large stone house with a slate roof. Wim said it was the oldest house in the Dubious Hills. The path leading up to it was of slate too. Alongside the path and in every crack it offered, the crocuses, like Arry's, were blooming. All of these were purple. Vand and Derry's three black dogs lay in the sun by the front door. None of them got up, but their eyes followed Arry. She banged the knocker, an iron bee with outspread wings, onto the iron sunflower intended for this purpose.

Derry opened the door, and smiled at once. "I wondered where you were," she said. "You three must be getting hungry. Come in." She was very tall, and large as well, with short black hair and blue eyes and a nose like the curved bill of one of her known birds.

"I wanted to ask you some things, too," said Arry, following her into the kitchen, which the builders of the house had put at the front. On the wooden table were a bag of oats, a crock of honey, and a large wheel of cheese. Arry felt cheered.

"You forgot your basket," said Derry, putting the kettle on the stove and opening the oven door to poke at the fire.

"Oh, I did—I took some of Con's clothes to Sune in it."

"I'll find you an old one." Derry spooned tea into a green pot and sat down at one end of the table. "What did you want to know about wolves?"

"Well," said Arry. It struck her that she wanted to know only about those aspects of the wolf that Halver might manifest. "Just what you'd tell the children if Halver asked you down to school."

"Didn't you listen the last time I came?"

"That was the day Zia ate the nightshade."

"Of course," said Derry. "Well, then." She folded her large hands under her chin, and her face grew vague. "Wolves live all over the world," she said. "In the mountains of Druogonos, on the plains before Worms-reign, in the far frozen wastes both north and south, in the forests of the Secret Country and the jungle of the Outer Isles and in our own hills. They are of the family of dogs and foxes and jackals, as can be seen by the skull and the foot and the tooth of all these. They may hunt alone or in little groups or in packs of many. They run their prey until they have tired or trapped it and then they kill."

"Oonan said you said that the things that got his sheep didn't kill like wolves?"

"So they did not, though sheep seem made for just this; they are so easy to panic, and where one goes they all follow. But these creatures were much quicker about it. Oonan wondered if very hungry wolves might do otherwise than a wolf ought, but I know not. Also, if they had been hungry, they would have eaten."

"What sort of predator does behave like that?"

"Killing and not eating?" said Derry. "We do."

"We?"

"Not here; we know better. But people in the world, they do kill and not eat."

"Do all of us here know better?"

"I would expect so, but you'd best ask Mally."

The kettle was boiling. Derry poured the water over the tea in the green pot, which revealed itself by the sharp smell to be raspberry leaves and lemon verbena. Arry drank hers gloomily. She was tired of asking Mally; and anyway, Mally so seldom gave you a straight answer. Know better, she thought, nodding from time to time and smiling when it seemed necessary at Derry's account of how cats hunted. We all know better than to kill and not eat. How do we?

She put her mug down. Halver did not know better. If he ever had, now he did not. He did not know what even the wolves knew.

"More tea?" said Derry. "Or home to your hungry ones?"

"Home," said Arry. "Thank you." She waited while Derry put the food in a flat willow basket, thanked her again, and went back outside. The wind had died. It was warmer, though not a patch on the beanfield. Arry walked carefully through the crocuses. Clothes, she thought, food, ask Derry, ask Sune, ask Mally. Mally might answer better when she was not sweating in the beanfield and supervising twenty-five children. After supper, then.

Arry went home and baked scones.

WHEN THE SCONES were done and cooling, she
swept all the floors and, now that Con seemed resigned
to using it, began trying to make the kitchen habitable
again. All the abandoned messes and projects made her
gloomy. She thought she might scrub the pillows the
cats had thrown up on and leave it at that. Oh, doubt,
what a pity there *was* no doubt what all that dried stuff
had been before it was eaten. She began to think hard
to distract her own stomach, which was unhappy with
the pains of the voles the cats had caught.

Halver was, of course, the prime thing to be thinking
about. Arry wondered whether it was worth the trouble
to go to bed tonight. Possibly Halver had made the reve-
lation he wished to make and would be satisfied; but just
as possibly he would want to argue with her again. Of
course, he could do that in the daytime. Unless he was
now sleeping all day. Possibly, too, what the wolf did and
what the man did had no necessary or probable connec-

tion. If he turned up tonight in the one form, she would certainly ask him in the other. It would help her decide whether she must do anything, whether his actions fell within her province.

Con and Beldi came home. Con seemed smug and Beldi exhausted. Arry washed Con, who had apparently preferred wallowing in the dirt to firing off beans like stones from a sling, fed both of them, and sat them down to their lessons. Beldi had brought milk, herbs, potatoes, and, unexpectedly, a large sack of walnuts that, he said, Zia had insisted on giving him when he fetched Con from the beanfield. Arry suspected some less than benign intention on Zia's part, but Con had only looked mysterious, not put-upon. Just the same, it seemed better not to leave them and go ask Mally questions. Tomorrow would serve well enough.

Arry curled up in the chair, Sheepnose under it and Woollycat in her lap, and thumbed through the last of the stories Mally had given her. This collection was the strangest of all. It was all in verse, like spells, but it was not spells; or at least, while you could have used bits of it for magic, each piece of verse seemed to be a story of one sort or another: people acted, spoke to one another, lost or found things. Reminding herself to think of change and its effects, Arry began to read.

> "There lived a wife in Usher's Well
>   A wealthy wife was she
>   She had three stout and stalwart sons
>   And sent them o'er the sea."

The sons were lost at sea; whereupon, in a spell Arry could tell was a powerful one, the wife threatened to make storms until they returned to her in earthly flesh and blood. When the nights were long and dark, they did return (Arry wondered what all the wife's neighbors had thought of the wind's never ceasing, nor flashes in the flood, all that time). The returning sons' hats were made of bark. Their mother blew up the fire and brought water from the well and everything was as it had been, until the blood-red cock crowed and then the gray, and the sons said it was time they were away, that they must go from Usher's Well to the gates of Paradise. So they did. If their mother made more storms, the story didn't say anything about it.

> "The King sits in Dunfermline town
>    Drinking of the bluid-red wine
>    O where shall I get a seely skipper
>    To sail this valiant ship of mine?"

A bonny boy who sat at the King's right knee said Sir Patrick Spens was the very best sailor who ever sailed upon the sea. Sir Patrick, when they came and told him, said he didn't know a thing about it, but he took the King's ship anyway. He saw the new moon with the old moon in her arms, and there was a dreadful storm, and the ship sank. Arry untucked the foot that had fallen asleep and tucked the other one under her. The white cat jumped down and bit the black one's tail; the black one hissed and they both tore across the room, and back, and into the kitchen.

The cats made more sense than the story, thought Arry. She felt exasperated. But why? Things happened, after all, and history told of them. Sune and Mally said so. Because these stories rhymed, or because Mally

had told her to read them, she wanted them to make
sense.

> "It little profits that an idle king,
>   By this still hearth, among these barren crags,
>   Matched with an aged wife, I mete and dole
>   Unequal laws unto a savage race
>   That hoard, and sleep, and feed, and know not me."

The idle king had been far from idle, it appeared: he
had been to places that sounded as if they came from
the same language as those in the curse Oonan flung at
the wolves; he had sailed and fought and governed. He
meant to leave the savage race to his son to rule and sail
off again with all his mariners, even if the gulfs washed
them down. He did not speak of his wife again, though
he had said that old age had still its honor and its toil.
He sounded, in his characterization of his subjects, like
Halver on a very bad day.

Arry shook her head, and read on.

> "Daylight's on the windowsill
>   Come you who are faithful still
>   Celebrate the work of will"

Arry did not understand most of it, but it rocked her on
to its ending, thus:

> "Though their elders shield the eye
>   Trembling as He passes by
>   Children know they cannot die."

Arry sat looking at this one for some considerable
time. She had not the faintest notion of what it might

mean, but it made the hair stand up on the back of her neck as if Con had left the door open in midwinter. She even got up and looked, but the door was shut, and bolted, and all the windows closed and shuttered too. She read again the lines that had made her go looking for the cold draft:

> "Children on the streets alone
> Wearing masks of black and bone
> In the shapes of things unknown."

Not if I can help it, thought Arry. She saw then that somebody had—of all the doubtful things—written in the margin of the book, just beside those lines, in a small square script: "Once out of nature."

This story made even less sense than the previous one, but it certainly had change in it. Once out of nature, what? Children would wear the forms of things unknown? Out of nature, thought Arry. Was that what Halver was? And yet shapeshifters were natural. Would Sune understand being asked if the same were true of the Lukanthropoi? She had better try it.

> "O what can ail thee, Knight at arms
> Alone and palely loitering?
> The sedge has withered from the Lake
> And no birds sing!"

The Knight replied that he was sad because he had met a beautiful lady in the meads, who took him up on her horse, fed him honeydew, sang to him, and kissed him, none of which seemed sad to Arry. But then he fell asleep, and dreamed he saw pale warriors, who cried,

"La Belle Dame sans Merci thee hath in thrall," and he woke up on the cold hillside.

In her warm chair, Arry hugged herself. She thought of the cruel stepmothers. Some of them were just cruel; some of them spoke kindly and then were cruel in the background. But the stepchildren had not seen any starved lips in the gloam, with horrid warning gaped wide. The Knight was luckier. But he was sad just the same. She turned the page.

> "And what was she, the Fairy Melusine?
> Men say, at night, around the castle-keep
> The black air ruffles neath the outstretched vans
> Of a long flying worm, whose sinewy tail
> And leather pinions beat the parted sky . . ."

Arry fell asleep, in the chair, pondering, and did not dream. One moment she was reading the long, difficult tale of the Fairy Melusina and her sons and husband, and the next somebody was making a doubtful racket and Con was pulling her sleeve and saying, "Arry, somebody's at the door."

Arry sat up, rubbing her eyes. The fire and the candles still burned bright. Con was still dressed. Arry got up stiffly. Somebody was indeed pounding on the door. Beldi stood staring at it, with the poker from the kitchen fireplace in his hand. He was wearing his nightshirt, and his hair stuck up all over his head.

"Who is it!" Arry yelled over the pounding.

"Oonan!" came the answer.

Arry unbolted the door and opened it a crack. Oonan, looking wild; nothing and nobody else. She let him in, slammed the door, and looked at Beldi, who leaned his poker against the wall and shot the bolt again. Oonan's chest hurt from running, his throat tasted like blood, he had a stitch in his side. He sat down on the nearest cushion and put his head between his knees. Behind the expected and familiar distresses of somebody who has run too far were pains Arry tried her best not to distinguish. Oonan had already made it quite clear that he did not want her identifying them.

"Con," she said, "get him some tea. Never mind if it's cold."

"I can heat it up," said Con, dashing into the kitchen. She came back cradling the large blue mug that Frances had drunk hot chocolate from, when there were milk and chocolate enough to make this feasible. She was crooning to it, "Oh for a beaker full of the warm South."

Oonan's tangled head came up sharply. He looked at Arry. She shrugged. "Con—" she said.

Con handed Oonan the mug. He thanked her gravely and sniffed at it. *"Con,"* he said. "This isn't tea."

"It's the blushful Hippocrene," said Con, quite smugly.

"And what do you suppose the blushful Hippocrene is?" said Oonan.

Con pointed at the mug.

"Con," said Arry.

"I don't know," said Con. "Yet."

"You may as well drink it," said Arry to Oonan. "It won't hurt you if that's all of it you drink."

"No?" said Oonan.

"Con," said Arry, "what made you think Oonan would like it?"

"It's for when your heart aches, and a drowsy numbness pains your sense," said Con.

"Con, that's a harvest spell," said Oonan. "You really mustn't misapply it."

"Who says?" said Con.

"Jonat and Niss say it's a harvest spell."

"Who says I mustn't?"

"I do," said Oonan, with great firmness. "You'll break it."

Con looked him hard in the face for quite some time. Finally she said, "Give me back the cup, then."

Oonan made a gesture at Arry and handed Con the cup. Con took it back into the kitchen. Arry let her breath out. Oonan had been right, she had been about to remonstrate.

"That's the question, isn't it?" said Oonan.

"What is?"

"Who says I mustn't?"

"I don't think it's my question," said Arry, carefully. He was very much put about, and still out of breath.

"In a moment," said Oonan; he seemed to be listening. Con was clattering and splashing in the kitchen— the kitchen she had refused to enter not so long ago. Arry looked at Oonan. He had his breath back. His throat still hurt a little, and his side; and whatever had made him run like that was still boiling in there.

Con came back with a steaming mug, which she delivered to Oonan. "Thank you, Con," said Oonan gravely.

Con gave him another long, hard look. Beldi called her from the back of the house, and she turned without a word and went out of the room. Oonan took a sip of his tea, and burned his tongue.

"What did she give you?" said Arry.

"It's just peppermint. However she may have obtained it."

"That's all right, there was some in the kitchen," said Arry.

Oonan put the mug down on the floor and ran both hands through his damp red hair, so that it looked more like a bird's nest than ever.

"What happened?" said Arry.

"The wolves came again," said Oonan. He almost always peered intently at the person to whom he was speaking, but he addressed these words to the floor. "They left the sheep alone this time. They ran me up and down the meadow until the sun came up and after, until the moon went down."

Arry felt as if she had been running herself. "What then?" she said.

"I can't tell you," said Oonan.

"But the moon was down."

"Yes."

They looked at one another. "All three wolves?" said Arry.

"No, the two smaller ones." Oonan was talking to the floor again.

"The large one came here last night," said Arry. "And took me for a walk to—and made me stay with it. Until the moon went down."

"I think you should watch with me tomorrow night," said Oonan.

"Or you should sleep with me," said Arry.

Oonan laughed; after a moment, so did Arry.

"I'm afraid," said Oonan, "that if they come to the sheep and I'm not there, they'll do more damage."

"Are you?" said Arry. He still would not look at her. She added, "I'll come by—when?"

"I think just after sunset should do nicely," said Oonan. "Grel says the moon doesn't properly rise at all tonight."

"Did they hurt you?"

"You know they didn't."

"There's something going on inside you."

Oonan raised his head and looked at her much as Con had just looked at him. "Have you talked to Mally?"

"I have. She wasn't very helpful."

Oonan hit his forehead lightly with the heel of his hand and looked stubborn. "I can talk to her again," offered Arry, with a despairing thought about what she could do with Con this time.

"It won't break anything," said Oonan.

"I will, then. Do you want something to eat?"

Oonan started to shake his head, and then looked at her. "I think I might," he said.

"Whom shall we ask?" said Arry, and leaving him laughing she went into the kitchen. Scones, cheese, honey. If Con really wanted to be helpful, she ought to speed up the process, whatever it was, that was the reason one soaked beans overnight before cooking them. Arry put three pounds of beans to soak and came back out with a tray. Oonan, his eyes closed, had leant his head against the wall behind him. His face was hollow, like a field after harvest. Arry put the tray down quietly, and he opened his eyes at once.

"I'm going to try to put Con to bed," said Arry.

"I shall stifle my natural instincts, then, should I hear screams," said Oonan.

Arry found Con asleep at the foot of Beldi's bed, wrapped in her towel. Beldi was in Con's bed, curled up tightly, her bed being too short for him. Arry thought he was asleep, but when she bent to blow out the candle left reprehensibly alight, she saw the gleam of his eyes.

"I'm sorry I fell asleep," she whispered. "You should have waked me. Was she much trouble?"

"Not as long as I did what she told me," said Beldi, also quietly.

"Did she tell you not to blow out the candle?"

"It's in a saucer of water," said Beldi.

"Do you want your bed back?"

"I'd like it back tomorrow."

"You shall have it, then. Go to sleep."

"Go to sleep yourself," said Beldi, as Arry had always said to their mother.

"Put your nightcap on the shelf," said Arry.

"Put your heart in sleep's soft hands."

"Loose your mind in dream's dread sands."

Beldi smiled and closed his eyes, and Arry went back to Oonan. He was feeling better, but his heart still thumped. Arry sat down.

"Arry," said Oonan. "Are you thinking of having a baby?"

Arry blinked at him.

"I was," she said, "but it would be such a lot of trouble. And Con and Beldi wouldn't like somebody else's moving in with us." She added, since Physici, Akoumi, and Gnosi must be honest with one another, "And it would hurt."

"You're too young," said Oonan. "No," as she frowned at him, "I don't mean you are too young for it to happen, I mean you are too young for it to happen well. Your body isn't settled."

"Well, good," said Arry, "since I'd decided against it for now anyway. When would I be old enough?"

"Four or five years, or six."

"Is this everybody, or me?"

"It's you, certainly," said Oonan. "It's everybody in varying degrees. Not many girls should have a baby at fourteen."

He was looking at her intently. Arry tried to stare him down, until she realized what really concerned him, and began to laugh. "No," she said. "I'm not falling in love with anybody, either. Who is there, really?"

"It's a question that has exercised me for for several years now," said Oonan.

"Shouldn't it be exercising Mally?" said Arry, a little absently. Then she said, "There's nobody for you either, is there? Or for Halver. Why?"

Oonan said, "We know too much."

## ❧ 12 ❧

WIM CAME BY the next morning while Arry and Beldi and Con were eating a belated breakfast. Con let him in and brought him into the kitchen. Arry had decided they might as well go back to eating there, but she wished Con had not brought a visitor while the cobwebs and dust of the room's long neglect were so tawdrily displayed by the bright sunshine. Wim was tall enough to get cobwebs in his hair, and wide enough that the piles of discarded objects were in danger from his elbows.

Arry offered him some tea. He thanked her and sat down, which made the room seem bigger, if no less tawdry.

Con had been staring steadily at him ever since she brought him in, and now, just as he lifted his mug to his mouth, she said, *"You* don't need walnut juice.''

Wim drank some tea and put the mug down. Of course, he had small children too; in fact, he had Lina, and Tany, and Zia herself. Nothing Con could say was likely to make him so much as blink. He said, "It makes a good dye for wool.''

"I mean *you* don't need it," said Con. "You're brown enough."

"Who says so?" said Wim, flicking a glance at Arry. Her mother had sometimes looked like that at her father, when one of the three of them—usually, as now, Con—said something strange or outrageous. She felt suspended between being a parent and being a child.

Con said, with a fair degree of impatience and less courtesy than Arry would have liked to hear, "Zia does."

"Ah," said Wim, and drank more tea. "It's Zia who sent me," he added, giving Arry a glance of a sort she did not, this time, recognize. "Since school won't start until the moon changes, she has a plan she needs you for."

Zia's plans were invariably dirty, disruptive, and productive of other plans that, in the end, led to loud disappointment on somebody's part, often Con's. Arry didn't care. They were proposing to take Con off her hands—and Beldi's—for an entire day and possibly, if past experience could be a guide here, the night as well.

"I'll come right away," said Con, and started to scramble down from her stool.

"She says you must have had a good breakfast first," said Wim, not looking at Arry at all this time. He addressed Beldi. "She needs you, too, Beldi, if your elder sister can spare you."

His elder sister had not considered it one way or the other. She nodded vigorously. Beldi looked less than willing.

Hurt again, thought Arry. She said, "I do need him, but I can manage by myself, if he wants to go."

"Zia says it's a very large plan," said Wim. He did not

seem apprehensive. "She's asking for Tiln and Jony and Elec as well; children of all sizes."

This was probably what had been making Beldi reluctant: not knowing if he would be spending his day with five or ten Cons. He said, "If Arry can manage, I'll come."

"I can," said Arry. "Do go."

Beldi nodded, and went back to his oatmeal. The three of them went out shortly after that, Con chivvying the other two along and leaving Arry with a table full of dirty dishes. She went out to the well, frowning.

The outside was much warmer than the house, and damp, and full of green sappy flowery scents. The birds were as noisy as children. There were more crocuses under the pine tree than there had been yesterday, vivid and precise and delicate as one of Tiln's paintings. All around the well the white starry flowers of Bedlam and the small blue squills were blooming, that yesterday had looked like so much rank grass. Arry trod as carefully as she could, getting her water.

When she turned back to the house she saw that the ivy her father had planted and the woodbine her mother had made them leave alone when they found it climbing up the house had both come out in tiny leaves. The woodbine held the new ones bristling over the bed of red leaves it had dropped the autumn before. Con had raided the red leaves even before they came off the vine, in an attempt to make a pair of boots out of them; but she had not taken them all.

Arry took the water back inside to the stuffy kitchen, started the water heating, and opened all the windows. By the time she had washed and dried and put away all the dishes and repaired or disposed of a great many objects, the kitchen looked the same except for an area of cleared floor about two feet by three, and she was both ravenous and very disinclined to stay inside any longer. She took cold potatoes and a selfishly large lump of cheese and a couple of withered apples, of the same vintage as the red leaves, and sat down on the front step to eat it all.

The black cat came down out of the pine tree, stretched all four legs in four directions, yawned, trotted over, and hooked a pawful of cheese out of her hand. Arry looked at her. "Are you pregnant again?" she said. Sheepnose, having bolted the cheese, turned her back and began washing her whiskers.

Arry sighed. When the Woollycat had her kittens, Con and Beldi had taken the cat up to Oonan, and Arry had gone as far in the other direction as she could walk in a morning, following the river until it disappeared thunderously down a rocky falls. When Sheepnose had her first litter, Arry's mother had still been here, and had attended to everything, with Arry crouched in the bedroom, pillow over her head and fingers in her ears, though the only noise the black cat made was panting, and the minute cries of the kittens had been untroubled.

She rolled an apple core over the rocky ground to Sheepnose, who sniffed it, gave her a look of profound disgust, and went back up the pine tree, never crushing a single crocus.

Arry sighed and got up. Another round of visits, asking questions and getting new questions, or the answers to questions she had not asked. Sune first, she supposed, and then Mally.

Most of the mud had dried. New flowers were everywhere in the rocks, all the early blooms you would expect in March or April now hurrying to catch up with the weather. And where there had been brown stalks, or rusty red seed heads, or nothing, were new green and yellow-green and new dark red, where later flowers would open. Stonecrop, yarrow, goutweed, alyssum, rock cress, wormwood, bellflower, tickseed, willow grass, fleabane, catmint, soapwort, sage, meadow sage, lavender, goldenrod, lambsear, thyme, and speedwell.

Arry fetched up with a violent jerk, as if she had missed her step on a rocky slope. The path was flat and solid. She sat down on a rock and shut her eyes hard. No wolves, she thought, and almost giggled. No flowers? If Halver could turn into a wolf, could he turn into a clump of alyssum? She opened her eyes and looked back along the path. The long, feathery leaves of the yarrow were known to her, at this moment, not because Jony had said so every spring, but because she knew. Maybe she should talk to Mally first. But looking the other direction, she saw Halver's house looking back at her, all its windows shuttered. Sune was just down the next hill. Arry got up and went on.

She went past Halver's house in a hurry, with her breath and heart pounding as if she had been running for miles. She felt better, for no known reason, once she was out of its long morning shadow. She went on down the hill, admiring the daffodils that edged this part of the path, and the new chickweed sprawling where the mud had been. Jony said chickweed was good in salads, but Con wouldn't touch it. Arry stopped walking. She looked at the chickweed again. Jony said that was chickweed. Arry knew nothing about it.

"I hate this," said Arry, invoking Con; and she went

on up to Sune's door, which was shut. It had no
knocker. Arry banged on it with her fist. In Sune's willow tree a lot of house finches were squabbling. After a
few moments she knocked again, and this time felt as
hard as she could for any sign of hurt. Nothing. The
house finches burst in a body out of the tree and flashed
off like a batch of Lina's bubbles, in brown and white
and reddish-purple. Arry went down to the willow, and
around its massive trunk.

Sune was sitting in the grass, leaning on the tree, still
spinning. She felt fairly awful, but nothing was actually
happening. She glanced up, saw Arry, and looked as if
she might have been startled if she could have found
the energy.

"That isn't very comfortable," said Arry.

"What, lumpy cold damp ground underseat and a
great willow root pressing one's spine the wrong way?
It's much the same whether I'm here or in the rocker."

Oonan and Mally both said, and Arry was beginning
to know, that pregnant women often knew about discomfort, though not usually pain. Arry wondered, for
the first time, if this said something about the exact nature of the spell that blessed them all, or about the nature of pregnancy. This was probably not the time to ask
Sune about it.

She sat down on a fallen branch. The deep grass was
scattered with snowdrops, though it was late for them
according to Jony. Bluebells were up but not blooming
yet. Jony said they were late this year as well.

"If you're coming every day about the baby," said
Sune, "I don't mind, you needn't invent questions."

Arry said, "Well, I don't invent them, they just arrive."

"Ask away, then. How is the baby, though? I'd like to know."

"Crowded," said Arry. "Not hurting at all. You could ask Oonan, though, to be certain; he could tell you more."

"I don't wish to hear that much, perhaps," said Sune.

Arry looked at her. Worry, like a teardrop or a candle flame, of which the blurred or bluish edges were fear. It made the heart feel heavy somehow, it was as bad as a stomachache. Unlike most stomachaches, it seemed to have no cause, or none she knew how to distinguish. Arry blinked, and the sudden dislocation of her knowledge, like a step missed on a rocky path, almost made her fall off the log.

"What did you want to ask?" said Sune.

Arry blinked again, and steadied herself with one hand on the damp rough surface of the log. "Are the Lukanthropoi out of nature?" she said.

"Are they what?"

"Mally gave me a story about children in the forms of things unknown and it had written in the margin, 'once out of nature.' " Arry did not look at Sune; she was afraid of what else she might see that she was not supposed to be seeing, that lay outside her field of knowledge.

"Yes, I know both those stories," said Sune readily. "The writer means death."

"That's what out of nature means?"

"Well, it's all I can think of. Whether the Lukanthropoi are a made race or are enspelled, they partake of the nature of things."

"But the dead don't?"

"No. Death is natural, but what comes after is indeed out of nature."

"What does come after?"

"I don't know," said Sune.

"Who would?"

Sune shook her head. Arry tried to think of some way to ask Sune who else might know about nature at all, but realized that she would be seeming to doubt Sune if she did this. She looked cautiously at Sune, ready to look away at once; but all she knew was that Sune's feet were swollen and her back painful and various parts of her complaining, more or less loudly, about being pushed out of their proper places. She said, "Is there anything I can do for you while I'm here?"

"You can tell me why you want to know about the Lukanthropoi."

"Derry says the wolves that got the sheep didn't act like wolves."

"Ah," said Sune.

Arry said, "What does that mean?"

Sune looked slightly startled, but she answered. "It means, of course, I should have remembered." She moved both hands over the baby, which kicked her gently. "One gets preoccupied," she added.

"I suppose one would," said Arry.

"You aren't thinking of finding out for yourself, are you?"

"First Oonan, now you," said Arry, half amused and half annoyed. "Is there a way you people can tell when you should ask? Ought I to worry?"

"Maybe Oonan has a way," said Sune. "I haven't. But because of young Knot here, I've been remembering my own growing up, and today I was thinking about the summer I was fourteen.''

"Did you want to have a baby?"

"No," said Sune, smiling, "but what I did want would have got me one.''

"There isn't anybody, really," said Arry.

Sune seemed to be thinking this over. The baby kicked her again, rather hard, but she didn't notice. She said, like somebody listing the items to be taken on a journey, "You were the only baby born in your year; I remember everybody's remarking on it. Boys mature later than girls. Even then there's only Tiln. Oonan is your uncle." She looked up. "Halver?"

"No," said Arry, before she had decided whether to speak or not.

Sune seemed to accept this. "Well, you know, your father had to go to the Hidden Land to find your mother," she said.

"Why are you trying to find somebody for me to have a baby with if I'm too young to have a baby in the first place? By the time I'm old enough Tiln would be, too."

"I'm thinking about displaced energies," said Sune.

"What?" said Arry, and realized with irritation that she sounded just like Con.

"What *do* you think about?" said Sune.

"Con and Beldi," said Arry. "The cats. The house. The weather. The planting. The songs Bec used to play. Why leaves turn yellow in the fall. Whoever's hurt. What hurt means, really, how many kinds of hurt there are, what's to be done about them all."

"Ah," said Sune again.

"What should you have remembered now?"

"That I'm not like you. When one knows what one reads, one needn't define one's knowledge in the same way, finding the boundaries. Almost it has none."

"How strange," said Arry, again involuntarily.

"You seem strange to me, too," said Sune; she sounded a little wistful.

"We all seem strange to one another," said Arry. "Mally says so."

"She would," said Sune. She shifted her body and braced herself with her arms. "If you would help me up, I think I'll go inside and attempt to be useful. Would you like some tea?"

Arry declined on the grounds that she had a great deal to do yet today, and helped Sune get off the log. Standing up made Sune's back hurt. She walked Sune back up the slope to her house and saw her safely inside. Then she set off for Mally's house. It was almost hot out now, and the air felt heavy. Arry stopped at home to get a drink of water. The empty house felt strange, and, after the huge spaces of the spring sky, small and a little musty. The cats were nowhere in sight. Arry stood in the kitchen drinking absently out of Beldi's breakfast mug and trying to formulate her questions to Mally in such a way that Mally might actually answer them.

The water tasted odd. Not flat or spoiled; a little sweet, almost bubbly, like the cider Wim sometimes made when there were too many apples. Arry supposed it was the blushful Hippocrene again. She would have to speak to Con. Whatever was the matter with Con, getting her magic back did not seem to have helped it. Arry left the mug on the table and went to see Mally.

The door was open today. The black dog slept in the

shade of the lilac bush. There was a great deal of noise in the house, laughter and trampling and shrill children's voices. Oh, no, thought Arry, Zia's plan. She put her head around the edge of the door, cautiously.

All the furniture had been pushed to the walls. Tiln sat just to the right of the door, in a carved chair much too big for him. On the other side of the chair was the kitchen table. Lined up from the table all around the room and through the door into the kitchen were what what seemed like every child in the whole village. They were all clutching something, sheets and rolls of paper, dolls, jewelry, garden tools, clothing. Beldi was in the middle of the line, looking resigned. He had one of their mother's blue plates. Arry couldn't see Con, or hear her either, which was remarkable. Zia seemed to be missing as well.

The far end of the line was disorderly, with shoving and shrieking and consequent crumpling of paper and tears and recriminations; there was also a lot of laughter and at least one game of chess. The children closer to Tiln were quiet, peering over one another's shoulders to see what he was doing.

What he was doing, just now, was looking at a doll held by his sister Mora. Her face was deeply worried. Tiln just looked thoughtful. The doll was one of the rag ones that Rine made, according to Mally, when she got bored. They all had black wool hair and blue embroidered eyes and red embroidered lips; they were made with various kinds and colors of cloth all stained a uniform color with walnut juice, and dressed in red smocks, trousers, and boots from a lot of cloth Arry's mother had had sent from the Hidden Land but not, when she saw it, cared for the quality of.

"Zia says it's ugly," said Mora.

Tiln picked the doll up by the waist and stared at it. He seemed uncomfortable. Arry thought for one appalling moment that he had something severely wrong with his stomach; then she realized that he was at least as worried as Mora, and that worry made his stomach hurt.

"No," said Tiln flatly.

Mora snatched the doll from him and galloped into the kitchen, shouting, "Ha! Ha, Zia! Ha!"

Tiln did not roll his eyes as a brother might; he just looked miserable. Arry cleared her throat. Tiln jumped and stared at her, and all the children clutching their objects hushed and stared too.

"I'm sorry to interrupt," said Arry, "but I wanted to speak to Mally."

"I'll show you where she is," said Tiln, and got up with alacrity.

He gestured Arry back out the door and took her around the house to the goat barn. Mally was sitting on the fence scratching the smallest goat behind the ears. She turned and saw them. She said to Tiln, "You needn't go on with this if you don't like it."

"It's easier than listening to Zia."

Mally grimaced. "Tell her no. A little noise won't hurt us."

"Will it?" said Tiln to Arry.

"Not physically," said Arry.

Mally looked at her for the first time. Mally was underslept, though less severely than Halver, and her joints were a little sore from planting all the beans. "Still worrying at that, are you?" Mally said.

"Didn't you know I would?"

"If you hadn't had a satisfactory answer, yes." Mally looked back at Tiln. "Shall I tell Zia?" she said.

"Of course not," said Tiln. "I have to go back now, or they'll be all over Wim."

He turned around and trudged over the new grass to the house as if he were going up a very steep slope indeed. Arry and Mally both watched him. Arry said, "What's Zia doing?"

"She claims," said Mally precisely, "that she is helping his knowledge to unfold faster by having every child in the place bring him objects and ask him whether or not they are ugly."

Arry found herself shivering. "I'm glad she wasn't born yet when I found out what my knowledge was."

"Truly," said Mally, "you are."

"I talked to Derry about wolves," said Arry. "And she said that wolves know better than to kill and not eat, and so do we, here in the Dubious Hills; but that people outside don't."

"Of course they don't," said Mally. "That was the whole point of the spell that makes us different. What do you think war is?"

"How should I know?" said Arry.

"Well, come to that," said Mally, "how should I? But that's what Sune says. What were you really asking me?"

"If everybody here really does know better. Than to kill and not eat."

"Certainly," said Mally.

Arry leaned on the fence and rubbed the goat's back. Wolves knew better; people here knew better; yet when Halver was a wolf, what did he do but kill and not eat. She sighed.

"That's not what's worrying you," said Mally.

Even I know that, thought Arry. She said, "Everybody has started asking if I want to have a baby and then pointing out that there's nobody for me to have one with."

"Who is everybody?"

"Oonan and Sune. They also say I shouldn't have one, so I don't see why it matters that there isn't anybody to have one with."

"But?"

"But Oonan and I realized, there isn't anybody for Oonan or for Halver either. And I wondered why."

"Did Oonan wonder why?"

"He said we knew too much."

Mally laughed. She laughed so hard she affronted the goat, which twitched itself from under Arry's forgetful hand and tore across the yard to the other side, where it thrust its head over the fence and began eating a branch of lilac. Mally said, "First, you should remember that if, like Sune, you just want a baby, anybody here will do for that. If, like Oonan, you want a companion, then matters become more difficult."

"I don't want either at the moment," said Arry. "I'm too busy. But I wondered why they both brought it up. Why did you laugh?"

"What Oonan said was so like Oonan," said Mally.

"Was he wrong?"

"I don't know. But he was very like himself when he said that," said Mally, and chuckled again.

Arry leaned on the fence. The sun poured down on everything like honey. Around her feet bloomed grape hyacinths that the goats had not yet eaten. "Was he very like himself when he brought the matter up?" she said.

"I think so," said Mally. "You seem thoughtful and

fretful by turns, and very full of questions. It's a restless age, fourteen. Oonan will try to fix it, when the only answer is to live it.''

"Do people who are fourteen think their knowledge is larger than it is? Do they imagine it covers things it doesn't?"

"Not generally," said Mally.

"Because," said Arry, who had not specifically planned to say anything about this, lest it impinge on her promise to Halver, "I sometimes think I know things I can't. The names of flowers."

"Jony has told you so often that you remember."

"But I thought I *knew* them. The names just came.''

Mally bent and pulled something from under the flat leaves of the grape hyacinths: a round yellow flower with five petals, no bigger than the end of her little finger. The leaves looked like clover. "What's this?" said Mally.

"I haven't the faintest idea," said Arry.

"Jony says it's sorrel," said Mally.

"Oh."

"What else do you think you know that you oughtn't?"

"Hurt that's not of the body," said Arry.

"Now that I might expect," said Mally. "That might be a genuine broadening. But the flowers, no. Surely that's just memory doing its dance."

She did not sound sure. Arry felt too tired to pester her further. After a moment Mally said, "Shall we go see how the torment of Tiln is progressing?" And they walked back to the house, with Mally plaiting the sorrel into her short white hair.

MALLY AND WIM asked the entire youthful population of their house to stay for dinner, including Arry. She spent a little time telling children what did or did not hurt, finding one actual sliver in a foot (Mora) and one actual bump on the head (Tany), and then went into the kitchen to see if she could help Mally. So many children made a tremendous racket. They were never so noisy in school, that she could remember. She wondered what Halver's secret was, and then shivered.

Mally was making root and cabbage stew, with bacon, and accepted an offer to cut up the turnips.

"They'll be back in school soon," said Arry, slicing vigorously. She needed to either bring all their own knives to Inno for sharpening, or ask Con to see to it.

"Do you know what's wrong with Halver?" said Mally abruptly.

"No," said Arry, truthfully, since shapechanging was not a form of injury; but she felt a little strange about her answer just the same.

"Does Oonan?"

"He may," said Arry. She looked over the table to where Mally stood at the big sink scrubbing potatoes. "Don't you?"

"No," said Mally. "It is therefore not a defect of character."

"Might something be worrying him?"

"It might," said Mally. "But when that happens, he talks to Sune, or Oonan, or sometimes Wim."

"And he hasn't?"

"He has not."

"If he were worried *about* Sune or Oonan or Wim, then what?"

"He must be worried about Sune *and* Oonan *and* Wim, then," said Mally.

If I see him tonight, thought Arry, I'll ask him.

Luckily, finding things for Tiln to judge the ugliness of had tired Con and Beldi out. Arry got them home and washed and abed and asleep just after sunset. She shut the cats in the house, put up all the shutters, and went up the hill to Oonan's in the windy spring dark, trying not to step on any flowers.

Oonan's door was shut, but a great deal of light bloomed in all the windows. Arry knocked, and he let her in at once, into a room that looked as if Con had been at it with her new light spells. Oonan looked as if something had been at him, too.

"You're early," he said, shutting the door behind her. "Do you want some spoonbread?"

"You should take a nap," said Arry.

"Oh, no, dear Physici," said Oonan. "Think again. In this nutshell of a house here we have very bad dreams."

"Have you been reading too?"

"What need reading, when wolves that are not wolves are so obliging as to chase me up and down my own sheep meadow?"

"Are you running a fever?"

"You tell me," said Oonan, stopping in his pacing of the room.

"No," said Arry, who had known this even as she spoke but was utterly at a loss as to what else she might say.

"I wish I could see now," said Oonan, beginning to pace again, "if we would meet my wolves, or your wolf."

"Both would be better," said Arry. "Then we would have seen all the same things, and we could talk about it."

"Do you think that would help?"

"Let me tell you what Derry says about wolves and what Sune says about shapeshifters and the Lukanthropoi."

"Why not?" said Oonan, falling into the nearest red chair, which creaked alarmingly. "Let us talk on the edge of ruin, for it will come will we or nill we."

"*Oonan,*" said Arry, considering his blood and brain. "Have you been at the ale?"

Oonan laughed, which, as it often did, made him feel much better, at least while he was doing it. "Would that I had," he said.

Arry sat down in the other chair and considered him. "Will I find out why tonight, if your wolves come?"

"Oh, yes," said Oonan.

"Could we talk about something else until then? Unless you think there's something you ought to be doing?"

"Let's eat something, then," said Oonan, getting up with the same abandon with which he had just sat down. Arry followed him into the kitchen, shaking her head.

Oonan's kitchen made Arry's seem even worse. It looked as if nobody ever used it—which might, of course, be the case: people Oonan fixed often gave him food, and he did not actually look as if he ever ate anything. In fact, while he gave her a very good soup made of beans and odd early-spring greens of the sort Jony could always find, and an excellent barley bread with cheese melted over it, he ate very little himself. Arry began to wonder with increasing apprehension what could be so much worse than finding out Halver was a wolf. That was what she knew would happen to Oonan tonight, and she was perfectly able and happy to eat a second supper. What did Oonan know was going to happen to her that made him lose his appetite? What had he found out from the two wolves who had visited him that could be so much worse? That Mally was a wolf; Sune; Wim, Niss, Grel, one of the children?

When she had finished eating and Oonan had finished breaking his bread-and-cheese into bits and losing the bits in his soup, Oonan made some tea and they went back into his front room. Oonan gave the soup to his cats, and for some time the only sound was the hiss of the lamps and the minute laps of cat tongues picking their way around all the greens to find the cheese. Arry finally grew restive and began telling Oonan about all the stories Mally had given her to read.

Oonan gave every appearance of listening to her, but he had nothing to say except, "What happened then?" and "I see," until she came to the strange story of daylight on the windowsill. That made him sit up straight and look at her. He made her recite as much of it as she could remember, which was easier than she would have expected: maybe it was a spell of sorts after all. The note in the margin made him frown.

"Once out of nature," he said, when she was done. "What is the work of will?"

"Nobody's ever said," said Oonan. " 'Hail the Lord of Human Fears'—that sounds like the way Sune says they speak of death in the Outer Isles."

"I asked Sune what out of nature was," said Arry.

"What did she say?"

"Dead."

"Really."

"Well, what would you say?"

"Not my province," said Oonan.

"But you think something, even if you don't know it." Oonan neither confirmed nor denied this. Arry said, "Does everybody?"

"Ask Mally."

Arry made an impatient huff, as if she were Con thwarted in some grand scheme.

"Where's your jacket?" said Oonan. "We don't want to miss our visitors."

Arry's jacket felt rather too hot. The air was still damp and hardly cooler than it had been in the afternoon. The smells of water and earth and green things lay heavily all around; when they passed a patch of grape hyacinth the scent made Arry want to sit down under it and rest. She trudged on after Oonan.

Oonan led her into the hut, left the door open, and began to pace. It was much colder in the hut, but just as damp. Arry sat on the hard bed and said, "Do you think they'll run us up and down the meadow?"

"I am hoping," said Oonan, "that now I have seen them and shown myself willing to converse, they will, as Frances used to say, abjure the preliminaries."

He very seldom mentioned Arry's mother. She looked at him, but in the darkness of the hut there was nothing to see except the impatient line of his shoulders.

"Maybe they won't come until the moon sets, then," said Arry.

Oonan stopped pacing, and probably stood looking at her. "I had thought of that," he said. "Grel says that will be between two and three hours after the sun rises."

"We should have brought a chess set," said Arry. "Or a whistle."

"Or our spinning," said Oonan, irritably.

"When's Sune's baby coming?"

"In five or six weeks, most likely."

"I think she's worried about it."

"She reads too much," said Oonan, more irritably. "That baby is fine and strong and not too large. *Sune* is fine and strong and large enough. She's been filling herself up with horrors and then, you see, she knows them. Even though I know she won't encounter them."

"She doesn't know that she can trust what you know?" said Arry.

Oonan sat down on the floor; Arry could feel him staring at her. "Nobody has ever said it in quite that way to me," he said. "Do we all know that, that we can trust what others know?" He paused, and Arry saw the pale movement as he pushed one hand through his hair. "What others *say* they know," he said. "We don't know they know it—except for Mally."

"I've never thought about it quite in this way either," said Arry. "It's because of Con, and wondering if there are hurts not physical. Each question seems to make more."

"And what made Con behave so that you wondered?"

"I think it was my parents' leaving."

"And Mally doesn't know?"

"She doesn't say, anyway. She gave me all the stories."

"About wolves?" said Oonan sharply.

"No, I asked Sune for those. About children whose parents leave them. But none of the things that happen in the stories has happened to Con."

"No," said Oonan.

Arry waited, but he was silent. Arry was tired of talking around and around questions she had no answers for. She tried to think of what they had talked about before she started wondering about the kinds of pain. Gossip, small news, games, music, dancing, the weather, the sick and hurt people they both dealt with, Con's mischief, whether Beldi was too quiet. It all led back to the same questions.

Arry thought her mind must be tired. It would not, in a sensible fashion, lie down and rest. So she let it go where it liked. It wandered slowly around the dark hut, noting how her eyes had adjusted so that she could see Oonan's face and hands and the ragged outline of his bird's-nest hair against the darker wall, and the gleam of his eyes, and the moonlight falling through the open door to make strange and fantastical the bits of straw and clods of mud that lay on the smooth-packed dirt of the floor.

"Floor," though you might not realize it from hearing it, was a Unicornish word. In that language, which assigned genders to its nouns, the feminine form meant a field or meadow, while the masculine form meant what one normally would think of as a floor.

Arry's foot jerked as she fell down a step that was not there, in a walk she was not taking. She heard herself make a noise like somebody poked suddenly by the cold nose of a cat.

"What?" said Oonan.

"Oonan. Who knows about Unicornish?"

"Sune, I suppose."

"That's all?"

"I believe so. Frances did, of course."

"That wasn't her knowledge, was it?"

"Language was," said Oonan.

"Was that why she never lost her magic?"

"Possibly. I'd ask Mally."

"Why don't you ever *ask* Mally, then!" snapped Arry. "My asking her doesn't do an oatgrain's worth of good."

"*I* don't want to be informed of all these things," Oonan snapped back.

Arry let her breath out and rubbed her eyes. The light falling in the door was brighter. "Did I wake you up?" she said.

"Maybe a little," said Oonan, in a smiling voice.

They sat on in silence. Arry was afraid to let her mind wander, lest somebody else's certainties flood it again. She supposed she must ask Mally about this. She blamed it on Halver, but that might not be right. "Oonan?" she said.

"What now?" said Oonan, sleepily but not unkindly.

"Who knows about the workings of the mind?"

"It's a field of knowledge that's divided into small plots," said Oonan, still drowsily. "I know somewhat, Mally knows somewhat, so does Sune; so, of course, does Halver."

"So he does," said Arry.

Oonan sat up; she could feel him looking at her.

"Afterwards," said Arry.

Oonan stood up all the way and began pacing the floor again. Arry watched him. They did this for a very long weary while. Arry's chin bumped her chest. She pulled her head back up, blinking. A great dark shape came through the open door, darted past Oonan, and seized the blanket of the bed in its jaws. Arry shot off the bed. The large wolf gave her a brief considering glance, curled its lip at her, and dragged the blanket back out the door.

"What was that all about?" said Oonan. He had stood quite still while the wolf came in. "Was that your wolf?"

"Yes," said Arry. "And you'll see in a minute." She remembered the wolf's leading her to Halver's house and vanishing into the other room so that it could reappear clothed. People bathed in the streams all summer with nothing on whatsoever; but perhaps wolves felt differently about such things.

Nothing happened for some time. Then Arry twitched all over and almost fell off the bed, and at the same moment Oonan tripped over something and bumped the wall, or at any rate that was what it sounded like. They had not heard the wolf come, but in the quiet after Oonan bumped the wall they heard the sound of a bare foot stirring the gravel, and then someone was standing in the doorway, blocking all the light.

Oonan went into one corner and lit a lantern. He stood up, holding the light out before him, and made a sound as if somebody had hit him in the stomach.

"Oh, yes," said Halver. He had wrapped the blanket around himself, and looked rather like Beldi playing Prospero in the autumn celebration of the Descent of Doubt. "It's I, O Akoumi. And how will you fix this?"

"What's to be fixed?" said Oonan; this was a ritual response, but he moved suddenly after he said it, as if he had not meant to speak, and then he put the lantern down in the middle of the floor and said sharply, "Shut the door. It's getting cold out."

"Is he cold, Physici?" said Halver to Arry.

"Very," said Arry, almost at random. Why, she thought, they don't like one another. She felt cold herself.

Halver shut the door.

"Arry," said Oonan. "Is this the wolf you saw before?"

"Yes," said Arry.

Oonan said to Halver, "Where are the other two?"

"Hunting," said Halver, calmly.

"Release me from the oath I swore them."

"I cannot."

"Then tell me one sufficient reason that I should not break it here and now."

"Because you are not a breaker," said Halver.

"You swore Arry to secrecy as they did me?"

"I did," said Halver.

Oonan took two awkward steps and sat down next to Arry. "What did he tell you?" he said. "What happened?"

Arry said, "I'll tell you later, in the light. Halver, what do you want?"

"I am a teacher," said Halver, "and I will teach as I must."

"How did this happen?" said Oonan.

"Why, Akoumi, don't you know? Cannot you tell merely by looking what it is that has deranged my form and so disposed my hours that I must sleep by day and in the night prowl with the fox, the barn owl, and the shrew?"

Oonan moved beside Arry, and she looked at him. In the light and shadow made by the lantern his eyes were very wide; he was biting his lip and staring less at than right through Halver. "Tell me how it happened," he said, not quite steadily. "When children fall and skin their knees, I know what's to be done, but I still ask. And I ask you."

Arry did not recognize that line, but it too had the flavor of ritual. Halver seemed to think so too. He raised his chin a little, so the shadows moved over his face. "In the pursuit of my duty," he said, "I went out last month with Sune and Wim to consider the motions of the moon."

"Sune shouldn't have been tramping about the hills," said Oonan indignantly. Arry put her elbow gently into the nearest available part of him, which turned out to be his own elbow; she winced and he twitched, but he didn't say anything more.

"Sune turned back early," said Halver, with no matching indignation. "Wim and I went on. Then Tiln came to say that Zia wouldn't go to bed until Wim had told her the thirteen-times table. So Wim made sure I remembered what he had told me and what Sune had read to us, and he went home with Tiln."

He sounded more like himself now. Arry tried to listen as if he were ill or injured. He did not sound either. He was tired and rather cold; the blanket was scratchy and his hand still itched. He was neither sweaty nor feverish nor afflicted with a headache. He was saying, "I climbed up to the top of the cliff there, and sat on the edge to watch the moon rise. I was running over in my mind what I would teach tomorrow, thinking especially about Con. You may remember, Arry, that she was not amenable to learning to count past ten."

Arry nodded. Halver said, "They came up behind me as silently as the moon rising, and one of them bit me here," and he put a hand up to the right side of his neck, "where the neck joins the shoulder."

Arry put her own hand up to where her neck joined her shoulder, and clenched her teeth. Halver sounded as if he meant it.

"Then they sat, one on either side of me, and did not let me get up," said Halver.

"Did it bleed much?" said Oonan, in his brisk, reasonable way, not at all the tone he had been using. "You haven't a scar—I don't recall seeing a wound at all. You didn't consult either of us about it."

"No," said Halver, with a tinge of mockery in his voice that Arry did not much care for, "it didn't bleed much. They sat with me until the moon went down; then they trotted off into that clump of aspen, the one Mora fell out of last October," he said to Arry, "and just as I had stood up and was rubbing the bite and wondering what to do, two people came out of the aspen; and they talked to me until dawn.''

Does he think I don't remember what he said to me, thought Arry, or does he think I'll keep quiet to see what he says, or does he know I can't tell Oonan afterwards no matter what I say I'll do? She did want to see what Halver would tell Oonan, and she did keep quiet.

Oonan said, ''Talked to you of what?''

''Disenchantment,'' said Halver, softly.

Next to Arry, Oonan had become perfectly still, not something one could often observe in him. He was a fidgeter; he had as much energy as a five-year-old. Arry blinked, hard. No, she thought. Whatever you are doing, whoever you are, no. That's Mally's province. It isn't mine. Pain's mine; where is your pain?

Oonan said, just as softly, ''Whose disenchantment?''

''Those who choose,'' said Halver. ''Or are chosen.''

''Which do you propose for us?''

''I have given Arry the means to choose already. I give it you also. What Physici, Akoumi, and Gnosi wish to do with the rest of them, we have the power to effect.''

''Or will, should we choose disenchantment.''

''Or will,'' said Halver.

''Yet you've chosen us already.''

''Mally always said you should have been a poet,'' said Halver; his tone was light but not, thought Arry, as pleasant as he would have liked to make it. ''I chose you that you might choose, if you like.''

''You won't bite us, then, as you were bitten?''

''Do you think that is the mechanism, then?''

"I know it," said Oonan, and all the fine hairs on Arry's neck stood straight up.

"And what does that avail you?" said Halver.

Oonan continued very still. He did not answer. Halver stood where he was, with the lantern making his yellow hair shine, and said nothing either.

Arry said, "What about the breaking of history?"

She made Oonan jump. Halver did not move.

"What about it?" said Oonan.

Arry looked at Halver, who said, in precisely the tone he would use at school, "How does our history begin?"

"With the War of the Sorcerers' Schools," said Arry, almost without thinking.

"Go on," said Halver. "You had this, I believe, two years ago; let us see how your memory has kept it."

He always said this, or something very like it; but there was a sound in his voice that made Arry look hard at him. He was still standing on the other side of the lantern in the dusty gray blanket, arms folded across his chest, as always when he was awaiting a recitation. Arry swallowed carefully, and began.

"Four hundred years ago, the four schools of wizards were fighting each other, for reasons nobody is sure of to this day, because whenever anybody tries to find out, the wizards all start fighting again. Four hundred years ago, they had been fighting for seven years, and some of them got tired of it." She paused. "Sune says," she added.

Halver shifted his bare feet on the hard earth floor, in a movement, when performed in boots on the carpet of the schoolroom, that usually meant you had waited too long to attribute your sources. Arry didn't think she had. She went on.

"These some—there were eight of them in all—went quietly away to the Kingdom of Dust, which has no wizards, and there they sat in some tents lent them by the Dusters, and all through spring when the desert bloomed and summer when it blazed and autumn when it bloomed again briefly, they talked about what made people fight at all, and how they might make people stop. Sune says all of this," said Arry, "and Karn and Grel and Wim say the weather in the Kingdom of Dust's desert is indeed like that and has been so for perhaps six hundred years.

"And when they thought they had found a way, they went to the Dubious Hills, which then were just a place that the Dusters did not claim because the water you could find there was not worth the weather that made it, and the rocks were bad for their horses' feet. It was also a place the Hidden Land did not want because they thought it would grow only oats; and a place the people of the Forested Slopes held in derision because all its trees were stunted. It was called the Sheepcots, when anybody bothered to talk about it, Sune says, and so do you, Halver."

This got her no reaction at all. She added, "You said that the people here called it the Small Hills, because, Sune said, they came from the mountains north of the Secret Country and the hills looked small to them."

"And they did," said Halver, in a curious tone Arry had never heard from him before; she wished Mally were here to label it. "Indeed they did look small."

Arry waited to see if he would say more, but he just

sat down abruptly on the floor, rearranged the blanket, and said, "Go on," just as he always said it.

Arry collected herself and did so. "The Sheepcots had wizards, but these were not wizards who had ever gone to school, and they were too busy raising sheep and coaxing their oats along to bother about the fighting wizards. Sune says.

"The Eight thought this country would suit them perfectly. So they put on all the people there the spells they had drawn and written and sung and carved, to make the nature of people such that people would no longer fight."

Arry stopped, and Halver said, "Well?"

"So we are as we are," said Arry. "And we don't fight, either."

"Why, then, didn't the Eight put this same spell on everybody? On the people in the Hidden Land, and Fence's Country, and Druogonos?"

Arry had never thought about it before. "Nobody ever said," she answered.

"No, indeed nobody did," said Halver. "And why not, do you suppose?"

Oonan made a restless movement, and Halver's gaze, even in the flickering light of their single lantern, seemed to fasten on him as if Halver had walked forward and taken Oonan by the collar of his jacket. "You may answer instead, Akoumi," said Halver.

"I know nothing of this," said Oonan formally. Arry could feel how stiff he sat, and knew that he was offended, and then wondered if offense were a form of hurt, which seemed unlikely. But if it were not, she should not know it.

"But," said Oonan, "I can offer speculation."

"It's all any of us has," said Halver.

That's not true, thought Arry. She kept quiet. Something was happening here.

"I am a healer," said Oonan. "I know that fighting makes breakage, and this is wrong. But it does not follow, as the Eight seem to have thought, that whatever makes us fight is itself a breakage in some mechanism intended to work in a different way or to different ends. There is that in us that makes wrong without being, to our natures, foreign, or broken."

"So there is no way to prevent war?"

"Of course there is," said Oonan irritably. "We live under one method. But it may be there are many ways to prevent it that all do damage to our natures."

"Doesn't war do damage to our natures?" said Arry, shocked.

"Indubitably," said Oonan. "But the spell we live under may do so also."

"Less damage, then?"

"Different damage," said Oonan. "So that the makers of the spell, once they saw it in its operation, perhaps thought that the peace they had bought was not worth the price."

"They thought," said Halver, "that the spell they laid on our many-times-great-grandparents was not a spell to be laid upon themselves."

"Who says so?" said Arry.

"Sune and Frances," said Halver. He seemed about to say more, but shut his mouth on it.

"What was it about the operation of the spell, then, that made them not wish to lay it upon themselves?"

"Bear in mind," said Halver, in his teacher's voice

again, "that the spell was laid doubly, on this place and on the people in it. Where it held sway, it became difficult, by the normal operations of human thought, to believe in anything whatsoever. After a number of unprepared visitors—chiefly warring wizards looking for allies or a last place for a desperate stand or sometimes just a drink of water—had come and immediately gone stark mad, the place began to be called the Dubious Hills, and visitors stopped coming."

"But our great-great-grandparents were well?" said Arry. "Or my mother—she came from outside."

"The people here when the spell was cast did not go mad," said Halver. "At least, not in the same way as the outsiders who came in."

"But my mother," said Arry again.

"This is the part no one teaches," said Halver, "because until last month at the full of the moon no one here knew it. Your mother knew it, Arry, but she could not see what to do about it. But now I know it."

Oonan moved impatiently, making the bed creak. Halver laughed up at him over the lantern. "When they saw what they had done, the Eight changed the spell," he said.

"But they still didn't put it on themselves?" said Arry. "Or anybody outside?"

"Well deduced, my student," said Halver.

"Why didn't they?"

"Because they chose to be free and endangered, rather than imprisoned and safe."

Oonan let his breath out in such a way that he was very close to making a snort or some other disgusted noise. Arry wondered what his knowledge, of wholeness and fitness or its absence, was telling him now about

Halver. Hers said only that Halver was unhurt, for the moment.

Oonan said deliberately, "That is outside your province, Gnosi."

"And so am I," said Halver.

Oonan started to say something, presumably, "Well, of course," and then straightened and looked at Halver. Arry looked in her turn at Oonan. His face was rather like Con's when Con first found out that their mother had left. Mally said it meant something like, "I can see such trouble."

Arry said rapidly, before she should think again, "Halver. If we had a blind child here—Oonan says we have had them sometimes—how would you teach it?"

Halver said, "I've never had one to teach."

Oonan turned his head and looked at Arry. She could see quite well now in the light of the one lamp; so, one supposed, could he. They were thinking the same thing. She had meant to let Oonan say it: he was older than she was. But he felt as if somebody had hit him in the stomach. He made a little motion of his head in Halver's direction, and Arry spoke to Halver.

"You don't know," she said.

"That's true," said Halver. "I do not, for the asking, know how to teach a blind child."

"But?" said Oonan, in a terrifyingly patient voice.

"I remember how I did teach. I can read. I can reason. I could do it, if I had to."

"But how would you know you were *right?*" said Arry.

"If it worked," said Oonan, in the same patient tone. It was not like him.

"If it worked," said Halver, nodding.

"You can't possibly," said Arry. "What if it didn't work? You can't go wasting a child as if it were a bad batch of yoghurt. You might as well say I could dose a stomachache with anything handy, just to see what happened."

"They do it outside every day," said Halver.

"We are not outside," said Oonan.

"But we might be," said Halver.

"Why?" said Arry. "Where's the benefit?"

"Try it and see," said Halver.

And he turned in his old gray blanket and walked out of the hut. Arry sat where she was. Oonan went out after him. He said something, and there was an explosion of growling. Arry jumped up, ran for the door, and collided solidly with Oonan as he came back in.

"He's gone," said Oonan, breathlessly.

Arry leaned her head on his chest and began to laugh. "Con would love that," she said. "Say your say, walk outside, turn into a wolf." She giggled.

"It's not funny," said Oonan.

"How do you know?"

Oonan started to laugh, and stopped, and stepped back from Arry. She sat down again, still chortling.

"And neither is that," said Oonan.

"They why are you laughing?"

"I don't know," said Oonan; and they both laughed until they cried.

## 14

WHEN THEY HAD finished laughing, they went soberly down the mountain to Oonan's house. The moon was behind a cloud; the dark felt warmer. Arry carried her mind along as if it were a bowl of milk filled to the brim. Nothing that should not be there fell into it.

Oonan put more wood on the fire and brought it back to life; then he took a spill and went around lighting all the lamps. His cats sat on the hearth and watched him. Arry sat in one of the chairs her mother had made and watched him too. He was upset. How do I know that, she thought? She consulted her knowledge, with considerable caution, lest things she did not and ought not know should sneak in. But she saw only the sober facts of her own province: heartbeat, breath, the slide of strange substances through the blood. Of course, she thought, when we get upset we make these substances and they make bodily reactions of the sort that I notice. Sometimes, anyway.

"I'm going to make some tea," said Oonan, in such a quiet voice that Arry didn't even jump, "and then I am going to break my word to Halver."

He went off into his kitchen, followed by the cats. Arry sat looking at the fire. Sometimes, she went on thinking, I say to myself, Con's upset, and it isn't because of bodily reactions; it's because once Mally told me that, when Con looks or acts like that, she's upset, and I remember. But that's memory, not knowledge. That's all Halver has now, memory: no knowledge. Why does he call that freedom? If I broke my oath to Halver, as Oonan is about to break his, I could ask Mally. That might be a question she could answer. Unless Halver is outside her province, now. But no, he wasn't outside mine: I knew when he had a fever and how his hand itched.

Oonan came back with the tea. Arry, who was thirsty from climbing the mountain, and arguing with Halver in the dust, and climbing down again, took a healthy gulp and almost choked on it. Oonan had made the kind of strong and bitter brew he would use to stay up for the lambing.

"Don't be so greedy," said Oonan sharply.

Arry glared at him, but he was staring at the fire, as she had been. He said, "I don't know what Halver said to you. He told me that he would deal differently with me, since you had denied him. But he didn't deal differently enough, did he? I denied him also."

"Denied him what?"

"He has a plan," said Oonan. "He wants to free us all from the hill-spell by making us shapeshifters."

"He wanted me to choose to be one," said Arry, "but he said part of the spell the shapeshifters said to him, he said it over me, and I felt it half working; it didn't seem much like choice." So easily she broke her word. The fire did not cower down nor the wind rise; her heart beat on quietly. Maybe it was more like a disease than an injury: the seed was sown but not yet sprouted. Perjury, shapeshifting: which was more mortal? "When it starts to work on you," she said, "it feels like almost falling asleep and half-dreaming you're falling, like the way you jump then, and wake yourself up. Has that happened to you?"

"Not yet. I think he's of two minds," said Oonan. "He can't tell how important the choice is. He would enspell us all in a heartbeat if he thought we would be as he is; but he doesn't know."

"He doesn't know anything," said Arry. It shocked her to say it, but she did, and more. "He's a child again. Only he has no magic." Fire is cold, she thought; water burns; fish fly and sparrows swim.

"He knows nothing now," said Oonan. "As the moon shrinks his old knowledge will grow again."

"Won't he change his mind then and stop wanting to make us all shapeshifters?"

"Remember he is in his second month of this. It has not happened yet."

"But you don't know?"

"That's Mally's province."

"We could ask her."

"Now?"

"Yes, I think so," said Arry.

"Drink your tea first," said Oonan. "You'll need it."

He would know, so she drank.

The wind had picked up when they went outside again, and ghostly clouds were sailing up over the dark lumpy horizon and into the clear and glittering sky. The air smelled of rain.

Mally's house was, not unexpectedly, dark and quiet. Oonan caught Arry's sleeve as she headed for the door to knock on it, and drew her around to the side of the house. He stood under a small round window and said softly, "Wake: the vaulted shadow shatters, trampled to the floor it spanned, and the tent of night in tatters straws the sky-pavilioned land."

Arry cast a wild glance over her shoulder, but the sun did not in fact seem about to spring over the hills. A light did flare after a moment in the round window, and Mally, looking even more like a dandelion puff than usual, peered out at them censoriously. Oonan pulled Arry into the new light, and Mally's face changed. She went away from the window, taking the light with her. Oonan and Arry went back around to the door, and after a moment Mally opened it, carried her lamp outside, and shut the door again.

"What's the matter?" she said to Oonan. She looked perturbed.

"One of my strange not-wolves is Halver," said Oonan.

"But he would swear you to secrecy, by his power as Gnosi," said Mally. Arry opened her mouth, and Mally added, "And you would break your word, both of you— why? What is he doing?"

"Go on," said Oonan, smiling, "you're doing well."

"Who are the other two?" said Mally.

"Now that, I cannot tell you," said Oonan.

"Why? Whom will it break?"

Oonan shrugged. Mally looked at him over her lamp. A few early insects came and danced around the light. Arry considered Oonan, his nerves and his joints and the pathways of his blood. Mally was considering others of his pathways. Arry thought, carefully, over what Halver had said to her. Not much, she realized; she had cut his speech short, perhaps. She thought over what he had said to both of them, to her and Oonan. Frances knew, he had said, although what he said she knew was not really in her province.

"Oonan," said Arry. "It's my mother. It's my mother, isn't it?"

"And your father," said Mally, still looking at Oonan. "Wherefore he would not tell you."

*"Oonan,"* said Arry.

Oonan looked at her. "I thought they would come tonight," he said.

"Halver would tell them not to," said Mally.

"I have to talk to them," said Arry. There is another hurt, she thought, an entire other world of hurt, and this is it, I am in it. "I have to talk to them at once," she said, as if she were telling somebody to apply pressure to a wound.

"I let Halver go," said Oonan. "They could be anywhere on the mountain, Arry, or anywhere for miles around. Wolves run fast and far, Derry says."

"I don't think you can talk to them until they want you to," said Mally. "They may have their reasons."

"What if they do want to and Halver won't let them?"

"There are two of them," said Mally reflectively.

"Halver is larger," said Oonan.

"Is he really?" said Mally. "Frances is taller than he is and Bec is wider."

They looked at one another again. Finally Mally said, "So Halver makes a better wolf."

"Are you surprised?" said Oonan.

And Mally said "No."

Arry gave up trying to think about Halver. I never wondered, she thought, I never wondered where they were. They were just gone; I wished they weren't gone. Why didn't I wonder?

"We'll think of a way to thwart Halver, so they may come to you if you wish it," said Oonan. "Now you should sleep."

"Now," said Arry, out of her aching throat, "we should consider what's to be done—about all of it."

"Not here," said Oonan. "Grel says this kind of sky and air mean rain."

Mally glanced around at her own front door, but said nothing.

"We'd best return to my house," said Oonan. "There's nobody there to wake up. Unless you're worried, Arry."

"Leaving Con to her own devices should worry anybody," said Mally. "If we sit in your kitchen, Arry, and speak quietly?"

"But no blushful Hippocrene, I beg you," said Oonan.

They all laughed, a little hollowly, and walked along to Arry's house.

"Waterpale has a town hall," said Oonan, "where anybody may consult at any hour and wake only the dogs. It has pillars carved with roses, and a spring in the courtyard. Sune says so; so did Frances."

"Waterpale is larger," said Mally, "and full of stone-workers. Frances said that, too."

Arry left them conversing companionably on the doorstep while she got a lamp lit and the kitchen fire built up and burning. She filled the kettle and hung it over the fire and got out the mugs and the morning tea. The cats came stretchily out of unknown sleeping places and sniffed her ankles and asked for milk, so she gave them some. The water boiled; she made the tea. She sat down at the table and drank a mug of it; then she remembered that Oonan liked honey in his, and got up and fetched the honeypot and put it on the table. She sat down again. The white cat got into her lap and settled down, purring and kneading Arry's leggings with both front feet. She leaned her elbow on the table and rested her chin in her hand.

They're not dead, thought Arry. They went off and turned into wolves. Or my father did and then my mother went to find him. Who turned *him* into a wolf? Did he choose? Did she? Why did they come for Halver and not for me? Maybe they don't like being wolves. But then why come for Halver?

Halver liked being a wolf. Halver required change and variety and new experience: this community, this whole country, was too small for him, although certainly being Gnosi and having new children to teach, and children who might as well be new because they were learning and growing, was the best occupation he might have had; it was a mercy his knowledge did not involve sheep or oats or the behavior of owls, which would have driven him to drink or murder in a month's time. If that were possible: one did not know, and could not think how to find out, whether one's knowledge was always congruent with one's nature.

Arry's elbow slid off the table, taking her tea mug with it, and the side of her face cracked resoundingly onto the tabletop. Woollycat sprang out of her lap and fled under the table, where she sat hissing. Arry sat up, rubbing her jaw: there would be an almighty bruise there by morning and probably a big bump, too, but the hinge of the jaw and her teeth were unhurt. You could not say as much for the mug, which lay in three large pieces and a powdering of smaller ones on the flagged floor.

Arry got up and had taken two steps in the direction of the broom when her mind began to work again. She ran out of the kitchen and through the front room to the doorway where she had left Oonan and Mally.

They were gone. Arry thought she felt her heart stop, though in fact, and of course, it did nothing of the sort; there was a kind of constriction of the muscles around the chest, and a matter of breathing, that was all. She stood in the doorway, peering at the dark yard. It had started to rain, very fine and misty. Deciding what to lock and what to take out into the dark on her search made her decide to call first. She drew in her breath for a huge bellow, and Mally, still carrying the lantern, came around the corner of the house followed by Oonan.

"What doubtful way were you going?" said Arry vehemently.

They blinked at her.

"Come in, for certain sake; the tea's getting cold."

They squeezed past her damply, and stood dripping on the floor while she shut and barred the door.

"There were wolf tracks," said Oonan, "or something very like them; I didn't want to go waken Derry. We were following them." His hair was beaded with small drops, like the redbushes up the mountain with their white berries.

Arry stalked past the two of them and into the kitchen; they followed her, sat down at the table, and began pouring the tea.

"Where did the tracks go?" said Arry; as in dealing with Con, it was better to let them get what concerned them out of their heads before turning to their transgression.

"Down to the stream," said Oonan, glumly, "and perhaps through it, or along it; but a healer and a soul-knower with a single lantern could see no more."

"Were the tracks fresh?"

"Yes," said Oonan, positively.

"How do you know?"

Oonan opened his mouth, and closed it again. He looked at Mally. "Were they fresh?"

"How should I know?"

"But how should I?" said Oonan. "For I did."

"It's been happening to me, too," said Arry. "I think it's the wolf-spell."

"But why?"

"That's what Halver meant," said Arry. "About the breaking of history." She was pleased with herself for a moment, but then she remembered. "But he didn't have his own knowledge," she said.

"If the wolf-spell is a spell of ignorance," said Oonan, "then maybe this is our own hill-spell fighting back. We'd have to ask Niss."

"What are we going to *do*?" said Arry.

"Whose province is it, that's the question," said Mally. She frowned, and ran both hands through her hair. "It may well be Niss's, now that I think of it. Halver is very likely under a spell, after all." She yawned. "I wish I'd thought of that an hour ago," she said.

"I could bring her up to the hut tomorrow night," said Oonan, wearily, "and see which of them pokes its whiskers in."

"I want to come too," said Arry. Or do I? she thought. What if they came here, tonight, and found I was gone? What if they come back here? What if they come back here tonight?

"Bring some beer and a fiddle," said Oonan, standing up. "We'll have a celebration." He put his mug down on the table and walked out. Arry heard the door open, and close again.

She looked at Mally, who was draining her own mug and fastening up the jacket she wore over her nightdress. "Is that all?" said Arry. "Let Niss look them over, and ask her?"

"It may be her province," said Mally, standing. She considered Arry's face for a moment, and added, "I'll think whose else it might be, if it isn't hers; we could talk to them tomorrow and see what they think." She put her hand lightly on Arry's head. "Go to sleep," she said. "Before Con wakes up."

And she left, too.

Arry did not go to bed. She almost fell asleep where she sat; then she went into the front room and opened the door wide, and sat in the largest chair, listening.

## &15&

WHEN SHE WOKE up it was full bright sunny day, and
the black cat was standing on her chest and yowling.
Arry sat up in the chair, rubbing her eyes. The cat
jumped down, still yowling, and began pacing around
the chair. Arry had been sitting on her right foot, and it
was asleep. She untucked it laboriously and leaned forward, rubbing it. Sheepnose came around the side of
the chair and stood in front of her, still yowling. She was
standing by a pile of dead mice, quite a large pile, thirty
or forty of them.

Sheepnose yowled again, and then hissed. Arry recognized that this was not the mighty-hunter cry, but a
serious protest. She supposed the white cat might have
brought the mice in, but it seemed unlikely. Woollycat
was lazy. Besides, while both cats might have caught all
those mice in a night's work, it looked more like the
product of dozens. It could take Sheepnose a week to
clean out a moles' nest, after all.

Arry climbed slowly out of the chair, wondering if this was how Sune felt every time she had to stand up. She gathered her breath and bellowed, "Con!"

Con came in the front door immediately. "I thought you'd never wake up," she said. "Look at all those mice."

"Did you see Sheepnose bring them in?"

"No."

"Or Woollycat?"

"No."

"Somebody else's cats?"

"I just woke up and came out and they were there," said Con. "When's breakfast?"

"Let me take a bath first," said Arry. "Where's Beldi?"

"Doing his lessons," said Con, scornfully. "He says we have to go back to school tomorrow. How would he know?"

"Asked Wim, I expect," said Arry, heading for the washing room. "Con, could you take those mice outside? They already smell."

"Sheepnose," said Con sternly. "Take those mice outside again right now."

When Arry came out drying her hair, Sheepnose had done nothing of the sort; neither had Con, who was nowhere in sight. Arry went out the front door and almost tripped over the white cat, who was sniffing deeply and repetitiously all around the path. And no wonder, thought Arry, kneeling for a better look. The soft dirt was pocked with very large tracks, a great many of them, heading for the door and going away again. Arry stood up and followed them. These did not go around the back of the house and down to the stream, as Mally and

Oonan had said the ones they had followed did. Arry could see the single line Oonan and Mally must have seen. But the overlaid and multiplied tracks went the other way, past the pine tree and down the hill and up and down again, into one of the water meadows where there were, indeed, a great many mice.

"Not any more," said Arry, giggling; and then shivered in the warm sun and bright open spaces of the water meadow. She had not heard them, not one of them, as they came in the door and laid those mice at her feet.

She went home in a hurry and made oatmeal pancakes and cheese scones and tea. Beldi emerged as she was taking the scones off the griddle, and poured out the tea for her.

"Where's Con?" he said, sitting down.

"Oh, heavens," said Arry. "I don't know. Not in the water meadow."

She made a swift search of the house; Con was not, of course, in it. She put her head in the kitchen door and said to Beldi, "Come help me find her."

Beldi put a scone whole into his mouth and got up willingly enough. He choked, however, when he saw the pile of mice. Arry hurried him outside and then stood in the sun, at a loss. Con had said nothing that might give a clue to where she was going. Arry had asked her to remove the mice. She might have gone to get somebody to help her, or to do it for her.

"Run on over to Mally's," she said to Beldi, "and see if she's there. And bring her home if she is."

Beldi gave her a reproachful look, swallowed the rest of his scone, and went off over the hill. Arry started to go the other way, to Halver's house, and then realized that if Con came home and nobody was there, she might wander off again. Arry called her a few times. Then she bethought herself of the other line of wolf-tracks, and followed it down to the stream. The path was scuffed here and there and some of the tracks half gone, but small children did not weigh as heavily on the ground as grown wolves, and Con usually walked in the grass or climbed on the rocks anyway. Arry called her again.

Nobody answered. But when Arry came down to the bank of the stream, she found Con sitting in the sunniest, shallowest part of the water, trying to catch minnows in her fingers. The sunlight glittered on the water, and on the silver specks in the gray and pink rock, and on the smooth gray pebbles in the streambed, and even in Con's tangled black hair. The hazel bushes on the far side of the stream were coming into leaf. All the ground under them was covered in daffodils. No wolf had gone that way, or the flowers would be crushed.

"Con!" yelled Arry.

"Well, now you've ruined it," remarked Con, standing up in her dripping smock. "You scared all the fish."

"Don't wander off without telling me!"

"I come down here all the time," said Con.

She did, too. Arry swallowed. What was in my head, she thought. "There are wolves about," she said.

"Not in the *daytime*," said Con, in the same tone she had used about Beldi's doing his lessons.

"Who says?"

"Zia."

"What does she know about it?"

Con pondered. "Well. She might have asked Derry."

"Well, next time you ask Derry, or at least find out if

Zia did. Zia's got a brain like the Autumn Dance, Mally says so. You mustn't just believe her.''

"I don't believe anybody really," said Con, climbing out of the stream and joining Arry on the grassy bank. "Mally says so."

Arry bit back her laugh just in time. "Let's go eat breakfast," she said. "And then we'll take those mice outside."

"Maybe we should eat them," said Con, accompanying her by jumping from rock to rock.

"I can't make mouse stew," said Arry, a little absently.

"Mother could," said Con. "She said they eat it in Fence's Country; but only in the winter."

"I thought I remembered that," said Arry. She added carefully, "Have you been thinking about her lately?"

"I think about her all the time," said Con. "I just don't talk about her."

"Why?"

"Mally says I don't like people to see what I'm thinking."

"Who does?" said Arry.

"Beldi wishes you would," said Con.

Arry stopped and stared at her sister, who was sliding down the last rock before the path went up the hill their house stood on. "Did Mally say that?"

"Mmmmm," said Con.

They started up the hill. "Con," said Arry.

"I don't remember," said Con.

When Beldi came home from Mally's, he brought Tiln with him. Arry had made more pancakes, as a consolation for having sent Beldi all the way to Mally's when Con was just down by the stream. He and Tiln sat down and ate all of them. Tiln looked peculiar, both exhausted and exalted somehow.

"Mally and Wim ask you to my celebration tonight," he said when he had finished eating. "Halver says we won't begin school until the day after tomorrow, so we can celebrate unimpeded." That sounded exactly like Halver, thought Arry. Although the thought of another day chasing Con alarmed her, and the notion that Halver might have something else he would prefer to do in that extra day frightened her, she smiled at Tiln and said they would all be happy to come. And how do I know that, she thought. Well, she didn't, of course. It was just a manner of speaking.

"What do you know?" asked Con, who had been staring at Tiln ever since he came in.

Tiln smiled. "What's ugly *and* what's beautiful," he said.

"Con," said Arry. "Don't go asking him. He's had enough of that."

"Only if it really matters to you," said Tiln to Con.

"Everything matters to me," said Con.

"That's not what Mally says," said Tiln; and as Con continued to stare at him and did not even open her mouth, he made a little bow to Arry, as Halver had taught them all but none of them ever bothered actually to do. "We'll see you with pleasure at sunset," he said, and left the kitchen.

Arry said, "Let's get those mice out of our house."

"Tiln must have walked right over them," said Beldi.

"We should have asked him if they were beautiful or ugly," said Con, scrambling out of her chair and making for the front room.

The pile of mice was still there. Arry wondered a little that the cats had not dragged them off somewhere, or eaten them on the spot. Maybe it was the smell of wolf.

"We must put them somewhere the crows can get them," she said.

"We need a box or a bag," said Beldi.

"Let's use the milk pans," said Con.

"No," said Arry.

"You could even stew them in the milk pans," said Con.

Arry went off into the kitchen and found, among the piles of discarded objects still to be dealt with, a wooden milk bucket acquired when they had kept a goat. She brought the bucket and the fire tongs back to the front room and began lifting mice out of the pile and dropping them into the bucket. Con demanded to try, and after dropping a mouse onto Beldi's feet and one onto Arry's, got quite fast and accurate at it. Arry sat back down in the chair she had slept in and tried not to watch. The mice were certainly in no pain now, but they made her flinch just the same.

When Con was finished, she sent Con and Beldi to carry the bucket up to the top of Windy Hill and spread the mice around for the crows. She herself got water and soap and the brush and knelt to scrub the stain off the floor. At least wolves were tidier than cats. Cats would have left all those mice on the rug, at the very least. She held the brush dripping over the floor, and paused.

Where the drops of water had fallen, lines of bright, beautiful, and unnatural green showed on the smooth gray floor. Arry dripped more water, and more, and finally scraped very lightly with the brush over the mess the mice had left. The brush did not take off the green, so she applied it a little harder. When she had cleared all the soapy mousy mass of water off that patch of floor, the green lines revealed themselves as blocky letters, which said uncompromisingly, "Keep the wolf far hence, that's foe to men."

It was part of a burial spell Oonan had taught her. She had not even been born, he and Wim and Mally all said, the last time anybody here had had to use it, but tears came up in her eyes and ran down her cheeks. When one of them dripped down onto the floor, all the green letters winked out like the stars at dawn.

Arry wiped her nose fiercely on her hand and scrubbed the entire floor, much to the annoyance of Sheepnose, who came in halfway through, and Woollycat, who came in just as she had finished cleaning up Sheepnose's dirty pawprints. She wiped up the new prints, and emptied her bucket, and washed and dried the bucket and the brush and hung them in their places.

Then she sat in the front door, staring at the crocuses under the pine tree, waiting for Con and Beldi to come back so she could disobey the message left her. Her brain must be slow, but it had finally occurred to her that, while wolves might sleep in the woods or out on the mountain, her parents were, presumably, wolves only when the full moon was up. Where would they take shelter, then, during all the days? She meant to go around to all the possible places, and find them.

She spent some time wondering what to do with Con and Beldi, and finally decided that she would just take them along. They had a right to see their parents too, after all, surely they must.

When they got back, Con looked flushed and triumphant and Beldi distinctly frazzled. Arry told them she needed to go visit Sune and that she meant to go all around the hills picking flowers. Beldi said he would rather do his lessons, and looked pleadingly at Arry, so she set off with just Con. It was almost hot, and after the night's rain rather sticky. All the early leaves had doubled their size since yesterday, and the late ones had come out vigorously. Larks and robins and sparrows and wheatears sang madly in all directions; the mockingbird made cat noises, as if the concert of its fellows had disconcerted it.

When they got to Halver's house, Arry suffered a pang of cowardice, and said to Con, "I want to speak to Halver for a moment. Will you run down the hill and tell Sune I'm coming?"

"What about?" said Con.

"The baby," said Arry, patiently.

"Halver doesn't know anything about babies."

So much for misdirection. "I want to talk to him about Beldi." Which was true as far as it went.

"Oh," said Con, and ran full tilt down the rocky hill. Arry winced, and turned her back, and knocked hard on Halver's door.

It was strange to be knocking to be admitted to school. Nobody admitted her, either. She knocked again. Then she went around the house knocking on all the windows she could reach. The ones in the back, where you would expect people to be sleeping, were all shuttered—in this weather. She would have shouted, but she was afraid Con and Sune would hear her; the wind was blowing down the hill from Halver's house to Sune's. There was no sound from the house, but Arry thought she felt somebody listening. She went back to the door and tried it. It was bolted. She tried the low schoolroom window, and it swung open easily. Arry looked over her shoulder at Sune's house, saw nobody, and climbed in.

The schoolroom was dim and cool and tidy, and smelled of oil paint and sawdust. Arry marched across the red rug before she could think about it, and almost failed to stop in time when she saw that the door between schoolroom and Halver's part of the house was shut. She pushed at it. It was bolted from the other side. Arry thought, and shook her head. No. She could remember no bolt on that door. But he *is* the wolf, she thought, why should he bolt *his* door? She heard herself laughing, and stopped. But something had moved on the door's other side.

Arry retreated to the window, picking up the largest of the wooden geometry blocks on her way. They can't be wolves in the daytime, she thought; but her heart was beating as fast as it ever had and she could hardly breathe. She wasn't hurt; this was fear.

There was the creak of a wooden bolt withdrawing, and the door opened. Arry opened her eyes as wide as she could.

It was only Halver. He was blinking and tousled and wearing his nightshirt. He had no fever, no headache, no sore joints or muscles. His hand still itched.

"It's me," said Arry.

"I thought it might be," said Halver, mildly. "What do you want?"

"I want to see my parents."

"They aren't here," said Halver.

"Where are they?"

"Choose," said Halver, in a gentle and reasonable tone that made Arry shiver, "and I'll take you to them when next the full moon rises."

"Very well," said Arry, "I choose not to be a wolf."

Halver smiled. "You wot well what I did mean," he said, in the accents of Arry's mother.

Arry put down the block, lest she throw it at him. "I'll find them myself," she said, and with no regard to dignity at all she climbed back out the window and ran down the hill to Sune's house.

**16**

CON WAS IN fact at Sune's house. Sune was sitting in her rocking chair and spinning; Con was sprawled on the floor with Sune's button box. She must have been importunate, or Sune must be very tired. Sune was certainly tired. Con had probably been importunate as well.

"There's tea in the kitchen," said Sune.

"Thank you, but I can only stay a moment."

"Con's settled for hours," said Sune.

Arry looked at her, and Sune nodded. Arry widened her eyes, and Sune nodded again. "Thank you," said Arry. "I'll be back in a hour perhaps. Can I bring you anything?"

"Strawberries," said Sune, reflectively.

"Too early," said Con, without looking up from her buttons.

"I know, chick; I was being funny."

"There's the strawberry wine," said Arry.

"Don't tempt me," said Sune. "Oonan says a bit of wine wouldn't do harm, but I have read such things."

"I'll be as quick as I can," said Arry. "Don't be a nuisance, Con."

Neither of them made any response to this. Arry left hurriedly and made for the high meadow as fast as she could. On the way she passed Tiln and Zia gathering flowers for the party, and Wim playing his flute, and Derry crawling along the ground like a dog after some especially delectable smell. Arry climbed off the path, which was rather steep just here, and came up behind her. Wolf tracks. They had come this way, then.

"Derry," said Arry.

"They are certainly wolf tracks," said Derry, sitting back on her heels and wiping her face.

"Derry, do wolves catch mice?"

"Yes," said Derry. "And eat them too. This happens especially in the far north, when the herds of snow deer move to colder places than the wolves care to follow. They eat mice then, waiting for the deer to come back. And a mother wolf with cubs who cannot hunt yet, she will find mice close by and bring them back."

"I thought so," said Arry. "Have they killed any more sheep?"

"No," said Derry. "They don't seem to like to come near Oonan's, though they've been all up and down most of the hills. And they seem to have gone up to the high meadow again, though there are no sheep there now."

"Is that where you're going?"

"I'd like to," said Derry, "but Vand needs help with the bees."

"I could go look for you," said Arry. "At least, I

could tell you if there are tracks like these. How many wolves have been by?''

"Just two," said Derry, "the smaller two. Don't go toiling up there in the heat just for me, Arry."

"I want to gather plants anyway," said Arry, more or less at random. Luckily Derry was not the one to question her about which plants, or whether any of them would be growing yet, or be gatherable at this time, in the high meadow.

"Do just keep an eye out for the tracks, then," said Derry, "and if they don't go where you're going, just remember where they branch off."

Arry said she would do so, and Derry turned and went off to her own house. Arry went on as fast as she could without running, which might attract attention and would leave her unable to speak when she got where she was going.

The high meadow was full of daisies and sunlight and the shadows of birds. Derry might have been able to find the wolf tracks amid the grass and rock and flowers, but Arry was bewildered. She made for the shepherd's hut instead. It was cool and dim and empty. Arry scuffed her foot over the straw and dust on the floor, and the bright green letters glowed at her like strange lamplight seen through a dirty window. She cleared the floor, and read, "Neither yield to the song of the siren nor the voice of the hyena, the tears of the crocodile nor the howling of the wolf."

"I won't if you'll let me *see* you!" cried Arry. Nobody answered her. She went back outside and sat down on a rock. It was warm from the sun, almost hot. A white butterfly dipped over the daisies and soared away out of sight. The birds sang fiercely. In the shadow of the rock scilla bloomed as blue as the empty sky. Arry tried to empty her mind, to catch whatever other knowledge might be waiting to move into it. Nothing came.

When she thought it must be time to go relieve Sune of Con, she got down off the rock and walked over to Derry's house. Derry had finished helping Vand with the bees and was churning the first milk from their cow. Arry asked her what the siren, the hyena, and the crocodile were.

Derry frowned, her strong brown arms moving up and down. "The crocodile is in my province: it is a river-going reptile of the remote south."

"Does it cry?"

"No," said Derry.

Arry thought she would ask Sune about crocodile tears. She looked expectantly at Derry, who said, "The hyena is on the margin of my province; it is a companion of predators, feeding on carrion. It is related to the wolf and the fox, but rarely kills."

"What's its voice like?"

"Raucous," said Derry.

"And what's a siren?"

"The siren is an arcane and intelligent creature, according to Sune; it's outside my province."

"What does Sune say it's like?"

"A woman with the tail of a fish, and a beautiful voice; they sit on rocks and sing sailors to their deaths."

"Ah," said Arry.

She went along to Sune, who told her that crocodiles affected to cry and then snatched up and ate the sympathetic bystander who got too close. Arry put this away to think about later, and took Con home. They spent the afternoon peacefully making a present for Tiln. It was hard to think of something suitable, given what his knowledge was. It was Beldi who hit on the idea of giving Tiln the means to make beauty. He suggested making paint, as their mother had used to do for them. "Tiln says he never has enough," he said. They also found a collection of their mother's brushes, and cleaned and repaired them. It gave Arry a pang to let them go, but none of the three of them painted, and it seemed that Frances did not want to come home.

They ate a very sparse supper, since they were going to a party, and at sunset shut the cats inside and went off to Tiln's house.

Oonan joined them on the way, and Derry and Vand and Niss and Jony and Elec. As they climbed the hill to Tiln's house they were hailed by Grel and Rine, whom nobody had seen since the solstice. Everybody else seemed to be already inside. Tiln was greeting people at the door, gravely. The whole house was full of people and food and music. Arry went about smiling and nodding and collecting a plate of food, but what she really wanted was to find Halver. He would have to leave before the moon rose, and she intended to follow him when he did.

She finally found him sitting in a corner with Sune, glaring at Oonan over Sune's head. Sune looked extremely tired, and felt it, but the walk didn't seem to have done her any harm. Arry felt disinclined to watch Oonan and Halver argue any more, so she went to find Niss. This was not easy either: Niss was about Beldi's size, and though she had red hair, which ought to make her more visible, she usually covered it with a black scarf.

Arry edged out into the kitchen, and found Mally making nutcakes. "Did you talk to Niss yet?" demanded Arry.

Mally stopped smiling. "No, I did not," she said.

"Can I do it?"

Mally scooped the nutcakes off the griddle onto a board, and slapped the next batch onto the griddle. "If you'll put it to her as a hypothetical," she said. "I take your word seriously, even if you don't."

"I broke it already," said Arry impatiently.

"And the sky didn't fall?" said Mally. "If you promise not to throw rocks, is throwing one as bad as throwing a hundred?"

"As well be hung for a sheep," began Arry.

"That's about law," said Mally. "This is about you."

"If I put it to her as a hypothetical, will she be able to answer properly?"

"Better," said Mally. "Responsibility makes her nervous."

"How hypothetical must I be?"

"Don't mention Halver's name," said Mally, "and don't tell her what the spell is."

The party overflowed into the kitchen at this point, as the musicians came into the only open and half-quiet space left to try to tune their instruments and agree on the first three dances. Arry nodded at Mally and squeezed by Wim and Jony and Grel and Tany and her own brother, who was clutching a drum and looking pleased. She grinned at him.

Niss was not in the main room; she was not in any of the bedrooms. Arry went back outside. Jonat and Zia and Con were building a bonfire. She walked around the house, finding nobody but the dogs; and when she came back to the door, Oonan stepped swiftly out of it and made her jump.

"Did you find her?" he said.

"No," said Arry.

"I don't believe she's here at all."

"Did you ask Jonat?"

"Where is he?"

"Right there, making the fire."

Oonan walked over to the pile of wood and said, without preliminaries, "Jonat, is Niss here?"

"She had something to see to," said Jonat, without glancing up. "Con, I'll need the moss now. Thank you. But she said she'd be here for the dancing."

"Thank you," said Oonan.

They walked down the path a little way.

"Let's go to her house, then," said Arry. "I want to know what to do before the moon rises."

"Is there some hurry?" said Oonan.

Arry did not want to discuss her parents with him. She said, "Once the moon changes, nothing can happen for another month; we can't find anything out, can we?"

"Why not?" said Oonan.

"You feel the same way," said Arry.

"I do," said Oonan. "But I mistrust the feeling."

"What can it hurt to go?"

"That's your province, I suppose," said Oonan.

"Come on, then," said Arry.

They went up and down, through the Little Marsh and up again, across a long narrow meadow full of rocks, and down and up one last time. Niss and Jonat and the children who lived with them had a small stone house with the only thatched roof left in these parts.

There was a light in it, not the yellow of lamplight, but a vivid, beautiful, and unnatural green.

"Oh," said Oonan, stopping and staring up at the house. The green light fell on his sweaty face and the bright untidy spikes of his hair. He looked bemused.

"They're in there," said Arry, and made for the door.

She was pulled up short with a jerk that felt just like the wolf-spell hitting and bouncing away again, but it was just Oonan grabbing the tail of her jacket.

"Wait just a moment," he said. "You wouldn't like it if she interrupted you in your work, would you?"

"I think my parents are in there and I want to go in there *now*," said Arry, prying at his fingers.

Oonan let go of her, but he said, "There's only one door to that house."

"There are windows," said Arry, and ran across the rocky yard and into the house.

It was very green inside, which somehow made it hard to see. Arry stopped short. A cat yowled somewhere. Something clattered.

"Stand still and be silent," said Niss's light voice, very sharply.

Arry stood still, biting her lip. She saw the hearth, on which burned the green fire; she saw two cushioned chairs, three hard chairs, a table, pots and pans hanging on the walls, a striped rug, the black-and-white cat, a stack of firewood, herbs hanging from the rafters, a broom, a wooden puzzle shaped like a sheep. No wolves. She could not see Niss, and then, as she thought the name, she saw the little human figure standing to one side of the fire with a bunch of flowers in her hands.

She was looking at Arry, and when Arry had stood

still and silent for what seemed like a very long time, she went back to breaking off flowers and tossing them into the fire. It died down to yellow each time and then blossomed back to green.

"From the hag and hungry goblin," said Niss, tossing flowers, "that into rags would rend ye, and the spirit that stands by the naked man in the book of moons defend ye."

Oh, no, thought Arry.

"From noise of scare-fires rest ye free," said Niss, "from murders benedicite. From all mischances that may fright your pleasing slumbers in the night, mercy secure you all, and keep the goblin from you while you sleep."

What's a goblin, thought Arry, she keeps going on about them.

Niss tossed the last blossom onto the fire, which turned slowly red and gold again, like any wood fire on a cool spring evening. "Come in," she said.

Arry walked over the threshold, with Oonan behind her. "Did you see the wolves?" said Arry.

"Wolves?" said Niss, startled. "No; not a one."

"Why were you doing that spell, then?"

"Something's amiss," said Niss, "and I was setting it straight, that's all."

"What was it?" said Oonan.

"Things that should be firm were shifting," said Niss.

Arry wondered if this meant Halver would not turn into a wolf tonight after all. She meant to be there to see, in either case. "What things?" she said.

"The ones you've come to ask me about, I expect," said Niss coolly. "Would you like some tea? The pepper-

mint's come up on the south side of the house, so you
won't have to settle for old chamomile."

"Weren't you coming to Tiln's party?" said Oonan.

"There's time for tea and then for that," said Niss.
She made a small pile of pinecones at the front of the
fireplace, lit it from the larger fire, and put a kettle on it.
Then she looked at them. It was difficult to make out
her expression.

"Mally said I had to put this to you as a hypothetical," said Arry, baldly; she could not think well enough
to be clever or cunning or even, she feared, properly
courteous. "What we need to know, Oonan and Mally
and I, is whether a particular matter is your province.
But I think you've shown already that it is."

"I cannot tell you all I would," said Niss, slowly.

Arry looked at Oonan, where he still stood in the
doorway; the firelight glinted in his eyes as he stared
back at her and nodded his head. "Nor can we tell you
all we would," he said.

"But is it your province?" said Arry. "Are you dealing with it?"

"I'm doing what I may," said Niss, "but it seems
larger than provinces. Spells are my province. You
named Mally; surely it is to do with her also, the character of those enspelled? And if you and Oonan are worried, then there must be danger, whether of hurt or of
damage."

The kettle boiled, and Niss padded her hands with a
towel and lifted it off the fire and poured the water into
a shallow bowl. The smell of peppermint filled Arry's
head.

Arry said, "But if it's all caused by a spell, can't you
just counter it?"

Niss laughed, heartily, and handed her a smaller shallow bowl of tea. "If it's all caused by pain," she said, "can't you just counter it?" She gave Oonan his bowl. "If you perceive it's broken, cannot you fix it?"

Arry felt obscurely put upon, as if Con had talked her around to something. "Aren't spells different?"

"No," said Niss, flatly. She perched on the edge of the table, her feet dangling, and gestured with her bowl at the rest of the room.

Arry sat down in a hard chair, and Oonan in a cushioned one. They sipped tea for a while in silence.

"But it's partly your province," said Arry.

"Yes," said Niss.

"Will you come with Oonan and Mally and me, then, at moonrise?"

Niss shook her head. "There's will involved," she said. "What magic alone can accomplish to safeguard us, I have done. The rest is talk, or action; it isn't magic."

"But—" said Arry.

"You're free to choose," said Niss. "That is what I have done. The rest is not mine."

"What about you? Are you free to choose too?"

"I have chosen," said Niss. "To be as I am."

"Will what you've done keep them from biting us in our sleep and making our choice for us?"

Oonan moved in his chair but said nothing; Niss slid off the table and said, "Is that the mechanism, then? I was told otherwise."

"I don't know," said Arry. "I thought you would."

Niss rubbed her hand over her head, pulling off the black scarf. Her hair fell down her shoulders like a second fire. "No," she said. "I can't tell, I can't see. It must be other than magic, the essential operation must be of character, or of knowledge, or of the body itself. It isn't mine.''

Mally tried to give the job to her, thought Arry, and now she's giving it back to Mally. She looked at Oonan, who put his bowl down and stood up. "Will you walk back to the party with us?" he said to Niss.

Niss nodded, and wound her hair up again in her scarf. Then she said to the fire, "Some must watch while some must sleep." The fire contracted itself and turned green again. Niss ushered them out of her house, and shut the door firmly.

Lagging behind the other two, who were talking amiably about whether any spell in heaven or earth would really keep a sheep from straying if it wanted to, Arry looked over her shoulder at the house. It glowed dimly under its thatched roof, like a green luminous mushroom with greener spots.

The bonfire was roaring when they got back, and both inside and outside the dancing had started. The musicians were crammed into the doorway so that everybody could hear them. Arry found Beldi at once, dancing with Zia; both of them were laughing, and they danced a great deal better than Arry would have expected. It was Vand, next to them, who tangled the long line going through the arch by forgetting to turn around twice before his partner swung him.

But she could not find Con. If Con was not watching Zia, plotting with Zia, or playing with Zia, it was hard to think where she might be. Arry went around to the kitchen door, which was open; out of the doorway came a lovely odor of baking honeycake. She went in. Con was sitting at the table, listening intently to Halver. His back was to Arry; Con had just to turn her head to the right to see her sister.

Arry stood still. Halver was saying, "This is the only way to know everything."

You did not have to be Mally to understand what Halver was doing.

Con scowled as only Con could. "How do you know it's the only way?"

Arry would have grinned, if she had not been afraid that any movement would make one of them see her.

"I don't," said Halver, readily. "But it's the only way for you, here and now."

"Mother said anything worth having was worth waiting for."

"You have been waiting for it," said Halver. "You needn't wait any longer now."

"What if I'd rather?" said Con. Halver had managed to make her suspicious—not a difficult thing to do, but she had probably never in her five years had better reason to be suspicious than now. Arry tried to think what to say. If choice were all it took, standing here in silence was not the best of courses.

Halver had been teaching Con for two years now; he too knew her suspicious mood. He said mildly, "Well, you know, if you go on waiting for the new bread long enough, it's day-old bread and then old bread and then it's stale, and you can't have new bread until next week."

"A week's not long," said Con.

Arry did grin. They didn't notice.

Halver grinned, too, unfortunately. "Very well," he said. "When Mally brings the birch candy back from Waterpale, if you don't eat it, it's gone until next spring."

"It tastes strange anyway," said Con.

Arry bit her lip. She wanted to laugh. At the same time she knew she must do something. Con was interested, or she would not be sitting here when there was music and dancing and food and Zia all just a few steps away.

The smell of honeycake was growing darker and stronger. Either it was going to burn, or Mally would be in here any moment, interrupting. Arry scuffed the sole of her boot on the floor and moved forward briskly. Halver had twitched at the sound and frowned almost as ferociously as Con could. Con went on looking at Halver.

"Are you supposed to be watching these?" demanded Arry, opening the door of Mally's oven and looking around for something to protect her hands.

"No," said Halver. "We just wanted a quiet place to talk."

"Well, they're about to burn," said Arry, using the wadded hem of her skirt and maneuvering the hot trays out of the oven and onto the racks awaiting them. She looked from Con to Halver and took a risk. "Shall I leave now?"

"No," said Con, still looking at Halver.

"Arry knows all about it," said Halver.

"She does not," said Con, with considerable scorn.

Halver, Arry was interested to note, was momentarily confounded. His mouth dropped. Then he turned red.

Then he laughed, briefly. "I misspoke myself," he said. "I did tell her, Con, about being a wolf."

"Arry doesn't want to be a wolf," said Con, in the pitying tone that often succeeded her scornful one.

"Why don't you ask her?" said Halver. He pushed his chair back, stood up, and left the room without further ado. He still looked a little red.

"Do you want to be a wolf?" said Con, turning to regard Arry.

"Not Halver's sort," said Arry. "What did he tell you, Con?"

"Is Halver a sort of wolf?" said Con.

"When the moon's full he is. I saw him. Derry said his tracks were wolf tracks, but that he didn't act like a wolf. A sort of wolf is exactly the phrase."

"You never tell me anything," said Con.

"Halver made me promise not to."

"Oh," said Con, disconcerted. She pondered. "He didn't make me promise."

"That's because you really never do tell anybody anything. He knew you'd want to keep it to yourself."

"Only Mally knows that."

Now I'm doing it, thought Arry. "Mally would have told him, don't you think, when you started school?"

Con abandoned this line of discussion by saying, "If I'm a wizard, I can be a wolf or anything else either, whether the moon is full or not."

"Probably you can," said Arry.

"So why should I be Halver's sort of wolf?"

"No reason in the world," said Arry firmly.

"But he thought I should. Why did he think so?"

"Well, what did he say?"

"He just said I'd *like* it," said Con. "Because then I'd know everything."

"Well, he's been a wolf and he doesn't know everything, does he?"

"That's what I told him," said Con.

They must have been around the subject several times before Arry got there. She could not think how to ask if Halver had mentioned their parents without actually mentioning them herself. "Why else did he say you'd like it?"

"He said I'd like the other wolves," said Con. "Better than people. And he said I could run far, and go all up and down the mountains and all the way to the Hidden Land and Fence's Country." She paused, fixing Arry with her big dark eyes. "If we were wolves," she said, "could we find them?"

"Did Halver say we could?"

"No. I just wondered."

Clever Halver, thought Arry. And here I thought perhaps being a wolf had made you less able to cope with your charges. "I don't know, Con," she said.

"Well, who does?"

"If we could think who knew," said Arry, "I think we'd know ourselves. Since there's no province for finding lost things."

"Why isn't there?"

Arry shook her head. "I want you to promise me something, Con," she said. "If you decide to be a wolf, tell me first."

"I don't want to be a wolf."

"If you change your mind."

"I don't want to."

*"Con."*

"If I'm a wolf," said Con, sliding out of her chair, "you can be a wolf too." And she ran out of the room, laughing.

WHEN ARRY CAME into the front room the musicians had stopped playing and Mally was just beginning to organize the giving of the gifts. People kept streaming in and streaming in. It was hot, from the lamps and the people. Sune was exactly where she had been—her feet hurt even sitting down—and Halver had gone back to sit next to her. Arry found Oonan hunched into one corner of a settle behind the table the presents were on. She couldn't talk to him or even approach him until the gifts had all been dealt with. She was worried about moonrise, but Halver had far more reason to worry than she did. He looked serene.

Arry went and sat on the floor next to Beldi. "Has Halver been talking to you?" she whispered.

"No," said Beldi. "Am I supposed to talk to him?"

"No, it's all right, never mind."

Beldi looked resigned.

Mally finished piling objects on the table and brought

Tiln in from outside. He was blinking a little in the strong light, sweaty and breathless from the dance; but smiling. People smiled back at him, and the talk grew less. Mally sat him down at the table and looked around the room, and everybody stopped talking. Mally thanked everyone for coming. Then she said, "We have a problem in manners here. It's customary for one receiving a gift to say, 'Thank you, it's beautiful,' but Tiln can't say that if it isn't true."

"I could say, 'It's just what I've been wanting,'" said Tiln, with none of his usual hesitance. "I don't know any more about that than anybody else does."

"No, but I do," said Mally, ruffling his hair.

"I shall say, 'It's very nice,' then, shall I?"

"I think that's sufficiently meaningless," said Mally. Her eyes moved around the room.

She's looking for my mother, thought Arry. Whose province was language. Do wolves have language? Nobody said anything. After a moment, Mally nodded to Tiln, and he began to accept his presents.

Spring was a good time to come into your knowledge. Good things to eat were coming back into abundance; people had been working all winter on this or that frivolous or useful or strange thing, inventing new games and toys, fooling with the shape of a sleeve or the set of a button, wondering how that recipe would taste with walnuts rather than currants. Arry watched Tiln carefully, and thought she could tell, if not which things he thought were beautiful, at least which ones he had been wanting. When he got to the paint and brushes, he opened every pot and dipped a finger in it to see what color it held; and then he smiled.

The last thing he took from the table was something

Arry had not recognized as a present at all. It was a long shaggy gray and cream and black coat; she had thought it was just a sort of rug or covering over the table top. It was from Halver. "So you can find beauty in the dead of winter without requiring Arry and Oonan's ministrations after," said Halver from where he sat by Sune.

"What is it?" said Tiln, running his hand down a sleeve.

Halver looked at Derry, who said, "Wolfskin."

Arry stopped breathing. She began again almost at once. Hides must be cured and treated, coats must be sewn; the wolf this had belonged to was a last year's wolf at the very oldest. But she still felt cold, in all this heat.

"It's very nice," said Tiln, in an awed tone.

Everybody laughed, and Vand started tuning his fiddle. People stood up and stretched, and went back outside, or into the kitchen for food and drink, or up to the table to look more closely at Tiln's presents. Arry sat where she was, staring at Halver. He was talking to Sune; after a moment she nodded, and Halver put his hand under her elbow and helped her stand up.

Arry got up too, swiftly. Halver had helped Sune walk here; how thoughtful of him to see her home again before he went and turned into a wolf. A wolf has no arm for you to lean on. Arry stifled a laugh. Sune and Halver paused to speak to Tiln, and then went out the door. Arry went after them, and paused in the doorway to give them a good start. She had thought of simply accompanying them on the grounds that she wanted to go home now, too, but they would wonder about Con and Beldi.

They kept stopping to speak to people, so Arry made

a quick foray through the house and found Oonan in the kitchen, cutting up a wheel of red cheese.

"Halver's taking Sune home," she said. "I'm going to follow him until moonrise."

"And what are you going to do then?" said Oonan. "Can you run as fast as a wolf? You can't follow him, Arry, unless he wants you to."

"Could Derry?"

"Ask her," said Oonan.

"I can't, Oonan, without telling her why."

"Then why bring it up?"

"I have to find my parents," said Arry through her teeth.

"I think," said Oonan, putting down his knife and regarding her gravely, "that they have to find you."

"They're telling me to keep *away*," said Arry; it was almost a wail, and she stopped talking and looked at the door.

"When; how?" said Oonan, coming around the table.

Arry told him about the green letters.

"Then do as they tell you," said Oonan. "They're your parents."

"They're not themselves."

"Who says so?"

"Oh, you're *hopeless*!" cried Arry, and bolted back through the front room and outside.

Sune and Halver were gone, but there was really only one path home, especially for someone so heavily pregnant, and she caught up to them without difficulty in the water meadow. They were about halfway across it when she came down the hill; she could see Sune's hair glinting faintly and hear the murmur of their voices.

Arry considered going to Sune's along the stream, which would be shorter, and then following Halver from there. She could think of no particular reason he should not wish to take Sune home and get out of sight before turning into a wolf.

Unless, of course, he wanted for some reason for Sune to see him do it. This was Mally's province; Arry had no idea why or whether he would do such a thing. The mere fact that she had thought of it at all made her uneasy. She stepped out softly into the water meadow after the two of them. If they looked back they might see her, since she was wearing a white shirt; but she walked on anyway.

They did not look back. They went on steadily on their way home, passing Oonan's house and Arry's and Halver's and moving slowly down the hill to Sune's small house. Arry came around the corner of Halver's house just in time to hear Halver say, "What in all doubt is that?"

Sune's house, like Niss's, showed green light through its windows and around its door.

"Niss said she might be by, with some kindly spells for young Knot," said Sune, placidly.

"Green's for warding," said Halver, not placidly at all.

They walked forward to the house; Arry came half-way along the downhill path and then sat down next to a rock and watched. Sune opened her door and the green light poured out like some strange form of melted butter and colored all the rocks and grass and flowers with itself.

Sune said something, and then laughed.

"What does it say?" said Halver.

He was keeping well back, Arry saw, and as much out of the light as he could manage.

Sune said, "And from the wolf I save thy soul, by my might and power, and keep thy soul, my darling dear, from dogs that would devour; and from the lion's mouth that would thee all in sunder shiver, and from the horns of unicorns I safely thee deliver.

"Mally says Niss is over-careful," said Sune, laughter still in her voice. "Unicorns indeed. Will you come in, Gnosi, and take some tea?"

"Thank you, no," said Halver. "If I hurry, I'll be back in time to hear Wim play the pipes." And he backed out of the green light and came quickly up the hill. Arry sat where she was. He plunged past her, almost running. Sune had gone into her house and shut the door. The green faded and went out, and plain yellow light lit up the windows. Arry got up and went after Halver.

His hand was itching furiously, and he was having more trouble with his breathing than she would have expected from somebody who had walked and run in these hills all his life. Arry ran lightly behind him, trying to be quiet but not worrying overmuch about it. Her feet seemed to know the path and to avoid rocks and roots of themselves. The air was growing lighter. Arry looked up and saw the moon shouldering its way over the hills. She was immediately shaken by a violent dislocation of everything, and just as it subsided she tripped on nothing and fell on her face.

So much for my feet knowing anything, she thought, sitting up and brushing gravel out of her leggings. She had torn her skirt, too, but was not herself hurt. She got up quickly and looked around for Halver. He had been at the bottom of the hill she was just rounding the top of, but he was nowhere to be seen. She ran down and up again and turned in a circle at the top of the next hill, looking for any movement, at man- or wolf-height. Nothing. She pushed her hands into the pockets of her shirt, thinking. He could not go to the sheep hut; possibly the whole meadow was barred to him: she didn't know the extent of Niss's spells.

"I wonder," said Arry to the rising mist, and she turned and trudged all the way back to Halver's house and up to his shut door. No green light. She knew he had eaten quite a lot at Tiln's party, but she did not know if his wolf-stomach needed feeding separately. What did he do when he wasn't killing sheep and dragging people about to witness his transformation so he could try to talk them into sharing it?

"Bother," said Arry, and went back to Tiln's party.

She stopped at her own house first. It did not glow hugely as Sune's had, but there was a faint wavery almost-light about it, like the reflection of sunlight off water on the shady underside of a bridge. Arry supposed the warding was still working. There had been nothing like that around Halver's house.

The party, when she got back to it, had shrunk but grown denser, like paper crushed tightly. A number of parents had taken their children home. Most of the remaining party was playing charades in the front room; Beldi was with them. Arry slipped behind Tiln, who appeared to be enacting a drunken cow with a broom, and went into the kitchen. To her great relief, Con was there, rolling out little balls of dough into circles so Zia could put spoonsful of honey and nuts on them and

Tany could fold them into crescents and give them to Mally, who was frying them in fat. If everything were only the way this kitchen smells, thought Arry vaguely.

She sat down on a stool out of the way.

"Why do they puff up when you fry them, Ma?" said Zia.

"Dough-sprites," said Con.

"I say so," said Tany.

Mally said, "The heat of the boiling fat expands the liquid in the dough. Grel says so."

"Can't we have dough-sprites?" said Zia.

"We can if we want to," said Tany.

"Maybe in yeast," said Mally, lifting a strainer full of little brown crescents out of her kettle and emptying it onto a towel.

"Let's make something with yeast in, then," said Zia.

"I don't think this is going to be that long a party," said Mally. "People won't stay for breakfast."

Arry took this to mean that Mally hoped they wouldn't. She was tired, and her arms were speckled with little burns from the spitting fat. Arry was tired, too. Con and the other children were emphatically not tired in the least. I should send all of them after Halver, thought Arry, except that he could eat them in one bite if he fancied eating a child. I wish I could tell if he did fancy it, if he could. But no, he wouldn't want to talk them into becoming wolves if he wanted to eat them. Unless it's to prevent himself eating them.

"Do wolves eat children?" she said aloud.

"Not if they can help it," said Mally, very quickly; Arry suspected that reassurance was more on her mind than the truth. But she added, "I asked Derry earlier tonight. She said, not if they can find anything else, even mice or frogs."

Oh, fine, thought Arry, I'll come home tonight and find a pile of frogs on my doorstep.

"They can eat me if they like," said Tany, licking his fingers. "When I'm inside I'll make them run around."

"Does it hurt if a wolf eats you?" said Con.

"Extremely," said Arry.

Tany looked at her. He was very dark, but he had light blue eyes, which made him always seem to be thinking of strange things. On the other hand, thought Arry, given what he said sometimes, perhaps he really was always thinking of strange things. He said now, "Not if they eat me."

Arry looked at him. What a mercy he was not her child. "Just you wait," which was what she usually said to similar pronouncements by Con, did not seem precisely appropriate here. She was still thinking what to say when a jolt of pain as if Mally had emptied the hot fat over her went down her arm. She sprang off the stool. "Somebody *is* hurt," she said, and ran out of the kitchen, through the startled players of charades and into the windy moonlit darkness.

"Oonan!" she yelled belatedly, peering around in the dark. She ran up the next hill, and collided hard with somebody coming down. It was Jony, and her arm was torn open from the round outside bone of the wrist right up to the elbow.

"What happened?" said Arry, ripping at her skirt since it was torn already. Oonan must sew this up, she thought, it will make a terrible scar even with a great deal of marigold, but I don't think the muscle is hurt; that would feel different. *"Oonan!"*

"It was a wolf," said Jony. She sounded annoyed, but she was also quite shaky. It was hard to tell, but there seemed to be a lot of blood. Arry was not equipped to tell where it was coming from or how much of it there was really.

"It asked me if I'd like to be a wolf too," said Jony, "and I said I would; but then it started to change me, and I was looking at, right exactly at, a clump of thyme, and I didn't know what it was, or where it grew, or when, or what its uses were. So I said I'd changed my mind."

"And it did this?"

"And ran off."

"The *wolf* spoke to you?"

"I thought it did," said Jony, hesitantly. "Wolves don't talk, do they? Where's Derry?"

Where's Oonan, thought Arry. He had shown her some of the places to press to stop bleeding, and what he had shown her seemed to be working. But she wanted him to look at this before she did anything else. He would know how best to avoid the scarring, not to mention inflammation and what, if anything, you could catch from a wolf bite.

"Can you walk?" she said. "I want to let Oonan look at this."

"Of course I can, it didn't bite me in the leg," said Jony. She consented to lean on Arry, and they started down the hill. "Does it hurt a great deal?"

"It certainly did at first," said Arry. "Now it's more throbbing."

People were finally coming out of the house, demanding to know what had happened.

"Where's Oonan?" said Arry.

"He went home," said Wim. "Lina's fetching him, she's the fastest."

"She'd better be," said Arry furiously, "there's a wolf out there that just got Jony."

Wim and Niss and Grel went running down the path. Arry took Jony into the house, pressing the torn skirt against Jony's arm as hard as she could. She could feel the blood trying to get out, which seemed foolish of it. The arm was beginning to hurt quite a lot. She sat Jony down. Where was Oonan? She asked Mally for some willow-bark tea and gave it to Jony, suppressing a mad urge to drink it herself. She had tried this once, of course; drinking it herself did nothing whatsoever to dim the knowledge of somebody else's pain.

All the children crowded around and gaped at Jony and looked hopeful. Arry was sure they wanted her to take off the bandage so they could get a good look at the wound. She snapped at them, calling them vultures. Some of them laughed; the rest looked hurt or taken aback. Where was Oonan? Where were any of them? Eaten by wolves, probably. Arry got Elec, who was reasonably reliable, to go on holding the cloth to Jony's arm, and ran outside and up the path. She collided solidly with Oonan.

"That bad, is it?" he said, taking her by the arm and rushing her back inside.

Arry sat down hard on the floor. Her job was done. Oonan sent Mora for a bowl of water, which she spilled half of. With the other half he soaked the cloth off Jony's arm. He sent Elec for goldenrod cream and marigold essence; he washed the wound and prodded at it, making Arry flinch. He took thread and needle and Jony's own potato water out of his pouch and sewed the long wound up. The children crowded around. Oonan told them crossly not to breathe on the wound or he would sew their mouths shut too. They giggled and backed off.

Arry went outside and sat down on a rock.

"It's safe now," said Oonan at her elbow. Arry jumped.

"You should go home and go to bed," he said.

Arry stood up tiredly. "Delighted," she said. And then, "Where's Beldi?"

**18**

BELDI WAS NOT in the house, not asleep in a corner, not sitting quietly by the dying bonfire, not eating the last bowl of dried blueberries, not visiting the goats or ferreting out the nest of new kittens in the hayloft. He was gone.

"Leave Con with Wim," said Mally, "and I'll come with you." Oonan also came. Arry could hear Con clamoring to be brought as well, that she could tell where Beldi would go; but whatever Wim might have had to do to prevent her, she did not actually come after them.

"Maybe she *can* tell," said Arry uneasily, as they paused on the path that would take them to Niss's, or else back home.

"Better than I can?" said Mally.

Arry supposed not. "Where shall we go, then?" she said.

"Tiln saw Beldi last just when Jony left," said Mally. "He's such an obliging child, that's the difficulty, he would go with two wolves or with one. If it were Con, I'd know it had to be your parents."

"If it were, I wouldn't worry," said Arry. "I think we should assume it's Halver; that will prevent more harm."

In the still cool darkness all riddled with green scents, she could feel Oonan and Mally looking at one another as clearly as if they had all been standing in the sunlight and she could see them.

"What do you know about my parents?" she said to Mally.

"For all love, let's walk somewhere or other while we're arguing," said Oonan.

"We're arguing about where to walk," said Arry. "Where would Beldi go to begin with, so a wolf could find him without alarming the entire party?"

"The goat barn," said Mally. "You didn't look for tracks, did you, when you were out there?"

"It's mostly rock," said Arry.

"I'll get a lantern just the same," said Mally, and went back into her house.

"You know you'd feel it if he were hurt," said Oonan.

"It depends how far away he is."

"How far could he get in half an hour?"

"How far could a wolf get?"

"He's too heavy to ride a wolf," said Oonan. "I asked Derry, while you were looking for him. Con, now, if it were Con gone missing that would be a possible thing."

"I thought it would be Con," said Arry. "I always thought, whatever happened, it would be Con it happened to."

"Con makes things happen, that's why," said Mally; Arry wondered how long she had been standing there with the lantern. Arry was very tired and her mind seem to go in erratic jumps, like a spring lamb frolicking. She did not feel frolicsome.

They took the lantern all around the outside of the goat barn. There were no tracks. The path itself here was rock, and while some of the small flowering plants that grew in its cracks were bruised, there had been so many people walking here today that this meant nothing.

Arry looked up the dark hill. It was crowned with a clump of birch trees. Their patchy white trunks seemed to glimmer a little; their new leaves made a sharp and precise darkness between them and the sky. "Mally?" she said. "Might he go sit up there?"

"Very like," said Mally.

They all climbed the hill as fast as they could go. Arry found breathing difficult; she was filling up with a kind of thick dread that seemed to leave no room for air. When they got to the outermost tree she hung back, and Mally and Oonan went through before her, with a crackling of fallen twigs.

"Ah," said Oonan.

Arry craned forward, and took hold of the nearest birch trunk. It was cold. Beldi was curled up on the ground with his head in a pile of dead yellow leaves and Tiln's wolfskin coat spread over him. He wasn't hurt at all, any more than the leaves were.

"Wake up," said Oonan irritably.

Beldi raised his head and blinked in the light of the lantern. Arry almost fell down, although both her feet were firmly on the ground and she was holding onto the tree. Death was not her province, after all; but she had so thought Beldi was dead it had been almost like knowledge. She would have to ask somebody about fear.

"Where's Halver?" said Beldi. "I wasn't done dreaming."

"What are you doing with Tiln's coat?" said Arry.

"That isn't Tiln's coat," said Mally over her shoulder. "I saw Tiln's coat in the front room when I went back for the lantern. Besides, the colors are different. This one is mostly black and gray; his has more cream in it."

"It's Halver's," said Beldi, sitting up. He looked resigned and rather grumpy. He was not, in fact, hurt in the least, unless you counted a small pain in his arm where he had lain on a stone.

"What happened?" said Oonan. He sat down in the leaves next to Beldi. Mally loomed over them with the lantern. Arry stayed where she was.

"I walked away from the fire after the dancing," said Beldi. "Arry says I always get too hot and should remember to cool off. So I walked up the hill, and I met Halver coming down. He had the coat over his shoulder. He asked me if I'd like to be a wolf. I said I had never thought about it; I told him he ought to ask Mally. He told me that if I came into this place and covered myself with the coat and went to sleep, I would dream about being a wolf, and then I would know."

"He said just that?" said Oonan.

Beldi nodded. "I asked him if that would be my knowledge, then, what it was like to be a wolf. I thought that was strange, but I didn't think I'd mind. He laughed. He said that would be only the smallest part of my knowledge. And he said it was part of my education. That's his province; so I did as he told me."

"What was it like?" said Oonan. And when Beldi said nothing, he added, *"Did* you like it?"

Beldi looked at Mally.

"Not altogether," said Mally.

"Except that I wasn't finished when you woke me," said Beldi.

"What didn't you like?" said Oonan.

Beldi looked at Mally again, but she said nothing. At last Beldi said, "There was nobody to ask."

"You were alone?"

"Yes, but that isn't what I meant. There was nobody to ask, anywhere."

"How could you tell?"

Beldi scowled; momentarily, he looked just like Con. "I don't remember," he said. His face cleared a little. "It was a dream," he offered. "Niss and Sune both say—"

"Yes," said Oonan.

He and Mally looked at one another over the lantern. Arry could not really see what their faces were saying. She thought of Halver's face, lit by the lantern in the sheep hut.

"Perhaps we'd better not start school again tomorrow after all?" said Oonan.

"Truly," said Mally. "I believe it must be time to put in the oats. I'll talk to Jonat."

"Somebody should show that coat to Niss," said Arry. "And Tiln's too."

"Somebody should be certain Tiln doesn't sleep under his tonight," said Oonan.

"Why?" said Beldi, standing up and folding the coat. It was almost as big as he was. "I couldn't tell anything for certain," he said, delivering the coat to Mally, "because I haven't my knowledge yet. But Tiln would know, wouldn't he, if it would be a beautiful or an ugly thing to be a wolf?"

"The question is, is true choice allowed?" said Oonan. He relieved Mally of the lantern. "A question for Niss, in the morning, I assume."

"A question for Niss, now," said Arry. But her voice cracked, with fatigue and distress and bewilderment, and she could see, as plainly as if she knew it, Oonan and Mally's sudden alliance as adults against an overtired and importunate child.

"We'll keep Con tonight," said Mally; and, as Arry opened her mouth, added, "and keep a watch over her. Go home and sleep. You can fetch her after you've talked to Niss. Tomorrow."

Mally went off down the hill with the wolfskin coat, leaving the three of them with the light.

They walked home slowly, not speaking. There was a heavy dew, and the first few birds were talking to themselves by the time the three of them got to Oonan's house. Oonan handed Arry the lantern. "Come fetch me when you're ready to talk to Niss," he said, and turned away up his own hill.

Arry and Beldi walked on, squelching a little on the grassy parts of the path. Arry was wondering so hard why Halver had not tempted either her brother or her sister with their parents that she could not speak; she was afraid she would tempt Beldi herself. Beldi and Con were the only other people who would understand how important it was, yet she could not tell them, and not only because she had given her word. There should be somebody she could ask, she thought hazily, as they climbed the hill to their house, whether you could break your word to somebody who would hurt Jony's arm like that.

The house was faintly green, as Sune's had been.

"Tread carefully," said Arry to Beldi.

There were no frogs on the doorstep. Arry opened the door, and both cats burst outside, complaining and purring at once. Beldi went in first, and as he crossed the flagstones where the green letters had been, he staggered and put out his hand to the wall.

"What?" said Arry, leaping through the door and staring at him.

"I felt as if I'd put my foot down on a step that wasn't there," said Beldi. He pushed his hair back and blinked several times. "I must be walking in my sleep."

"Go to bed, then," said Arry. "Or do you want tea first, or something to warm you up?"

"No," said Beldi, "thank you, good night," and he went slowly across the front room and into the scrubbing room.

Arry looked at the floor. It needed washing, except for the spot where the mice had been, which was clean and gray. No green letters. Keep the wolf far hence, she thought. Just you do that. She shut the door, and went to bed.

She dreamed of the Fairy Melusine, who had a tail like a fish, and whose children all were monsters. What woke her was the smell of frying onions. Arry went sleepily into the kitchen and found Beldi making breakfast. He never cooked, because, he said, he could never be as good a cook as Bec had been. He smiled apologetically at her over his steaming pan and said, "I thought I'd make up for being troublesome last night."

Arry almost did it. She almost laughed and told him he was never troublesome. Half the laugh came out, but she squashed the rest of it and said swiftly, "Maybe you were a little. You shouldn't wander off without saying anything." She remembered that he had missed the uproar over Jony, and added, "Jony got bitten by a wolf last night: it might just as easily have been you who was hurt."

"I was with Halver," said Beldi.

"So you were. I forgot."

Beldi set his pan on the hearth and stirred the iron kettle. He must have made enough oatmeal for an army. Well, they could always make bread out of it, now that there was honey. He said, "I couldn't have bitten her, could I?"

"Wouldn't you remember?"

"It was very like a dream," said Beldi. He reflected, stirring. "I don't remember being angry, or hungry either, so perhaps I didn't."

"We can ask Niss," said Arry, "but I don't think, if you were asleep under a wolfskin, you could have bitten Jony. She wasn't dreaming, she was just going for a walk."

"Wandering off," said Beldi.

"It's been safe here," said Arry. "I think now it isn't."

"Breakfast is ready," said Beldi, spooning potatoes and onions onto Arry's plate. He stood and held it out to her, and suddenly looked stricken. "I forgot to make the tea."

"Never mind," said Arry, taking her plate. "I've had enough tea this month to last the rest of my life."

Getting everybody fed and washed and dressed was much easier when everybody did not include Con. It was only the middle of the morning when they walked over the green hills to Oonan's house. Arry had assumed they would have to wake him, but he was sitting on the stone wall of his garden with all three cats. He looked and felt very much as if he had not been to sleep at all. He was sitting on one wolfskin coat and had the other over his lap, stroking the thick stiff fur.

"Did you sleep under those?" said Arry sharply.

"I did indeed," said Oonan. He smiled crookedly. "As you might, perhaps, expect, even without asking Derry, a wolf knows not what is broken nor how it may be fixed. There is a certain sensation of wrongness in some circumstances, and a set of behaviors to go with them, but no knowledge."

"What did you do?" said Arry, and when Oonan only looked at her, she said, "As a wolf, in your dream, or whatever it was, what did you do?"

"I can't tell you," said Oonan. He lifted a fold of the coat over his lap. "After Niss has looked at these, you may wish to sleep beneath one yourself. If she says it will cause no harm."

"You'll risk harm but I mayn't?" said Arry.

"I was afraid of whom you might meet," said Oonan.

They both looked at Beldi, who was leaning on the wall with his resigned expression.

"Whom did you meet?" Oonan asked him.

"Nobody I can remember," said Beldi.

"What did you do?"

"It was like a dream," said Beldi, patiently. "I ran through the woods. I ran through the high meadow." He considered. "I chased sheep," he said.

"Good," said Oonan. "The sheep were here last night. I counted them then, and again this morning. You weren't chasing real sheep, unless you went to Waterpale or Greentree."

"I drank from the stream by Sune's house," said Beldi. He paused. "Sune's house smells odd if you're a wolf," he said. "So does ours. I didn't like the smell, I think."

And from the lion's mouth that would you all in sunder shiver, thought Arry. From the hag and hungry goblin, that into rags would rend ye. Good. Niss is doing as she ought. But why won't she consult with us; why won't she tell us what she's doing?

"Let's go talk to Niss," she said, taking the coat from Oonan's lap and folding it awkwardly. Oonan got up and collected the coat he had been sitting on, patted each of his cats on the head, and set off for Niss's house.

Vand was putting a new layer of whitewash on it. He waved cheerfully but said nothing. The door was open. Arry put her head inside, and Niss looked up. "Mally told me to expect you," she said.

They went in; Niss made them tea and gave them some oatcake to go with it; Niss's white dog looked hopefully at the oatcake, and Oonan fed her pieces while Niss spread both the coats out on her table and considered them. She ran her hands over them, she lifted them and let them slump back onto the table, she stared at them, she leaned over and sniffed them.

"Nice work," she said at last. "But I wonder—" She stared at them again. "Soul clap its hands, and sing," she said, "and louder sing, for every tatter in its mortal dress." Nothing happened, but after a moment Niss nodded. "This isn't wolf at all," she said. "It's hardly anything, truly. Cobweb and moonshine. It seems a wasteful way to go about it; you could put these properties into an ordinary wolf skin and have done with it."

"Maybe the maker hadn't a wolf skin to spare," said Oonan.

Arry felt both extremely grateful and extremely cold.

"Who is the maker?" she said.

"I can't tell," said Niss, rubbing her hands over the coats again. "Not an enchanter, I think." She stared into space for some time, and Arry fed the dog some oatcake. Finally she shook her head. "If wolves were wizards," she said. "It must have been a shapeshifter of one sort or another. This is not magic, not really; it's a thing natural to the doer."

"What does *it* do?" said Oonan. "Is it dangerous?"

"It confers essence without actuality," said Niss.

Oonan looked at her. Arry saw Beldi smile. Niss said, "Those who sleep under it will dream they are wolves." This did not seem to Arry to be at all what she had first said, but Niss always did say that magic was slippery. Maybe the language in which you spoke of it must be slippery also.

"Is it dangerous?" said Oonan.

Niss considered the coats again. "Not in itself," she said at last.

"Was it made with malice?"

"Oh, no," said Niss. "This is good work, very good indeed."

"Does it permit choice?"

Niss stared at the coats yet again; she laid both hands flat on them and leaned hard for some time. Finally she said, "Those who sleep thereunder may not choose whether to dream, but they may choose whether to be."

"Can they choose whether to sleep thereunder in the first place?" said Arry.

"It depends on who gives it them," said Niss.

Arry looked at Oonan. Oonan shook his head. Arry said, "What if Halver gave it?"

"Well," said Niss, "you must ask Mally, of course, but it seems to me that if Halver were the giver the choice would be what to learn."

"What did you learn, Beldi?" said Arry.

Beldi blinked at her. "How to be a wolf?"

"Probably not," said Oonan. "Can you catch and eat a mouse? Or a sheep?"

Beldi looked blank. "No," he said.

Niss sat down and drank all the rest of the tea. She was a great deal tireder than she had been when they got here.

Arry asked her, "Why have you warded some places and not others?"

"I do what's needed," said Niss, with her mouth full of oatcake.

"Did you ward our house?"

"No," said Niss. She sat up straight. "Why?"

"Somebody did."

"With what?"

"Keep the wolf far hence, that's foe to men."

"That's a Hiddenlander spell," said Niss. "I don't use it, myself, except for burials."

"Will it work?"

"Certainly."

"You didn't tell me about this," said Oonan.

"There are things you don't tell me, too," said Arry. Then she thought, no, the only way out of this is to stop keeping secrets. "The warding letters were under an enormous pile of dead mice," she said. "I found them yesterday morning."

"Frances," said Oonan. "She said—" He shut his mouth hard.

"Oonan, we have to break our word, both of us."

"She's your mother," said Oonan. "Halver is your teacher. They know what they're doing; they must."

"Halver's a wolf," said Arry. "His knowledge is all disrupted. He's doing harm, is what he's doing."

"That's your province," said Oonan.

Arry was so angry she could not speak. Then something in his tone made her think. She smiled at him. "So it is," she said. She thought, carefully. "I charge you, then, by the knowledge that is in me, to tell me what I must hear to deal well in my province."

"I thought you would never do it," said Oonan. "Niss, shall we go away and let you rest?"

"No," said Niss, heaving her small self out of her chair and heading for the kettle. "I fear this will be in my province also, before all's done. I'll make stronger tea."

# ❧19❧

OONAN WAS A good storyteller; he had learned how, he said, when everybody had the white fever, so that their bodies required rest but their minds were raging and required occupation. Arry thought, too, that he understood how hungry she and Beldi were to hear all they could about their parents. Sitting in Niss's little house and warming his hands on a mug of tea he never drank from, he told as slow and careful a story as any in the books Sune and Mally had lent her.

He did skimp a little on the opening, in which the two wolves had run him up and down the high meadow until moonset. Arry didn't blame him. He made clear enough the combination of terror and hilarity that all this galloping up and down and being snapped at by jaws that never quite met in his flesh, no matter how slow or clumsy he was, had caused him. Finally the wolves chased him into the sheep hut, which he was very reluctant to enter, he said, because then they would

have him cornered. But they chivvied him into it exactly
as if he were a sheep and they two very well-trained dogs.

He sat down hard on the floor, covered in sweat and
breathing like a bellows. The dust he had raised made
him cough. And then it felt as if the entire world had
taken a giant step sideways, as if it had been dancing on
a low platform and missed the edge. He could not fall in
fact, of course, because he was sitting on the floor already; but his mind felt as if it had dropped down an
unexpected step.

He rubbed his eyes, and when he looked up, Frances
was carrying a lantern into the sheep hut, and Bec came
behind her with a basket. He recognized them at once,
but the way they looked shocked him just the same.
Frances had cut off all her red hair; it was shorter than
Oonan's; she looked like a new-shorn sheep, only less
pleased. She was too thin. Bec looked much the same as
he always had, short and wide and dark-haired, with the
greeny-dark skin he had from his connection with Jonat
and Wim's families. But Oonan had never seen his
brother look other than cheerful, and now he looked as
little pleased as Frances.

"I cry you mercy," Frances said to Oonan, and she
set the lantern in the middle of the floor.

"I'll consider it," said Oonan dryly. "Where have
you been?"

"Give you good den, Bec," said Frances. She used
the tone in which she reminded her children to say
"please." " 'Greetings to thee, Frances; thou hast been
long away; it joys my heart to see thee once again.' "

"My house is yours," said Oonan, making a sweep-
ing gesture around the hut. "Dust, straw, and all: I pray
you partake."

Whereupon they all laughed, but Oonan did not feel much comforted. Frances and Bec sat down on the floor with Oonan, as if they were all going to play noughts and crosses in the dust. They were both wearing long coarse gray robes, and they were both barefoot. The clean soft state of their feet made it clear that they usually went shod. Bec opened the basket and took out strange foods from the Hidden Land: meat pies made with beef and cinnamon and cardamom, apple tarts made with pepper, honeycake made with rye rather than oat flour. He and Frances began to eat at once; they seemed very hungry. Oonan ate a little for the sake of courtesy, and finally asked them to tell him their story.

"When I left three years ago," said Bec, still with his mouth full, "I went as I always did, to Waterpale to see what the traders had brought in from the Hidden Land. There was one from Wormsreign."

"Where the people, the children and the very mice, are all shapeshifters," said Frances.

Bec looked at her, and she smiled and was quiet.

"He was sitting on a rug, like the others," said Bec, "but he had nothing with him, no goods at all. He wore red silk. I had looked at all the other goods, and seen nothing I wanted, and yet I was loth to go home with nothing. The children always hoped for strange things. So I asked him what he was selling. He laughed. He said he sold nothing, but would give to those worthy of the gift."

"They say, Travel not in the Hidden Land," said Oonan, "but I hadn't realized we must say, Travel not even so far as Waterpale."

"I asked him what worthiness was," said Bec. "He

said it was knowledge. I told him that in the Dubious Hills he would find both knowledge and doubt, and that sometimes those who sought the one might find the other.''

"Bec, Bec," said Oonan. "Didn't you heed what Sune told you about challenging Wormsreigners?''

"Sune also told me," said Bec, with perfect mildness, "that one might summon music out of the air.''

"Did you ask Niss?" said Oonan.

Bec went on as if he had not spoken. "We sat and talked the sun down the sky, about knowledge and memory and experience. He was himself a musician, though we at home would not have said that he knew music. He had a tongue like honey and a mind like an April day, always shifting. Fran will scold me yet again if I explain to you all the shifts he used on me, so I will say just this: he persuaded me that if I gave him my knowledge I would have it still, for all practical purposes, for I would remember it. And he said he would give me in turn the power to become a wolf at the full moon, and that I would then know, as Derry could not, as no woman nor man ever could, the wolf and all its thoughts and doings.''

Frances looked very much as if she would have liked to scold him anyway; all she did was to lay her hand on his knee and put on a resigned face, very like Beldi's.

"And I agreed with him to do this thing," said Bec.

"Why did you?" said Oonan.

"You would have to ask Mally, I suppose," said Bec.

Frances laughed. Bec looked at her, and then he laughed too. "Old habits," he said. "Though even now it may be that Mally could tell you what I cannot. But this is why I think I did agree. Mally told me once that I need new things: not large ones nor many, but new. There was nothing new in music, in the Dubious Hills. I thought, that if I wanted novelty in music, I must travel, to Wormsreign or even the Outer Isles; but if I changed my field of knowledge, I could stay home. Wolves are at home with us, after all."

"Did you plan how many of my sheep you would eat each full moon?" demanded Oonan.

"No," said Bec, mildly. "I thought I would make do with mice. As indeed we have, for the most part."

"They're better stewed," said Frances, making a face. "But then, no doubt mutton is better roasted also. We are not truly wolves; I think there, my love, he lied to you."

"He might not know," said Oonan. "Being a shapeshifter."

"Being a shapeshifter," said Frances, sternly, "he did know nothing. It was this that Bec forgot, when he sat in the sun all day and supped up the honey breath of a thing hath no one nature."

Oonan said quickly, "So you made the agreement with him. What happened? How did he do it?"

"It was the full moon that night," said Bec. "I met him in the pine wood above Waterpale. He said that, if I truly consented to this bargain, I must say a rhyme." He pulled his knees up under the gray robe and rested his arms on them. "I can't forget it," he said. "It was this: And then I hate the most that lore that holds no promise of success; then sweetest seems the houseless shore, then free and kind the wilderness. Elected Silence, sing to me and beat upon my whorled ear, pipe me to pastures still and be the music that I care to hear."

Arry saw Niss twitch when Oonan recited that spell.

Oonan saw too; he nodded at Niss and said that he did not care for the sound of that at all, but he had thought it best to keep quiet.

"And then," said Bec, "he said a rhyme himself. And this was it: Though they *are* fickle. Let one go alive, he will run to the bosom of another and tell lies: Adventures another had, or perhaps no one, or just a different tale than the one to you."

"Rhyme?" said Oonan.

"I said the same," said Frances, smiling a little. "'Rhyme it hath none.'"

"He spoke it so," said Bec, patiently. "Like a song or a spell. And then we sat and waited for moonrise. I fixed my eye on him, most constantly, for I wished to see a man turn to a wolf, and I wished to see what I might look like when I came to it. But as the moon rose, all the ground beneath us seemed to fall sideways; and when I recovered my balance, there was the wolf."

"And then?" said Oonan, though he really did not wish to.

"He trotted up to me," said Bec, "very much like a dog; and he sank his teeth into the meat of my shoulder, just there; and the whole world moved sideways again, very violently, and I was a wolf as well."

There was a long silence.

"What was it like?" said Oonan at last; he felt it was expected.

"No," said Frances. "That is not the question. The wolf-being is a play, it hath a kindness to't, any might wish to romp so for a night of bright moons. It is the coming to oneself after that shows the crack in the cup."

"Is that why you stayed away?" said Oonan to Bec.

Bec nodded. "I thought to send word," he said. "When she found me, I had a box of half-writ, unsent letters. I think I wanted her to come."

"Faugh," said Frances. "When I could not write to Arry either, did I wish her to find us?"

"Maybe," said Bec. "Maybe you did; though you knew she mustn't."

"She's bound to soon enough, if the sheep go on being killed, which hurts me," said Oonan. "What happened?"

"Halver," said Bec.

"Yes, I assumed as much; but how did he get into this?"

"I did bring him," said Frances, grimly.

"Why Halver?" said Oonan. "Why didn't you come to me?"

"Not your province," said Bec.

Oonan made a furious sound that shook the low roof of the dusty hut and made Frances, always inclined to slouch and lounge, come up off the floor onto her knees as if she were ready to wrestle.

"Province, province, province," said Oonan, passionately. "Why are we so punctilious about it?"

"That's war," said Bec, sounding faintly surprised. "People intruding on one another's provinces. We understand to stay out. We must stay out."

"All right," said Oonan, breathing through his nose like a woman giving birth, though presumably with less pain, and where was Arry when you needed her to approve your simile? "How is this outside my province, or inside Halver's?"

"Education, knowledge, the alteration of mind,"

said Frances. "That's Halver, Oonan; it might be Mally
also, but we thought not, then, that each person might
become a wolf differently, according to's character. Perhaps we should have thought. But we thought no harm,
nor saw none neither."

"There *was* harm," said Oonan, again passionately.
"I'd have known it before I knew anything. How could
you be so blind?"

"Not our province," said Frances, very gently.

"Faugh!" said Oonan, and jumped to his feet. "It's
change; change may be harm; you don't know, that's
why you have me, why didn't you *ask*?"

Frances looked up at him, her short red hair disor-
dered on her lined brow. "Because that is what we lost,"
she said. "That is the crack i'the cup."

Oonan sat down, hard, on the bed of planks. A little
dust puffed out and danced in the light of the lantern.
"Say that again," he said. He understood already, in his
heart; he remembered Halver's answer about teaching a
blind child, and he had used the word himself just now.

"We are outside now," said Frances. "Outside all
provinces save life and death. We remember, but we do
not know; what we were taught grows dim in us." She
gave the lantern a shake, and the flame flickered and
made all the dark shadows jerk and shiver. "Even for
practical purposes," she said, imitating Bec imitating
Halver's speech, and sounding very scornful as she did
so, "we have not our knowledge now."

"Yet you bethought you of Halver," said Oonan.

"Reason would do as much as that," said Frances.
"Reason is what we have now."

"So you told Halver," said Oonan. "What happened
then?"

Bec answered him. "He got enthralled. You know—you understand—you remember how he does. He walked up and down his room and talked and shouted. This was true learning, he said, this was education, what he had done until now with every child under his care was mere—mere—" Beck looked at Frances.

"Rote and eyewash," said Frances precisely.

"No, not that, I could remember that myself. The Draconian word."

"Ah," said Frances. "Indoctrination."

"What?" said Oonan.

"When the Dragons use it, it still means just education," said Bec. "But in Wormsreign it means otherwise, and that's what Halver meant."

"Where did he come by a word like that?" said Oonan.

"I told it him," said Frances. "Very long ago; the year Arry was born. He would ask me for words as a child asks for honey. Thinking them even less harmful, I gave him them."

"They aren't harmful," said Oonan absently, "in themselves." He slid off the bed and sat over the lantern with them again. His eyes met Frances's. "How can you live?" he said. "How can you live, not knowing?"

"People manage it, all over the world," said Frances, dryly.

"Well, but Halver wants us to manage it?"

"He does so."

"And yet you don't wish him to make us?"

"You don't wish to be forced to't, do you?" said Frances.

"Children don't wish to learn arithmetic, either,"

said Oonan. And hit himself gently in the forehead. "That is the very problem, of course," he said.

"Aye," said Frances, with the Hiddenlander accent surfacing very strongly. "Ye needs must choose, and choose his way."

"Or what?" said Oonan.

"He will teach how he may," said Frances.

That, said Oonan, made them all silent and gloomy. He collected his mug full of cold tea, and drank all of it down without stopping. Arry sat staring at him. He talked to my mother, she thought. I want to talk to my mother. "Why didn't they come talk to us?" she said.

"Well," said Oonan, "Halver swore them to secrecy, as Gnosi. And they think you are better here without them, than outside with them."

"Why can't they be here with us?" said Beldi.

"They can't live here now," said Oonan, patiently. "In them our spell is broken."

"Halver is living here now," Beldi pointed out. Then he looked at Arry, and said as if no one else were present, "She'd rather be with him than with us."

"Halver's living here now, Beldi," said Arry, "but he's sick most of the time."

"You have all of us," said Oonan. "Once Bec became a wolf and gave up his music, he had nothing except Frances."

"Why," said Niss, as if nobody else had spoken since Oonan finished his story, "does becoming a Lukanthropos break the spell we live under? There's no sense in that."

"If you don't know, Niss," said Oonan, "nobody does."

"It can't be the magical end of it," said Niss, stubbornly. "I told you, it must inhere in character."

"What's Halver going to do?" said Arry.

"What are we going to do, that's the question," said Oonan.

"Well, but we can't answer if we don't understand what Halver will do. Would Mally know?"

"You have to fetch Con anyway," said Oonan. "We may as well ask her, once more."

"How could Bec lack for novelty when he had Con?" said Arry.

"Mally always said she took after him," said Oonan. "Maybe she wasn't novel to him, if her mind worked as his did always."

They all stirred, and drank up their tea, getting ready to leave. Beldi said to Oonan, "What about the coats?"

Oonan shrugged. "Frances and Bec said nothing about them."

Everybody looked at Niss. "What kind of work are they, exactly?" Arry asked her.

"Oh, Wormsreign," said Niss, as if Arry had stood in the middle of a field at broad noon on a clear day and asked her where the sun was.

"Oh, Wormsreign," Oonan mimicked her; then he smiled.

"Faugh," said Niss, without heat. Frances had always said that, and had further remarked, as a private joke with Arry, that it seemed to be catching. Niss got up and went and leaned on the coats again. "In fact," she said thoughtfully, and stopped speaking.

Arry started to say something, but Oonan waved her to silence.

"This is truly good Wormsreign work," said Niss. "But there's something else." She ran one hand up and down the uppermost coat and shut her eyes. "Oh, *Halver*!" she said, exasperatedly.

"What?" said Oonan. He said it with a marvelous lack of emphasis.

"He's put it on those who dream under these coats to find him," said Niss. "Well, he's tried. Teacher or no, inside or outside whatever it is he's inside or outside of, he is not a wizard." She brooded over the coats a little longer. "Or is he?" she remarked. She opened her eyes suddenly and gazed at Oonan. "Somebody is," she said. "Never let me say again that children ought not to ask questions."

"What?" said Beldi, promptly.

Niss laughed. "Let me look a little further," she said. "This is clever, clever, but it is not good." She screwed her face up, like Con drinking buttermilk. "I spoke wrongly," she said in an extremely formal tone, and unscrewing her face she straightened up fast. "Whoso sleeps under either of these coats three times, by choice, must come to Halver to be made a wolf, or die."

"No," said Oonan.

"Oh, yes," said Niss.

"*Now* is it everybody's province?" said Arry.

"Where did he get them?" asked Beldi.

"Wolves run far and fast," said Niss. "Derry says so."

"We must fetch Mally," said Oonan, "and all of us must speak to Halver."

Fetching Mally was easy enough; she was home playing with Con and Lina and Zia and Tany, and Arry thought she looked as if asking Halver questions about a dire and hurtful plot would be easier. Mally set Tiln to watching the children, except for Con, whom they brought along rather than argue with her. Con and Beldi lagged behind. Beldi would be telling her Oonan's whole story, and there would be that to deal with along with everything else.

Fetching Mally was easy; persuading her was not. "I don't believe it," she said, at intervals more regular than the call of the cardinal. "Not Halver."

"The coats do what they do," said Niss, placidly.

"But not by Halver's will," retorted Mally.

They lagged, too, arguing, though not so far behind as Beldi and Con. Arry and Oonan hurried on, getting hot and thirsty all over again. Halver would give them all some tea, too, no doubt.

"What are we going to ask him when we get there?" panted Arry.

"I don't mean to ask him anything," said Oonan. "I mean to tell him several."

"You think Niss knows more than Mally, then?"

"I know less harm will be done by assuming so," said Oonan.

"You said that was my province."

"We share it," said Oonan. "A foolish arrangement, but there you are."

"Oonan, who does say what is whose province?"

"Well," said Oonan, stopping on the path that led up to Halver's house, "we suspect it, Mally confirms it, and then we all say it for ourselves."

They stood watching Mally and Niss stride up the hill, still arguing, and Beldi and Con struggle up behind them, not talking any longer. Con wore a distinctly lowering expression. Beldi looked resigned.

"Has it occurred to you," said Arry, "that many of these things were easier when we didn't think about them?"

"Yes," said Oonan.

Mally and Niss arrived. "We'll ask him, that's all," said Mally.

"That won't prove a thing," said Niss.

"Oh, yes, it will," said Mally. "Halver doesn't lie."

Con and Beldi labored up to them. "What are you standing around for?" said Con.

Oonan turned and walked up to Halver's shut door and knocked upon it.

"I want to see my mother," said Con.

"So do I," said Arry.

Oonan knocked again.

"She always had a good reason for everything she did," said Mally.

"And she's supposed to tell us what the reason is," said Con. Arry, focusing knowledge on her, saw to her surprise that Con was feeling far less hurt and hollow than she had been. Well, after all, Frances had not just looked for Bec, she had found him, and both of them were alive, and perhaps even well, bodily anyway, whatever might be wrong with their minds.

"She can't tell us the reason for not wanting to see us," said Beldi, "if she can't see us."

Oonan knocked again.

"She could have told Oonan," said Con, sitting down on a rock.

"I think she did," said Beldi, "only not in so many words."

"Well what is it then?"

Oonan walked around the side of the house, where he could be heard calling Halver and banging on windows.

"No school today?" said Niss to Mally.

"We thought it better," said Mally. "I suppose he might be helping them get the oats planted. It's not very like him."

Oonan reappeared around the opposite side of the house. "I don't think he's there," he said.

He was not visiting Sune, either; nor was he helping to plant the oats. He was nowhere. They looked for him; they even got Blackie and Oonan's two dogs to help them. But they did not find him.

**20**

EARLY AFTERNOON FOUND them footsore and bewildered back at Mally's house, eating cold leftover
party food and soothing a wild-eyed Tiln, who had been
left too long with too many small children. Mally de-
voted most of her attention to devising amusement for
the small children in question and in feeding everybody, but from time to time she would murmur, "I
don't understand what he's doing."

"Frances said they were outside all provinces but life
and death," said Oonan. "If Halver is also, then of
course you wouldn't know any longer what he would
do."

"I know that!" Mally snapped at him. "But experience, memory, and reason must be good for something."

"For all their sakes you'd better hope they are," said
Oonan.

"For all our sakes," said Mally, still snappish, "you

had better hope they are. It would take a powerful lot of knowledge, Akoumi, to repair this entire community.''

Arry got up from the table where she was sitting with them and made her way to the corner settle where Niss was eating her lunch and staring at nothing.

"Those coats,'' she said. "What would be best to do with them?"

"I can't disenchant them,'' said Niss. "I can keep them safely; there isn't, on the coats themselves, any compulsion at all, and the charm itself requires free choice to fuel its operation.''

"Could we burn or destroy them? They don't seem likely to to do other than hurt, do they?''

Niss looked rather shocked. "They're very fine work,'' she said. "And dreaming of being a wolf hurts nobody, does it?''

"I don't like the conditions,'' said Arry. "It's asking for trouble. Especially if Halver is going to disappear like this. Once people have slept under the coat three times, how long have they got to report to Halver before they die, for mercy's sake?''

Niss frowned. "Now there's a curious thing,'' she said. "I didn't notice; perhaps I was careless, but it makes me wonder.''

"Say that again,'' said Mally from the table.

Niss obediently repeated what she had said; Mally said, "Didn't notice what?"

"Arry asked about those who have slept under the coats, in what space of time they must report to Halver lest they die; but I couldn't say.''

Mally chuckled. Then she laughed. Then she leaned her head on her hands and wheezed. "Oh, Halver,'' she said finally, wiping her eyes.

The rest of them looked at her; Arry thought they all had expressions very like Beldi's. Mally said, "This is not a threat; it's one of Halver's lessons."

"Go on," said Oonan, a little blankly.

"Are shapeshifters immortal?" Mally asked Niss.

"Those of Wormsreign are," said Niss. "I don't know about the Lukanthropoi. I should have to look at one and see the shape of the spell—if it is a spell at all."

"Assuming they are," said Mally, "then the lesson is obvious." Seeing that they were all regarding her as blankly as Oonan had spoken, she added, "If you know Halver. Remember the traps in logic he used to lay, Oonan. If one does not report to Halver to be made a wolf, one will die—in time. Not as a direct result of failing to deliver oneself, but as the natural end."

"And yet of course it *would* be a result of not delivering oneself, if the wolf spell confers immortality," said Oonan.

"If it does," said Niss, "there's a price for it."

"Loss of knowledge," said Oonan. "Halver and Frances and Bec all told us that."

Niss frowned a little. "It's usually blood," she said.

"Mally," said Arry, "are you certain?"

"I'll sleep under Tiln's coat three nights running and not go to Halver after," said Mally.

"But will you let Tiln do it?"

"No," said Mally. "Any more than Frances and Bec would let you."

"Keep the wolf far hence," said Arry.

"I'd advise it," said Niss.

Oonan got up and walked the length of the room and back again. "Why has Halver vanished?" he said. "What sort of lesson is that?"

"From time to time he leaves his pupils on their own," said Mally. "This is not reason and memory, Oonan: this is knowledge."

Halver did, too, do just that: memory told Arry he did; but she felt uneasy, and she could see that Oonan was not altogether believing either. She thought about it, eating one of the honey-and-walnut crescents that Mally and the children had made last night, or rather early this morning. "Are immortal people out of nature?" she said.

Everybody looked at her; nobody answered. "If they are," Arry said to Mally, "would you know what they were like?"

"Nature has nothing to do with it," said Mally.

"It has everything," said Niss.

"How so?" said Mally; Arry had never heard her sound so haughty.

"Define nature," said Niss, like a flash.

Mally began to laugh again. "The nature I deal with is not the nature you deal with," she said. "Let be."

"Why are you arguing?" said Arry.

"Now that," said Mally, turning from Niss, "is a worthy question. I am arguing because I feel the foundations of my knowledge shook. Niss is arguing for precisely the same reason. And that is why you are asking such large questions."

"I'll ask you a smaller one, then," said Arry. "Why did Halver hurt Jony?"

"If he did," said Mally, "it was to teach her something."

"What?"

"I think you would have to ask Jony," said Mally.

"If you come along with me," said Oonan as he

passed them on one of his trips down the room, "you may do just that. I must look at that arm."

Arry got up. "Can Con and Beldi come too?" she said. She had some hope that Mally would offer to keep them longer. Oonan also looked at Mally; but she said nothing.

"Why not?" said Oonan at last.

Arry fetched them from the kitchen, where they were (they said) building a library out of all Mally's pots and arguing with Zia and Tany about where they would get the books to put in it. They did not seem to mind leaving. They ran ahead of Oonan and Arry, chasing the blue butterflies that were suddenly everywhere and shouting and singing the silly songs of spring.

"I don't feel somehow," said Arry, staying with Oonan's more sedate pace, "that we've accomplished anything at all; I feel as if we were going backwards. I'd have known better what to do a few days ago than I do now."

"Must you do anything?" said Oonan.

"There's hurt here, a great deal of it."

"Quite often, you realize," said Oonan as they came down the last slope before Jony's house, "when you find it, you turn it over to me to fix."

"You don't seem to know how to fix this kind."

"I'm not sure it indicates a breakage," said Oonan.

"Well, I can't abide it."

"Ah," said Oonan; and then they were at Jony's house.

Jony was sitting in a willow chair padded with blankets, scowling at a pair of knitting needles and a ball of blue wool. When Oonan called to her, she looked relieved; then, when she saw his entourage, she looked a little alarmed.

"You needn't offer us tea," said Oonan, dropping to the ground beside her chair, on the side with the bandaged arm. "Niss and Mally have given us plenty already. In any case, this is a visit of knowledge. May I look at your arm?"

Con and Beldi came up quietly on Jony's other side, big-eyed, not quite avid. Oonan looked at Arry.

"It's very sore," she said, "but not throbbing the way they do. I'd wager, Oonan, you won't find any infection."

"I wouldn't wager against you," said Oonan, unwinding the bandage. "This isn't the one I put on last night. Has Niss been at this?"

"She said you gave her such a scolding for not changing the one on Tany's foot the time he trod on the flint arrow, that she would change this one every hour and you could—" Jony stopped speaking, but she could not help grinning at Arry, who smiled back.

"That's not what I meant," said Oonan. "Has she been at it with magic?"

"What do you think?" said Jony. "It doesn't need Mally, surely, to tell you the answer to that?"

"I wish she wouldn't, until I've seen what there is to see," said Oonan, laying bare the long red wound all neatly stitched with black. "It puts a fog in my way."

He wrapped his finger in a fold of the bandage and prodded delicately at the edges of the wound. Arry flinched. When he looked at her, she shrugged. The pain was not bad, but the wound should be let alone.

Oonan did in fact let it alone after that, dabbing on a

little more of the ointment of goldenrod, rewrapping the clean bandage and warning Jony about a variety of things she should watch for. Then he said, "What precisely happened?"

Jony said pleadingly, "I told Niss already, and Mally, and Halver. I told you, too, Arry, last night."

"Halver?" said Oonan. "When did you see Halver?"

"This morning," said Jony. "I was looking for the early chives, and the watermint, down by Sune's part of the stream."

"What was he doing?" said Oonan.

Jony eyed him a little warily. She did not often hurt herself, and had not even as a smaller child; but it did probably seem likely to her that such questions were no part of the Akoumi's business. She answered him patiently, in the same way Arry had heard her speak to Tany. "Sitting on the bank of the stream eating an oatcake," she said. When Oonan did not seem satisfied with this information, she added, "He was dressed for climbing, and he told me that since Jonat's sudden determination to put the oats in had given him a holiday, he was going to walk as far as he liked and see where it took him."

"How did he sound?" said Oonan.

"Like Halver," said Jony.

Con and Beldi had gotten bored as soon as the bandage went back on. Arry made sure she knew where they were—making a pile of slate over where a great piece of it was crumbling out of the ground—and sat down on the ground by Oonan. "You remember Mally says there are at least three Halvers?" she said to Jony. "The jolly, the stern, and the quizzical?"

Jony nodded. "They run together at the corners,

too," she said, "like mint getting into all the bits of a knot garden. This was the jolly quizzical, I'd say."

"What did he say?" said Arry. If school were anything to go by, Jony had a good memory.

"He wished me a good morning," said Jony, apparently resigned to answering meaningless questions. "And he asked me why I had a bandage on my arm. I told him a wolf had bitten me. And he said, 'That was a nip in play, in passing; a bite in earnest would not have let you get up this morning, let alone gather herbs as ever.' I asked him who had told him this, and he got very stern for a moment; then he laughed and asked me who I thought. I said Derry, and he laughed again. Then he asked me what had happened with the wolf, and I told him."

"You'd better tell it again," said Oonan. "And if you can tell it to us just as you told it to him, so much the better."

"I was walking in the cool air," said Jony, "and sniffing for herbs, though it's too early for most. And I came around that outcropping of rock above Mally's house, the one where the good thyme grows. There was a wolf sitting in the middle of the path. It had deep yellow eyes, the color of wool dyed with dock. It was larger than any dog we have. I stopped. And it spoke to me."

"Did its mouth open and shut?" said Oonan; almost at the same time, Arry said, "What was its voice like?"

Jony frowned at her wool, rubbing her bandage a little. "No," she said to Oonan at last, "its mouth did nothing. And its voice," she said to Arry, "sounded like mine. I didn't remember until you asked."

"And you told Halver all this?" said Oonan.

"Yes. Except about its mouth and its voice, because

he didn't ask me. And I went on—shall I now?" Oonan
nodded, and Jony went on. "It said, 'Feet in the jungle
that leave no mark, eyes that can see in the dark, the
dark, tongue, give tongue to it, hark, o hark,' and then it
laughed. That's why I think its voice sounded like mine:
I think I have a funny laugh."

"How did you feel when it said the rhyme?" said
Arry.

"Odd," said Jony. "As if the ground had moved. I
said, 'Greetings, wolf,' not being able to think of anything else. It said, 'Greetings, wolf to be.' I asked what it
meant, and it said I could be a wolf for the mere recitation of a verse and the will to do it. I said No, thank you.
It laughed again. It said, 'Against the wolf courtesy avails
you nothing. Will you not come and run under the
moon? You may be restored to yourself long before
dawn.' And I said, No, thank you again."

"Why?" said Oonan.

"I should think you'd ask me why if I'd said yes,"
said Jony, with some asperity.

Arry touched Oonan's arm, and Oonan said to Jony,
"All right, go on."

"The wolf said, 'Do not refuse the third time; that
would seal all. No harm will come to you; you shall be
restored before dawn.' So I said I would." She looked at
Oonan, but he did not ask her why. She said, "And it
said the verse again, which felt even odder, as if there
were an earthquake. I was looking at the place on the
rock where the new thyme should be just starting under
the dead stuff; and I could see it suddenly, much better—but I didn't know what it was any more. And I said,
'No, thank you!' very loudly, and lost my balance and sat
down on the path."

She scratched at the bandage again.

"Don't do that, you'll make the scarring worse," said Oonan. "What then?"

Jony rubbed her ball of wool instead. "It ran at me and tore my arm in passing and ran on into the darkness. It wasn't like a dog, there was no warning. Why do they say in cold blood when blood feels hot?"

"They mean the wolf's blood, not yours," said Arry, not very coherently.

"I think you had your warning earlier," said Oonan.

"Nobody will tell me what I ought to have done," said Jony.

"I think on the whole you did very well," said Oonan.

"If I'd done very well you'd think I wouldn't be hurt."

"Would I?" said Oonan. "I don't know."

"What did Halver say," said Arry, "when you told him all this?"

"He said experience was a hard school but fools would learn in no other."

"Did he say anything else?"

"He said he must be off on his walk, and he would see me in one school or another when the time came."

Oonan stood up. "I think," he said to Arry, "that we must be off on our walk as well. I'll look at that again tomorrow," he said to Jony. "Tell Niss that if she must work more sorcery on it she's to speak to me first. And don't use that arm for anything much."

They walked over to where Con and Beldi had built a pile of slate pieces as high as Con's waist. "Where are we going now?" said Con. "When are we going to find them?"

"I think," said Oonan, looking at Arry, "that we need to ask Mally where they might go; and then go there."

If he thought he could fool Con into thinking a search for Halver was really a search for their parents, he was in for an unpleasant surprise, thought Arry. You might find them where you found Halver, but they did not seem to have been working together after the first night.

When they got back to Mally's house, Tany and Zia were throwing sticks for Blackie. Arry left Con and Beldi to help them and followed Oonan into the house. Mally was reading a book, and did not look overly pleased to see them.

"If Halver had a whole day to go walking in," said Oonan, with no preliminaries at all, "where would he go?"

"Up," said Mally. She considered. "And north as well, this time of year; the going's dryer and there's a clump of three oaks he likes."

"Can you show us on the map?" said Oonan.

Mally fetched the map and showed them.

"Con can't possibly walk that far," said Arry.

"I don't suppose," said Oonan to Mally, "that you've any idea of where Frances and Bec might spend their day, under the circumstances?"

"Watching Halver," said Mally, "if they could find him."

"Well, that makes things easier," said Oonan.

"Shall I make them easier yet and take Con off your hands?" said Mally.

"And Beldi," said Arry.

"He isn't any trouble," said Mally. She reflected.

"Though if we go on giving him the notion that being troublesome means being well-loved, he can think of trouble none of us dream of."

"I've been worrying about that," said Arry. "I'll take Tany and Zia and Lina for you, Mally, as soon as this business is settled."

"Oh, excellent," said Mally. "They can help Beldi think of trouble. Here, take some of these pies for your supper. And don't stop to argue with Con. Go out the kitchen door—quietly—and take the little path past the thyme rock. I'll talk to Con."

"I don't know what we'd do without you," said Arry, and hugged her.

"I do," said Mally dryly. "Go away, now."

They crept out the kitchen door and took the path through the pine woods. "It's a pity Halver isn't fond of these," said Oonan. "Going for a long walk on a spring day is not my notion of fixing things."

They walked and walked and walked. If one's mind were clear and happy, it would have been a fine day to do just this. It was warm and breezy. The tentative blue sky of spring was all laddered with thin white clouds. Their shadows sported over the hills like cats, chasing the sunlight over sparkling granite and dull slate, the bright dry grass and the small hidden gleams of water. The may was blooming, and the small wild cherry trees, and scilla and bloodroot and the strange leafless forsythia. Jony had pointed them out to Arry every spring since Jony got her knowledge.

Arry had never walked in these parts before. She let Oonan find the paths and stand pondering at the places where they crossed or disappeared. She was thinking about Halver and what to say to him. They came out of the woods and walked up long hills of blowing grass with an occasional lost-looking bush or gnarled tree for emphasis. They climbed crumbling slopes of slate and crossed little hidden meadows all starred with white and yellow flowers. Arry finished with Halver and began to think about her parents. Keep the wolf far hence, that's foe to men. They had meant Halver, of course, but they must also have meant themselves, or they would not have stayed away. Frances had said she wanted to write to Arry, but even that would not have kept the wolf far enough hence. Why, then, had she and Bec come back?

It was getting hot. They stopped to drink at the next spring they found. They both took off their jackets, and Arry took her skirt off as well; she could go on in her leggings and shirt. The skirt was cooler than the leggings, but not as easy to climb and walk in. Arry thought of Frances and Bec in their long gray robes, and wondered how easy they had found this path.

They rolled the clothes in a ball and tucked them under a rock. Oonan said that, with luck, they could come by here in time to eat their supper, just when the evening was growing cool and they would want the clothes again.

"I just thought," said Arry. "Mally gave us enough for five or six people."

"Yes," said Oonan.

They walked on; or climbed, mostly: things were getting more and more vertical, though from time to time they found another high meadow, blue with gentians. Experience is a hard school, thought Arry, but fools will learn in no other. Experience was what you had to go by if you had no knowledge. Halver had no knowledge now. Was he calling himself a fool? Or, as seemed more likely, had he been calling Jony one? But if what she had refused from him was not experience, then what was it?

The sun was three-quarters down the sky and Arry's feet and knees hurt by the time they trudged up one last bare slope and saw against the sky the three small twisted oak trees. The wind was blowing towards them. Arry heard nothing, and Halver would smell nothing. They kept walking. Halver could probably hear their breathing by now, but he did not come out. They passed under the shadow of the trees, which still held grimly to last year's brown leaves; they walked rustling around the three rocks drifted with more brown leaves and hollow acorns and twigs. Halver was not there. Nobody was there.

"Mally was wrong," said Arry. She said it almost to see if the words would come out at all. They did.

"We may just be late," said Oonan. "He may have been here and gone."

"Does it look like it?"

"No," said Oonan, reluctantly; "but I'm not Karn, after all."

He leaned heavily on a large gray rock. Arry walked around the top of the hill, peering here and there, looking for a tuft of wolf-hair, blackened rocks, ashes, a nest in the heaped leaves, gnawed bones. Wolf or person, he would have left some trace. He had had Karn teach them that much. She stood on the northern crest of the slope and looked north, at sharp hills piled ever sharper until they disappeared into the clouds. Nothing moved but a raven, and the shifting sunlight. A mind like an April day, Bec had said the trader from Wormsreign had. He had meant something more changeable than this, a day where it rained hard one minute and shone brilliantly the next.

"Or we may be early," said Oonan.

"Jony saw him this morning; he had hours on us. If he was here at all, he was here before us."

Oonan rubbed the sweat from his face, leaving a smear of dust. His mouth twitched. He began to laugh.

"What if Halver knew," he said, "that we would ask Mally where he would go? Then he would go somewhere else."

"But Mally should have known that, too," said Arry.

"Should she?" said Oonan, still laughing a little. "Or should we have asked a different question?"

"She's not a divining-game!" said Arry.

"No, I suppose not."

"We asked her what Halver would do," said Arry, "and she told us, and he didn't do it."

"If you can talk so much, you must be rested," said Oonan. "We have a long walk home, and dark before we get there."

# ❧ 21 ❧

THE WAY HOME was mostly downhill, but it did not seem easier or shorter. They wanted their extra clothes long before they got to them, and they had eaten their supper before they began to want the clothes. They came sorely and wearily out of the pine woods to find Mally's house all dark. But as they sat down at the edge of the woods to rest before the last little walk home, somebody got up from the bench next to the well and walked across the pebbles to where they sprawled on the lovely damp cool of the moss.

"What news?" said Mally.

"Halver wasn't there," said Arry. Oonan made some movement next to her, but said nothing.

Mally was perfectly silent. The dark solid form of her, between them and the lighter sky, did not move at all; even her wispy ephemeral hair did not stir. Arry was aware, more precisely than ever before, not of just perceiving, but of having herself caused hurt. And she had caused it with the truth.

She realized Mally had stopped breathing only when she started again. "He must have been there," Mally said, quite calmly.

"We started later than he did, Mally, and we were a long time getting there," said Oonan. "We probably missed him."

"But he's sleeping there," said Mally.

"Did he tell you so?" said Oonan.

"No, of course not," said Mally. She sat down rather heavily next to Oonan. "I knew he was there," she said.

"I thought you did," said Oonan. "That's why we walked so far." His tone was not reproachful; it was even soothing; but it hurt Mally even more than what Arry had said.

None of them said anything for some time. The night breeze lifted the hair stuck to Arry's neck and breathed the scent of the hawthorn into her dusty head. The stars stared down as they always had. A few bats skittered across the sky. It was so quiet that Arry could hear the faraway streams running over their rocks. Then something small rustled in the pine needles not far behind them, which made Mally jump; and Arry spoke.

"Oonan, I have to go. Mally, I'll come for the children in the morning."

"Oonan will take care of me," said Mally.

Arry got up, creakily, and walked away. Behind her Oonan said, "There's nothing *wrong* with *you.*" Mally laughed, and Arry walked faster. Mally was in Arry's province, well and truly in the very heart of it; and Arry was walking away. She broke into a run for a few steps, but she was too stiff and tired. She went on as fast as she could.

Niss's house was not dark. Niss liked to work at night, Mally had often said so; Vand, she said, could sleep through anything, and often did. What if that's wrong, too, Arry thought suddenly. But no, that's from before; it should be all right. She walked up to the open door, from which was issuing a less than pleasant red light. They had all been taught from a very early age never to interrupt Niss when she was working. One was to stand there until one was noticed; she would notice eventually.

Arry stood in the doorway, straining her eyes to see what was happening inside. She could not make the light and shapes mean anything, but presently she heard Niss singing. "What wondrous life is this I lead. Ripe apples drop about my head; the luscious clusters of the vine upon my mouth do crush their wine; the nectarine and curious peach into my hands themselves do reach: stumbling on melons, as I pass, ensnared with flowers, I fall on grass."

It sounded better than the hag and hungry goblin. Arry arranged herself comfortably against the doorframe. She had run through several arrangements and was wondering if sitting down on the threshold would be too distracting, when Niss said, "Who's there?"

"It's Arry."

"Come in," said Niss, and the red light went out. Niss added absently, "Look, the dawn in russet mantle clad," and the fire in the fireplace woke like a cat stretching, gathered itself and slowly fluffed up into a strong blaze.

Arry went in.

"Why abroad so late?" said Niss. "Sleep charms?"

"I need to borrow the wolfskin coat," said Arry.

"I can hardly keep Beldi's from you," said Niss slowly.

"In fact, I'd rather have Tiln's," said Arry. "Beldi's slept under his once, and I don't want him near it."

"Who should want you near either of them?"

"Halver, by the look of it," said Arry. "Might this be a way to find him? Could the coat summon him, after somebody had slept under it three times?"

Niss regarded her steadily in the flickering light of the fire. She had to tilt her head back to do it. I must have grown again, thought Arry. Niss sighed, and went to a chest in the corner, and opened it and took out the wolfskin coats. She said briskly, "Do you think I am easier to be played upon than a pipe?" Nothing happened, but after a moment Niss said, "The coat could summon him, certainly; but on what occasion I know not."

"I'll find out for you," said Arry, holding out her hands.

Niss dropped one coat back into the trunk and came across the room with the other one bundled in her arms. She looked reluctant. "It does seem," she said slowly, "that people ought not to go turning themselves into wolves without consulting me."

"I don't mean to turn myself into a wolf," said Arry.

Niss looked at her steadily. "Dying's not my province," she said, "but I don't advise it."

"I don't plan on it, any time soon," said Arry.

"Do you know what you're about?"

"Learning about pain," said Arry.

"Let me tell you a spell," said Niss, still holding the coat. "Don't say it unless you mean it. I can say them with or without intent, but I can't teach you that in five minutes."

"I understand you," said Arry.

"Listen well, then. Here it is. Mastiff, greyhound, mongrel grim, hound or spaniel, brach or lym, or bob-tail tyke or trundle-tail, Tom will make him weep and wail; for with throwing this my head, dogs leaped the hatch, and all are fled."

She repeated this several times, until Arry assured her that she would remember it. Arry said, "Must I throw my head?"

"No," said Niss, laughing.

"There's no wolf in the rhyme, Niss."

"I well know," said Niss, not laughing at all. "But I think the mongrel grim will serve."

She piled the wolfskin coat into Arry's arms. Arry thanked her, and went out. Halfway across the water meadow she finally put the thing on; it was much lighter to wear than to carry. The cats were milling about the front door when she got home, though this was usually their hunting time. They bounded into the house, complaining loudly, as soon as she had opened the door. The house smelled stale and stuffy. Arry opened windows, and gave the cats some milk, and heated some for herself, with peppermint in it for her stomach's sake. Three times, she thought, not three nights. And a good thing, too, now that Halver's found ways to make people want to be wolves without being a wolf himself. He must be in a hurry.

She sat down in the largest chair, with extra cushions, and laid the coat across her lap. She was afraid of it, though she did not really know why. At the worst, after all, she could let Halver turn her into a wolf, and then she could see her parents again. He was the only way she could think of to get to them, whether he turned her into a wolf or not. He also really could not be let to slink and plot all over the hills, tempting half the children and biting the rest, which was the way he seemed to want to go on. Or if Mally were right after all and this was just a lesson on a strange and grand scale, then she must do what she could. Halver always told them to attack a problem, not to stare at it and wait for it to resolve itself.

She stroked her hand down the sleeve of the coat, and Sheepnose leapt into her lap and settled down, kneading the fur and purring hugely.

"Well," said Arry. "Once can do no harm, in any case." She blew out her candle, wriggled further under the coat, rubbed the affronted Sheepnose behind the ears, and shut her eyes.

She fell asleep almost at once. She woke at dawn, when the birds were shouting their loudest. Sheepnose had retreated to sleep on a fold of the coat that had fallen to the floor, and Woollycat was stretched out on Arry's thigh, head laid flat along the coat like a sleeping dragon.

Arry moved her arm, which had gone numb, from under her head, shoved a cushion there instead, and tried to remember what she had dreamed. Nothing. "Oh, doubt!" she said suddenly, sitting up with a jerk and dislodging the indignant Woollycat. "Keep the wolf far hence."

That meant she would have to sleep under the coat outside. She got out of the chair and moved blearily to the window. The sun was lining everything with gold; the birds were as loud as a waterfall. Not now, she thought; she must have some real sleep before walking anywhere else with the heavy coat. She stumbled through the washing room to her own bed and went back to sleep on top of the quilt, with all her clothes on.

She dreamed she was Sir Patrick Spens, set upon a golden bough to sing to lords and ladies of Byzantium of what was past, or passing, or to come; except that she could not really sing at all and was concerned only with the fact that there was going to be a dreadful storm, whereupon the three sons of the Wife of Ussher's Well would come back with bark in their caps and find Melusina splashing the bath water about with her fishy tail. This would make the lords and ladies unhappy. She used her golden beak to pluck the bark from the cap of the youngest. "Look!" said everyone. "From the far side of the tree that grows in Paradise!" "Nonsense," said Frances. "Paradise is a Unicornish word for an orchard or park." Arry dropped the bark onto Frances's head. Frances smiled and thanked her. The lords and ladies began to harangue her for not singing. They sounded remarkably like Con and Beldi. After a while Arry realized that they were Con and Beldi. She opened her eyes.

Woollycat stared back at her from the pillow. Con and Beldi were not in the room, they weren't trying to wake her up at all. They were in the kitchen.

"You can't make pancakes out of the blushful Hippocrene," said Beldi; he sounded a little desperate. "You use buttermilk." There was a pause, punctuated with clattering and splashing noises. "Everybody says so."

"I don't," said Con. "I hate buttermilk."

Arry rubbed Woollycat's nose. "You probably could

make pancakes out of the blushful Hippocrene," she told the cat. "It's acidic, I think. But I can't imagine what they would taste like. Con really oughtn't to waste all that flour and milk." Woollycat jumped off the bed at the last word and sat on the floor making impatient noises. Arry got up. She was still dressed, however dusty and sweaty the garments might be, so she stopped only briefly in the washing room and then went into the kitchen.

They had not made much more mess than she might have, if she had been in a hurry. They had built a small fire of pinecones on the hearth, to boil the kettle, and were heating the griddle on its remains. The main fire was burning much too briskly to cook pancakes, but Con could presumably deal with that. The only alarming thing was the batter itself, which was a faint pink and suffered from an uprush of huge bubbles, as if it were being boiled itself.

"We were going to surprise you," said Con.

"You have," said Arry, peering into the bowl. It looked worse close up, though it smelled pleasant. She retreated to the table and poured herself a mug of tea.

"I told Woollycat not to wake you up."

"She didn't."

"I told you you were talking too loudly," said Beldi.

Con gave this remark no attention whatsoever. She said to the fire, "In thee I see the twilight of such day, as after sunset fadeth in the west." It shrunk itself into a bed of coals, and Con moved the griddle onto that. Arry bit her lip on a number of remonstrations. Con had protected her hand with a towel; and she was at this moment remembering to try the griddle with a drop of water. She dropped rounds of batter on it. They were of wildly differing sizes, but it didn't really matter. It was the pinkness that most required comment, but it was too late for that. As the pancakes cooked, they got pinker, as pink as Con's cheeks. The little bubbles that broke their surfaces were as red as raspberries.

Arry could not bear to look at them. She went down into the cold cellar and got a crock of apple butter and the honey Derry had given her. That had not been long ago at all; most of the honey was still there; but it seemed as if it happened in some other spring.

When she came back up Con had put a whole plate of pancakes on the table. Beldi was serving himself, looking glum. Arry got plates for herself and Con and served pancakes onto both. Con, she was astonished to see, was cleaning the griddle while it was still hot, a proceeding earnestly recommended to her by everybody in her family but never once followed before. Arry looked long and hard at her, but she had no fever, nor any other complaint of flesh. Of spirit it was harder to tell, but the kinds of pain Arry had found before did not seem to be present.

Beldi had taken a spoonful of pancake and was looking at it as one might regard a piece of good rotten bark, to see what might crawl out. Arry felt much the same.

They both watched Con. She hung the griddle back on the wall, which she had certainly never done before, and sat down in her chair. She grinned amiably at her siblings. "You forgot to put any honey on," she said. She spread honey liberally over her own pancakes, cut off a spoonful, and crammed it into her mouth. She chewed and swallowed it, and cut off another. Arry fol-

lowed the progress of the first mouthful as if she were
studying the action of poison on her dearest enemy. It
went down like pancakes.

She knew what Con was going to say, but felt com-
pelled to wait and hear her say it. Con finished her
plateful and took three more pancakes. Arry was relieved to see her use her fingers instead of the fork. Con
put apple butter on the pancakes this time. She looked
at Arry, at Beldi, and back at Arry. "Why aren't you eating?"

As if he too had been waiting for this, Beldi put his
spoonful into his mouth. His went down like pancake
too. He said, "Too dry."

"Put some honey on it," said Con.

Arry put her spoonful into her mouth. It tasted like
summer, late, full, old summer with harvest almost
upon it. It had, under its complex flowery grainy sunny
flavor, almost no actual substance; she could not imagine what Beldi had meant by calling it too dry. She swallowed it. "It's lovely, Con," she said, "but mightn't it be
a little too rarefied for breakfast?"

"It's a special breakfast," said Con.

"Yes, extremely," said Arry, and ate the rest of her
plateful.

"Because of Zia's plan," said Con.

Arry looked at Beldi. He said, "I made her tell you at
least."

"You did not," Con said, without heat. "You can't
make me do anything. You *persuaded* me that I ought,
and Zia helped you."

"Zia wanted you to tell me?" said Arry. "Why?"

"Because you've got Tiln's coat," said Con.

Angels and ministers of grace defend us, thought Arry. "What does she want with Tiln's coat?"

"You older ones always forget," said Con, leaning her elbows on the table and fixing her round dark gaze on Arry. In her clear high voice Arry could hear traces of Zia's deeper drawl. "But Halver teaches by games. If we lose the game, then he makes us learn the hard way. So Zia wants to win the game."

"And what's the game?"

"Being better wolves than Halver."

"Who told Zia," said Arry, with extreme care, "that Halver was any sort of wolf at all?"

Con looked at her pityingly. "Zia always finds things out," she said.

"Did Halver tell her?"

"Halver doesn't tell you when he's playing a game," said Con, still pitying.

Arry put the entire tangle aside for later consideration and said, "So why are you making us a special breakfast, again?"

"Because wolves can't cook," said Con.

"Halver isn't a wolf all the time."

"No," said Con, with enormous patience. "But to be better wolves than Halver, we have to be wolves all the time."

"Con, for mercy's sake. Do you want to be a wolf?"

"No," said Con, with her mouth full. "I didn't want to learn to read, either, but I liked it after."

"But if you become a wolf you'll lose your knowledge."

"Haven't got any," said Con, indistinctly.

"But Mally thinks you're going to be a wizard."

"I'll be a wolf wizard, then."

Arry ground her hands into her forehead. She reminded herself that she did not have to have this argument, that force would probably suffice, that she had the one coat and Niss the other, and what Niss would do for the Physici of the whole community she would not do for Con. On the other hand, to underestimate Con or Zia, or most especially Con and Zia, might be fatal, not in the rhetorical but in the true sense. And why in the world, thought Arry, can Zia persuade Con to anything while I can persuade her to nothing?

"There's no such thing as a wolf wizard," said Beldi.

"Sune says there is."

Oh, merciful heaven. "Con," said Arry. "You can't perform this plan at once. I need to study this coat, and Niss needs to study Beldi's. She must discover how they work, and I must discover if they can do hurt."

"Zia already asked Niss," said Con. "She said no, no child might have one." Con scowled. "And she hid it with the strongest spell she has. So we have to have this one."

"Not while I'm studying it."

"Well, when?"

"I don't know, Con."

"Well," said Con, scrambling down from her chair. "Zia said she'd think of a way to get the coat away from Niss. So we'll think about that, and if we can't you can give us Beldi's."

"Con, you are not to meddle with Niss."

"No, I won't," said Con cheerfully. "I'll just help Zia think."

"Whatever she thinks, I want you to tell me. I need

to see if it will do hurt. These coats are very powerful, Con.''

For once, the combined ring of authority and truth seemed to catch Con's ear. "All right," said Con. "But we can't wait very long, Arry, or Halver will win."

"Halver can't be a wolf at all until the next full moon," Arry told her. "I'll be done by then. Go take a bath, Con, it's been days since you did."

Con went off without demur, probably in the hope of finding towel-sprites. Arry looked at Beldi. "Will Zia let you in her plan?"

"She'll let anybody in who does what she says."

"Does Mally know about this plan?"

Beldi shrugged.

"Can you be my spy? Can you stick with Con and Zia and tell me what they're doing, what state they've got to?"

"She usually makes us promise not to tell," said Beldi.

"Well, promise me first; promise me you will."

Beldi looked at her.

"No," said Arry swiftly, "it isn't right. But it's as right as we can manage at the moment."

"Frances used to say that," said Beldi.

"She did, didn't she?"

"This isn't just a plot to make me watch Con, is it?"

"No," said Arry. "It is not. This is extremely important." She hesitated. Beldi could certainly keep quiet; but he was not very old. I'm not so very old myself, she thought. "Halver is trying to change us all," she said. "And while that's part of his province, I think there's something wrong. So do Frances and Bec. It looks as if they're trying to stop him, but I think they need help. And I certainly need help—not just to keep Con out of the way. She and Zia could wreck anything, you have seen them do it before. This mustn't be wrecked."

"Maybe you should ask them to help you," said Beldi.

"I don't want them. I want you."

She had thought this would please him, but in fact his face went very blank. "All right," he said after a moment. "I promise to tell you all about their plan, and not to tell them about yours."

"Thank you," said Arry.

Beldi nodded, and helped himself to the last of the pancakes. Arry drank her tea and thought. It would really be better to go talk to Mally again. But she did not think she could bear it; she was not sure that anything Mally could tell her would be of use; and she felt in a serious and terrible hurry. She took the last of the oatcake, the three remaining cold potatoes, and another large lump of cheese, shoved them into a pouch that had been her father's, and went into the front room to collect the wolfskin coat.

Both cats were sleeping on it. Arry wondered if sleeping on it three times would also cause some profound transformation; if it worked on cats; if it would work through Niss's warding. She shook the coat, and the cats sprang away, glaring. Arry rubbed each affronted head briefly and went out the front door.

It was warm again, and today the sky was perfectly clear and no breeze blew, which meant it would soon be more than warm. Arry stood under the pine tree, looking at the crocuses, which were a little wilted now, and would soon lose their blooms altogether and resemble striped grasses until they turned brown and disappeared. Where shall I go to nap, she thought. Lying down right amongst the crocuses would be pleasant, but not these crocuses, of course, so close to the house: She wouldn't be undisturbed for long enough to shut her eyes.

She walked away towards Halver's house, skirted the foot of its hill, and came to Sune's house. Sune was sitting outside in the sun, still spinning. She had quite a large mass of yarn by now, but she would have to knit fast if she wanted a blanket for Knot by the time Knot presented herself. Sune felt better today, though she did not feel very well. She waved, so Arry climbed the hill and greeted her.

"Have you been sleeping out?" said Sune, looking rather pointedly at the coat.

Arry realized that she had not bathed since she went on that long futile walk with Oonan; that she was still wearing her crumpled shirt and grass- and mud-stained leggings; that she had not even combed her hair, which was coming out of its braids and probably full of twigs. "I thought I'd see what it was like," she said. "Can I do anything for you?"

"You can, in fact," said Sune. "I haven't seen Halver today, or yesterday, either."

"I think he's devising some particularly strong lesson for us to make up for the holiday," said Arry, putting the coat and pouch down.

"I never found planting oats much of a holiday," said Sune. "Though there must be better ways of avoiding it than being pregnant."

Arry fetched her a great deal of water; brought her last sack of potatoes out of the cellar; moved the rocking

chair nearer the fire, since Sune said Grel had been by
to say it would grow cooler this evening and probably
rain; spread an extra blanket on the bed; and made a
pot of tea. Sune thanked her profusely. Arry professed
herself delighted, and in fact she was: she needed to be
tired if she were to sleep well outside.

She went on down to the stream and into the little
wood on its far side. No crocuses here, but drifts of scilla
in the clearings, and eyebright, and more may blooming. Arry finally tucked herself under a huge twisted
hawthorn, put her head on her pouch of food, spread
the coat over herself, and shut her eyes.

Her mind woke up at once. Is this once or twice
under this coat, she thought, exactly as she would when
measuring cinnamon for solstice buns. Extra cinnamon
never marred the buns, though Frances used to talk
about how much it cost. If something didn't happen
soon after her third nap under this garment, she would
just have to have a fourth. She hoped it wouldn't be like
kneading the cinnamon into the dough after it had already risen once. That was never entirely satisfactory.

Neither was being a wolf. She could see less than she
was accustomed to, and smell a great deal more. She
trotted dutifully about, sniffing; but while she knew that
a wolf would have been wildly fascinated with all these
scents, she could not make herself be interested. It was
like reading a bad recipe. Arry finally lay down and put
her nose on her paws and went to sleep, which had the
effect of waking her from her human sleep sooner than
she liked. It was still morning. She rubbed her eyes and
sat up. How long ought one to go between naps, she
thought. What Niss had told her really was just like a

carelessly written recipe, leaving too much for the experience of the cook to fill in. She cast off the wolfskin coat and sat with her knees under her chin, working the tangles out of her filthy hair and admiring the sun on the new birch leaves.

If it had been a very little warmer she would have gone and had a bath in the stream. She thought that, if she dreamed she was a wolf again, swimming might do to relieve the boredom. She could not believe that this was what Halver had had in mind. But then, after all, he had intended this coat just for Tiln, and the other just for Beldi. Niss might say that whosoever slept under them three times would suffer this or that effect, but it did not follow that everybody would have the same experience.

A cooler breeze moved through the trees. Arry pulled the coat over herself and lay down again. She watched the sunlight falling through the may blossoms, pink and white and gold. When she woke up a wolf, she did go swimming in the stream, frightening all the fish and making a great deal of noise. Then she lay down in the sun to dry. It was when she woke up in the sun in her own shape again, but still damp, and with the beginnings of sunburn, that she began to view the wolfskin coat with respect. She shook the dry grass and leaves out of it, and went back to her hawthorn tree to fetch the pouch of food. The strap was there, and a crumble of oatcake.

"Bother," said Arry. She was getting hungry; it was early afternoon now, and the pancakes of blushful Hippocrene had not been entirely filling. She stood turning the strap in her hands, frowning. This would be either the third time, or the fourth; it was either necessary, or not; and what her wolf-self was most likely to fill its time with would be in killing something.

Arry went home and finished cleaning the discarded oddments out of the kitchen. Con and Beldi came home at suppertime, and she fed them potato-and-onion pie. They were both preoccupied. Con declined offers, after dinner, to play chess, to be read to, to play with the cats, to be helped to make scones, and to see if Sune might like to make some music. She went off to her room. Arry looked at Beldi.

"Well?" she said.

Beldi was lying on the hearth-rug, and he addressed himself to the fire, which Con had spoken to with somewhat different intention before she went to bed. "It's very hard to tell with Zia," he said. "She likes—Mally says so—she likes you to think she always knows what she's doing, and she makes things up. Mally says she's the other half of Sune. Tany's even stranger. Mally says he truly doesn't believe in anything; she says he's like the people the Descent of Doubt first descended on, before they changed the spell—did she tell you about that?"

"I heard about it," said Arry.

"They don't talk like ordinary people," said Beldi. "Mally says you have to sift them."

"What, like flour?"

"Like flour with weevils in, is what she *said*," said Beldi, giggling.

"She thinks their thoughts are weevily?"

"Yes, very."

"What do you think?"

Beldi's head, outlined by the fire, moved a little; but

he did not turn to look at her. "I think," he said, with a certain relish, "that Zia has a plan, but she hasn't told anybody what it is. She isn't persuaded yet that she needs us, but she's keeping us interested with her false plan, or half plan, or a plan she'd like, even if it wouldn't work, until she can see what to do."

"She's only five," said Arry, a little taken aback.

"So's Con," said Beldi.

"Well, that's true. What does Zia want you to think her plan is?"

"Burn herbs at midnight in the pine woods, conjure the wolfskin coats up out of nowhere, run away to the highest meadow there is and sleep under them until we find out what's what," said Beldi.

"Can Zia conjure?"

"Mally says not," said Beldi; he sounded distinctly doubtful.

"Well, she knows, Beldi." Had they got wind of Mally's failure concerning Halver?

"She knows what Zia's *like*," said Beldi. "That's different from what she can do."

"Is it? I don't know."

"Well, I don't either, but I think."

"When was she going to do this?"

"We were going to do it when the moon is full next. If Zia decides to do it without us, or to do something else, then she'll do it any time she thinks is right."

"Does Mally know what she's up to?"

"Mally knows she's up to something." Beldi added reflectively, "Of course, she always is."

"Mmmmm," said Arry.

"What are you up to?" said Beldi.

Arry sat up straight, dislodging Sheepnose. Beldi so

seldom asked questions. She supposed it was only fair; he had told her what she needed to find out. "I'm trying to find Halver by sleeping under the wolfskin coat."

Beldi rolled over on the rug, thus dislodging Woollycat also, and sat up. "But Niss said—"

"I heard her."

"Do you want to be a wolf?"

"Not especially."

"But—"

"I think this is a lesson of Halver's. I don't think I have to become a wolf or die. I think there are other choices."

"But what if you're wrong?"

"It might be very useful to have a wolf for your sister," said Arry.

"A wolf and a wizard," said Beldi. He sounded glum, and sulky. Arry looked him over, inwardly. His pain was so unlike Con's, or anybody else's, that she was not entirely certain it was pain at all.

"You can be something too," she offered.

"My parents are wolves already," said Beldi.

"I won't leave you," said Arry.

"How do you know? What if that's what wolves do?"

"Derry says they are very familial," said Arry.

"I'm coming with you," said Beldi.

"Leaving Con alone in the house?"

"She's a wizard," said Beldi. "And she never wakes up, anyway."

"She's five years old."

"I'm coming with you."

"Then I'm not going anywhere," said Arry. "I can sleep under the coat on our doorstep, as well as anywhere."

"I'll watch you, then."

"That's actually a very good idea," said Arry. "I can't tell what happens precisely." She pondered. "If I turn into a wolf," she said, "and look at all menacing— or even if I don't—you must run back into the house and shut and bolt the door."

"Are you sleepy now?"

"No. Let's play chess."

Beldi won three games, and Arry decided trying to sleep would be easier than playing a fourth.

SHE DID NOT think she had slept, at first. The rustle of the wind, the small sound of Beldi's breathing, the rustle and click as he amused himself by playing both sides of a chess game, never altered. She stretched, finally, thinking she might make herself some sleepy tea; and Beldi turned his head and gasped.

Arry opened her mouth to speak, and closed it hastily. The wolfskin coat was gone: she must be wearing it indeed. Both cats were asleep in the hollyhocks, and neither of them stirred. She got down off the doorstep, which was no longer comfortable for the shape she was, and tried wagging her tail. Beldi sat where he was, very still, his head turned sideways. Arry moved very slowly and lay down on the other side of the hollyhocks. The cats never stirred. The night air was full of intriguing and unfamiliar smells. But the warm air wafting out of their house held a green and awful smell, as of potatoes gone very bad. It must be Niss's spell.

Arry and Beldi stared at one another. Arry supposed she could go back to sleep: that seemed to have the effect of cancelling the transformation of the coat. If Halver came now, she would not be able to deal with him anyway, unless she chose to tear his throat out.

She considered this thought. It had never occurred to her before. She could certainly not act on it without considering it again in her ordinary form; but it had an extraordinary appeal to it in her thoughts as she formed them now. She was not hungry; she had no thought of hurting or killing or eating Beldi, or Con; she did not want to run through the dark slashing at Jony; she did not want to chase sheep or pounce on mice. But killing Halver had a delicious smell to it.

It would hurt, thought Arry. You can't kill him without hurting him. She shut her eyes fiercely.

She woke up in her proper shape, in the sheep hut, which was where she had meant to go for her final sleep under the coat. She was herself again, and the coat was not with her, which was a pity, because, as Grel had said it would, the evening had turned cool. And Halver had taken the blanket from the bed on his last visit. She sat down on the bare planks, hugging her arms. Whatever Beldi was seeing, she hoped he was not afraid or alarmed.

She sat and waited, while the small sounds of the night established themselves and grew clear and distinct: frogs croaking, locusts sawing away, something small slipping through the grass, the half-heard high chittering of bats.

Frogs? thought Arry. At first she thought it was some remnant of the wolf-self hankering after a treat; but it was rather that the frog-chorus was wrong. This was not spring peeping, but the full summer song. The locusts, too, did not belong to spring, not to this spring. Arry got up and peered out the door of the hut. Warm air poured over her. The moon was high and small and full in the clean sky. The bright soft scent of the wild roses that grew in the rocks moved along the air.

This must be another dream, thought Arry. The fourth time must—must—I can't think what it must, I hope it isn't the terrors of the earth. I could go back to sleep. I could go home, and see what's there. That feels dangerous: there would be two of me. She stepped outside. The sheep were back, clumped in the spot from which the rock could fall on them. On the other hand, she thought, I could talk to myself; that might be useful. If this is the summer to come and not one gone by. If this is anywhere at all really. She squinted at the moonlight and the shadows, trying to think. She felt very sleepy, much more so than she had when it would have been useful.

Something dark was running across the field towards her, its belly low to the ground. Arry sprang back into the hut and snatched up the first piece of wood that came to her hand; but when she came back to the door, it was to find Blackie wagging and prancing and, when she spoke to him, rolling in the wild thyme and sending up mixed scents of herb and dusty damp dog. She rubbed his head. He leapt to his feet and began to growl. Arry took her hand away at once, but he was not growling at her. Somebody else was coming, who walked upright and wore a white or gray robe. The person was too thin for Bec and not tall enough for Frances.

"Well, of course," said Arry. She came out of the

hut, still holding her stick. Blackie accompanied her, pressed against her leg and vibrating with low growls.

Halver looked very bleached in the moonlight. His voice was rather thready. What he said, however, was entirely like him. "This is not," he said, as he had when Jony brought in a basket of stinging nettle to show a useful plant to the younger children, or when Tany said that Do What You Will was the whole of the law, "what I had in mind."

"It never is," said Arry, almost at random.

"Now that is untrue," said Halver. "You have been an excellent student. It's in the change from student to equal that we are, perhaps, having a little trouble. Why are you sleeping under Tiln's coat?"

"It was the only way I could think of to find you."

"Finding me is worth either becoming a wolf or dying?"

"I thought you wanted me to become a wolf."

"I thought you wanted very much the contrary."

"It hasn't been very interesting so far," said Arry.

Halver laughed. "That's because you're not Tiln," he said.

"I wondered if that had something to do with it. In any case, you did want me to become a wolf, so you ought to be pleased."

"I wanted you to make a choice," said Halver. "This wasn't it. What did you wish to see me about?"

"Two things," said Arry. "First, my parents. I couldn't think of any other way to find them, either."

"You won't find them with me," said Halver; his tone was mostly rueful, but there was something very bitter in his face. Arry wished Mally were here to interpret it, and then remembered that that might not serve at all.

"Why?" said Arry.

"They think we should let you be."

"We?" said Arry, with a sinking feeling.

"We who change shape under the moon, who have made a choice and abide by it, who are not trammeled by this spell that sacrifices wisdom for petty knowledge."

Who says that's what it does, thought Arry. She said, "Let who be? Con and Beldi and me?"

"The entire company of these hills."

"And what do you think you should be doing?"

"Freeing the lot of you."

"From what?"

"You never would do this in school," said Halver regretfully. "It's amazing to what lengths a teacher must go simply to provoke a few questions."

"Con asks questions."

"Oh, anybody under the age of six will do so. It's after that concerns me."

"I did ask you questions," said Arry. "I asked you about Con, about the nature and kinds of pain; but you put me off, Halver, you didn't answer them."

"I couldn't," said Halver. "It wasn't my province. And that is the heart of the matter."

"Can you answer them now?"

"Indifferently; I have had them under my study for very little time. But of a certainty there are more pains than the physical, and they are sometimes easier and sometimes harder of assuagement."

"I could have told you that much."

Halver laughed again. He seemed, in fact, in excellent spirits. Arry considered him. No fever, no head-ache, and his hand had stopped itching.

"If you wish to study these pains, you must come out," said Halver. "Come out from under this spell."

"How?"

"Choose."

"To become a wolf, or die?"

"Transformation is necessary," said Halver, "and this is the one I know."

"Why can't I choose to become a wolf, or not to become a wolf?"

"I teach the reluctant as well as the eager," said Halver.

"I don't see where dying enters into it."

"I put it there," said Halver.

"Why?" said Arry. She remembered the question about the blind child, and his careless answer, as care-less as this answer. She could not believe he had said it, or that he could mean it. It's one of his games, she thought, one of the advanced ones. She still felt out-raged. "Isn't there enough dying as it is?"

"That is the root of the problem," said Halver; he was pleased with her; she was being a good student. Arry wondered if the transformation were less thorough than he seemed to think. His province still concerned him. Or it might be that people's knowledge was indeed suited to their natures, and it was in his nature to be a teacher.

She said, "That sounds like the beginning of a long speech. Will you come in and sit down?"

"It's spring in there, and cold with it," said Halver.

"Come and sit in the wild thyme and lean on the welcoming rock."

Arry did so, cautiously. Halver sat down facing her. "Now," he said. "Pain was in the world from the beginning; we do ourselves no service by trying to rid ourselves of it. We are made to suffer it."

"Not here," said Arry. "Not here."

"Even here, *you* suffer it."

"There's a purpose in that," said Arry. "I suffer it, others don't—and I know what to do about it." She began to add, "And it doesn't frighten me," but that was not true and Halver had probably been told so. She said instead, "It's my province. It's large and strange enough."

"It's as small as these hills," said Halver.

Arry thought most vividly of her long walk with Oonan: hill piled on hill, the small woods, diminutive meadow after meadow, the deep pools and the gentians. She thought of the road to Waterpale, which had taken her father and then her mother to so strange a fate; she thought of the river crossing to the Hidden Land. "It's large enough for me," she said.

Halver let his breath out, ran a hand through his hair, and smiled. He had thought of another approach. "People are entitled to their own pain," he said. "It is itself a powerful teacher."

"They've *got* their own pain," said Arry. "The pain of the heart, the mind, the soul, whatever it is that is at the borders of my province, that makes Con say 'I hate this,' they can learn from that. They'd better; it must be good for something."

"They can't learn from it if they don't regard it."

"I'll show them to regard it, then. This is a life's work in itself, Halver; I've got plenty to do."

"You cannot do it under this spell," said Halver. "The pain of the heart is among those matters the Eight felt they must deal with, that there would be no more war. You cannot do it if you don't come out."

"How do you know?" said Arry.

She felt this was a telling retort, and for a moment Halver seemed to agree with her. He looked utterly blank; then he put his head in his hands. Arry half expected him to laugh, and admit defeat. Instead he dropped his hands and stood up. "I feared this," he said. "Under this spell the intelligence cannot choose. The heart cannot choose. That is why I have made the threat. Change or die, that is the choice."

"You're offering it to everyone?" said Arry. She felt cold and full of dread, but for a moment she almost laughed. What would all of them say?

"How else?" said Halver. He sounded, and suddenly felt, extremely tired. "I'd hoped to have Frances and Bec to help me, but they don't understand."

"They're free of the spell, they've been free longer than you, and yet they don't agree with you?" said Arry. "Is there no conclusion to be drawn from that?"

"That the world is wider than you can think," said Halver.

He stood over her, looking down; he reminded her of an owl on a fencepost. Arry got up. He was going to say something final. She said, "Why is it summer here?"

"I don't know," said Halver. "I assumed Niss was meddling with the coats. It doesn't signify. Go to sleep, and you'll be home again."

"And what then?" said Arry.

"We'll have school tomorrow," said Halver, "and I will tell everyone what's to be done."

"You can't," said Arry. "You can't possibly kill any of us."

"That's Mally's province, I would have thought," said Halver. "But she might well say the same, and if she did she would be right. It makes no matter. The wolf can." He turned and walked away across the meadow.

Sleep, thought Arry, oh, indeed. On a bed of planks and dust, with a head full of terrors. Well, it must be done. It could, at least, be done on a bed of thyme instead. She curled herself into the sweet sharp smell of the bruised leaves and shut her eyes. Blackie had vanished when she sat down to talk with Halver, and she had not heard him come in, but he was licking her face, with a very rough dry tongue for a dog. Arry put her hand out to push him away, and encountered Sheepnose's sleek short fur. She opened her eyes.

Inside the house the fire, obedient to Con's commands though now somewhat short of actual fuel, burned on. Beldi was asleep on the threshold. Arry pushed the wolfskin coat to the floor and got up. Beldi had probably seen nothing but his older sister snoring under a coat. Or no, he would have seen a wolf sleeping in the hollyhocks. The way for him to come with her was, of course, for him to sleep under the coat as well. It was probably better that neither of them had thought of that—but she would have been very glad of a witness.

Then again, tomorrow after school she would have all the witnesses she could ask for. She thought it over. Halver had said he could not kill the recalcitrant, but the wolf could; which presumably meant that he must wait until the moon was full again. Even the new strange Halver would be fair enough, in any case, to give people time to consider the choice he was offering them.

How do I know that? thought Arry. I don't, of course. And Mally may not know either. Nobody knows at all. It's possible even Halver doesn't. I'm going to ask Mally just the same. It can't hurt. And I want to talk to Niss, and to Oonan.

She went inside and sat down limply on top of Sheepnose, who had crawled into the warmth of her chair and gone to sleep again. Sheepnose made an irate noise and squirmed. Arry got up again and sat on the wolfskin coat. I don't want to ask anybody anything, she thought, ever again. I want to do something, just to do it quickly. Not, I daresay, a very good reason for wishing to do anything.

She put some wood on the fire; the fire consumed it instantly and then died down properly to a bed of coals. Arry woke Beldi up just enough to walk him into his bedroom. He would be indignant with her in the morning. Then she took off the clothes she had been wearing, had a bath, put on fresh clothes in case the very act of sleeping had become irretrievably enchanted, and went to bed in her own bed with harmless linen and wool as her covering.

She dreamed of nothing at all. What woke her was, once again, Con and Beldi quarreling in the kitchen. Arry put her shoes on and dipped her head in cold water before she went to face them. It was a cool gray dripping sort of morning, and Con was not, for a mercy, making pancakes, though somebody had made a pot of tea. Both of them whipped around when they heard her footstep, and Beldi, for a wonder, got his word in first.

"Tell her I didn't!" he said.

"Didn't what?"

"Ruin my fire," said Con.

"I put wood on it so it would proceed naturally," said Arry. "Beldi was asleep. What do you want for breakfast?"

"Relish sweet," said Con. "Manna wild and honey-dew." She marched out of the kitchen.

Arry looked at Beldi. "Did anything extraordinary happen while I was gone?" she said.

"I didn't even know you *were* gone," said Beldi. "You turned into a wolf while I was looking at the stars, and then you went to sleep. You snored a little. After a while I went to sleep too. What happened?"

"Are you awake? Can you remember what I tell you? Halver's going to tell everybody about it at school today, he says, but I want you to hear and remember what he told me."

"Let's make some more tea first," said Beldi.

"I'll tell you while the water's boiling; Con'll be back soon enough." She told him everything that had happened. He frowned several times during her recitation of the argument. Arry was not sure if this came from not understanding, or from understanding all too well. The water boiled; she made tea; she made oatmeal pancakes and fried potatoes; she and Beldi ate them. Arry got up tiredly at last and went to pry Con far enough out of her sulks to enable her to eat her breakfast before school. School was a wearing business at the best of times, and today would not be the best of times.

Con was not in the house. Arry was hardly surprised.

Beldi did not seem so either. "It's probably Zia's plan," he said.

"Well," said Arry, "you go along to school; we need one representative of the family there, at any rate, and I already understand what Halver will say. I'll go to Mally's and see if I can find them. Where were they going to burn their herbs?"

"In the pine woods," said Beldi.

"Of course, where else? In the place with the most flammable floor of all. Go on to school; we'll come when we can."

Beldi went slowly off towards Halver's house, and Arry pelted in the other direction as fast as she could go. She did not know why she was anxious, but it was better to run for nothing than to be too late for something. She went on past Mally's house and up into the pine woods, where she stopped to breathe and also to listen. Children's voices drifted with the wind and the smell of burning, over the crest of the hill. Arry crashed through the woods, climbing as fast as she could, gained the top of the hill, put her foot into a spring there, and slid down the other side next to the stream it became. In the first clearing she came to she found Zia and Con and Tany and Lina.

Lina had at least seen to it that they cleared all the dry needles away and surrounded their fire with rocks. She was sitting with her back to the fire, and to Arry, rather hunched up. Arry thought she understood how Lina felt. It was odd that the field of one's knowledge so often made one feel so, when you thought of it.

"Con!" she yelled.

Con straightened from helping Zia make little piles

of dried leaves and flowers, and regarded her with no expression at all.

"What are you doing?" said Arry, arriving breathlessly at the edge of their circle of rocks.

"Playing," said Zia.

"No, you're not. You're conjuring."

They all stood and looked at her. Even Lina stood up and came to stand behind Con, though she eyed the fire unhappily. They did not plead, or make excuses, or try any more lies or explanations. They just looked.

Arry looked back at them. Lina had scratched her hands moving the rocks; Zia had a bruise on her shin and another on her elbow; Tany had a burned finger, though there was no fire lit here as yet; Con was hungry. She looked harder. This is my province, she thought; this is my field of power; I know what I see. I know what hurts. I know what is hurting each of them, now and always. She looked harder still. We flinch from pain, she thought, whether we know it's there or not. I know why Con is doing this: she thinks it will get her Bec and Frances back; and why else did I sleep under the wolf-skin coat in the hope of finding Halver?

She looked at Lina, who was older than Con, Zia, and Tany but smaller than any of them, who wished her short sleek brown hair, like an otter's, would curl and spring all over her head like Con's or Arry's. She was afraid of the lightning and the lightning bug alike; she would eat all her food cold and raw if she could; Halver said her knowledge would not grow properly if she hedged it in so, but would warp and twist on itself like an oak high up in the cold wind. Such oaks were struck by lightning, in summer storms. He said Grel said so.

She looked at Tany. He was the only one there was.

The rest of them lived in his liver, that was why it was called that. He let them out when he was bored or lonely, though they never did much for the being lonely. He believed there were others somewhere, but whenever he thought he had found one it merely melted into himself at the moment he had the highest hopes. Halver said he could learn if he would think about it, but all the things Halver wanted him to think about were curled up already, tight as new ferns, in the parts of him named for them. He had asked Oonan, when he thought Oonan was another person, for the names of all the parts. But Oonan had the names wrong, which showed he was just Tany too. Halver said Oonan was right, which showed exactly the same thing.

Arry shivered and looked at Zia. At first she thought that everything that existed hurt Zia. But that wasn't it. Everything was hugely and fiercely important to Zia. When Con told Tiln, "Everything matters to me," she had been imitating Zia again. And who wouldn't, who wouldn't warm her hands at that fire? Even Lina followed her, if at a distance. Halver said she had no sense of proportion, and that nobody without one had ever become a wizard in the entire history of the world.

Arry sat down on one of their rocks. "You'd better tell me," she said.

"Why?" said Zia.

"Because I think I can help you." Halver is hurting them, she thought. Mally says he does that to teach them. But he's hurting them just the same.

"You want to beat Halver at his own game," she said. Zia nodded.

"You think his game is being a wolf."

Zia nodded again.

"But it isn't."

They all looked at her.

"He's telling them all about it right now, in school," said Arry. "He wants to make us all either be wolves, or die."

"Why do you think so?" said Zia.

"I slept under Tiln's coat and found Halver, and he told me."

"If we sleep under the coats, then he'll tell us, and we'll think so too," said Zia. "So you have to help us get the coats."

"That will take too long," said Arry. "He said he couldn't kill us, but the wolf could; and he'll be a wolf again when the moon is full. You don't think you can all sleep under the coats by then, do you?"

Zia looked at the other children, her thought plain on her face. But she did not voice it. "How can you help us, then?" she said.

"We could kill him first," said Tany. "If he wants to kill us, that's what we should do."

Arry's stomach contracted. Nobody else seemed alarmed at all. They looked calmly at Tany, and considered it. Lina said, "Niss said we mustn't."

"She said we mustn't do it with our own magic," said Zia.

"That's because we're too small to do it any other way," said Lina.

"It's what she said just the same," said Zia.

"Jony knows about poison," said Con.

"That'll hurt him," said Arry, before she could stop herself.

They all looked at her again.

"Put him to sleep first then," said Lina. "Jony knows about that too."

"Will she tell us?" said Con.

"I'll tell you," said Tany.

They all looked at him. "Catnip and valerian and hops," he said. "Hops are best. Nightshade if you're careful. It's poison, too, but it'll hurt him. Lavender works a little. Lemon balm does, too, but it makes you cheerful first. Passionflower. Sweet woodruff. Wormwood. Yarrow."

"You *can* learn if you think about it," exclaimed Arry. "Why did you think about all this, Tany?"

"I asked Jony a long time ago," said Tany. "In case things got too noisy inside."

Arry stared at him.

"What do we do after we put him to sleep?" said Con.

"Hit him in the head," said Zia.

"Put him in the stream," said Lina.

"Chop off his head," said Tany. "Or cut his throat the way Rista does with the old sheep."

Arry folded her cold hands firmly over her quivering stomach. "Chopping off his head would hurt even if he were asleep already," she said. "So would cutting his throat."

"Hitting him might too, then," said Zia. "So we must put him in the stream."

"Can we carry him?" said Con. "Even if Arry helps?"

"Give him tea by the stream," said Lina. "Then just tip him in."

Arry swallowed hard. She found herself remembering going up to the high meadow with Oonan, the night after Halver first killed those sheep. Oonan had used a spell Niss gave him. It had gone like this: "Hence loathed Melancholy of Cerberus and blackest midnight born, In Stygian cave forlorn 'Mongst horrid shapes, and shrieks, and sights unholy, Find out some uncouth cell, Where brooding Darkness spreads his jealous wings, And the night-raven sings; There under ebon shades, and low-browed rocks, As ragged as thy locks, In dark Cimmerian desert ever dwell."

That was a curse, and it seemed it had stuck on Halver. She had not expected to be bringing it about herself, and she had most certainly not expected to be letting the little children plan its execution. She looked at them in awe and fascination. They don't know, she thought. They haven't the remotest notion. When do we begin to have one? I can't remember.

"Would that hurt him, Arry?" said Con. "If we made him sleep and then put him in the water?"

"He would have to be very thoroughly asleep," said Arry. "I should ask Oonan, I suppose, to be certain." She stopped speaking abruptly. Old habits indeed, she thought. Oonan would be horrified.

"Arry?" said Con. "Who'll teach us, after we do this?"

"I don't know," said Arry. "Maybe we could go to school in Waterpale."

This met with rather mixed enthusiasm. Then Tany said, "After we do this we won't need teaching any more."

Nobody asked him how he knew.

"When shall we do it?" said Con.

Arry drew a very deep breath and steadied her voice. "This is very serious," she said. "Breaking Halver so Oonan can't fix him, that's what it amounts to. So it mustn't be done if there's any other way. We should go to school now and see if he's threatened everybody yet. And we must give everybody time to talk to him and persuade him not to kill any of us, even if we refuse to be wolves. But if he holds to his purpose, then we must do it before the moon is full again. Tany, if you could ask Jony which of those herbs work best together, and taste best, and which she has supplies of, already dried, that would be useful. Zia and Lina, if you could take a good look at the stream and find a deep pool with a good tea-taking spot above it. Con, I think when the time comes it's you that must invite him. You're fondest of him."

She held her breath; but Con must be given the reminder. Con merely looked thoughtful.

Tany said, "And then we can get the coats and be wolves."

He wanted to be a wolf, and she was taking his choice away. Arry clenched her jaw. It was not a true choice, it was a contrivance of Halver's. If Tany became a wolf he would never come into his knowledge.

Arry supervised the dousing of the fire. Zia packed up her piles of herbs again. All five of them walked up and down and up and down the hills until they came to Halver's house. The door was open, and they could hear excited voices from the bottom of the hill. The four little ones broke into a run and disappeared into the house. Arry sat down on the ground quite suddenly.

The voices went on. Halver must have issued a general summons: she heard Mally's voice, and Niss's, and

Oonan's, and Sune's, as well as those of the children. Grel's deep booming tones and Rista's melodious ones drifted down to her as well. Everybody was out.

It had begun to drizzle again. Arry sat in the grass and let the rain gather on her hair and run down her neck. She was so cold already that it made no difference. This is a broken thing, she thought; maybe Oonan can fix it. This is not like Halver; maybe Mally can tell him. This is sorcery; maybe Niss can deal with it all. Once he has told them all, in plain terms, what he wants to do, they'll have to stop him.

This is hurtful, she thought. I have to stop him.

**23**

ARRY DID NOT go back to school. Nobody remarked on this. She did visit Mally, who steadfastly insisted that Halver, either as man or as wolf, would not kill anybody. Arry was strongly tempted to ask her if Con and Tany and Zia and Lina would kill anybody, but if Mally realized the answer was Yes she might very well begin to think things Arry did not wish her to think. The four children were, after all, still solidly in Mally's province. Mally was harried and overworked: everybody came to ask her if becoming a wolf were a part of his or her character, a happy or convenient thing to be doing. None of them, she said irritably on the second day, asked similar things about dying.

Arry visited Niss, who said she would ward everybody's houses against wolves, but could not possibly ward everything if anybody expected to have a clean harvest and healthy sheep. She visited Oonan, who frowned worriedly at her every time he set eyes on her, and fed her a variety of herb teas that did more harm than good, because they recalled to her the conversation with her young conspirators. Oonan shared her opinion of what was likely to happen when next Halver became a wolf: what he did not share was her conviction that something definite must be done. Keeping Halver at bay until the moon waned was the only action he seemed to contemplate. "There's only one of him," he said reasonably.

"Are we to be besieged forever?" demanded Arry.

Oonan laughed.

"Besides, if people do decide to become wolves, there will be more than one of him."

"Bec and Frances didn't join him."

"They were wolves first," said Arry. "Niss says perhaps it matters who makes you a wolf, as well as what your character was to begin with."

"Well, let's wait and see," said Oonan.

His appearance was at odds with his insouciant speeches. He was thin and twitchy and worried. Arry tried to ascertain if he had some private plan; he finally snapped at her that he had nothing of the sort. Arry asked Mally if this were likely, and was told it was certain.

She visited Derry, who was almost as harried as Mally, as everybody demanded information about what it was like to be a wolf and exactly how being a wolf was likely to have taken Halver. She sent them to pester Sune instead. Sune was in a high state of discomfort and impatience, and tended to hand out books with a wild impartiality rather than bothering to tell anybody anything. "If this child doesn't arrive soon I'll become a wolf just to shock her into a sense of her duties," she said.

"Is that a good idea?" said Arry cautiously.

"No, of course not," said Sune. "If you want to watch Oonan turn the color of sour milk, just mention it to him."

This sent Arry back to Oonan, not to watch him turn the color of sour milk but to demand what he thought Halver would do if Sune had not had the baby by the time her choice must be made. This was how she found out that Oonan cherished a firm belief that Bec and Frances would somehow forestall Halver's entire plan, or at least defend everybody who held out against turning into wolves from his depredations.

Arry went back to Mally and demanded who was likely to wish to become a wolf, even at the expense of knowledge. Mally was washing lettuce. The first time Arry asked her, she just shook her head. When Arry repeated the question, Mally burst into tears, saying she didn't want to know, and fled the room. Arry sat dumbly at the table where Tiln had been when all the children brought him their things to be judged beautiful or not, and stared at the kitchen door that Mally had slammed. This house is full of pain, she thought, but in the body at least, nobody is hurting at all.

Arry walked home very thoughtfully. She had not thought of refusing knowledge before, but certainly if she were Mally she might not want to know these things either. If you knew, you might feel you had to do something about it, talk people out of it, and yet if you knew them, you would know when you couldn't. Of course it would hurt.

Arry did not visit her fellow conspirators. Beldi dutifully reported to her that Zia's interest in her original plan had become perfunctory; he was persuaded she was planning something else instead, and that Con was part of the plan as well, but they told him nothing. He did say they all seemed to be intending to become wolves.

"And what about you?" said Arry.

"I can't decide if I don't know what my knowledge will be," said Beldi.

"Surely whatever it is it's better than none?"

"But if it's very small and petty and useless."

"No knowledge is useless," said Arry, very sharply.

"If," said Beldi, not looking at her, "Bec and Frances are staying away from us so we don't become wolves, then if we did become wolves just the same, would they come back?"

"If we become wolves," said Arry, "they won't have anything to come back to. Everything will fall completely apart. Oonan says so; so does Niss."

"We could go live in the Hidden Land," said Beldi.

"Everybody will be *hurt*," said Arry, very clearly.

Beldi said slowly, "But we'll know it."

"Well?"

"Halver says that's how we learn."

"I say he doesn't know learning from jumping off a cliff," said Arry furiously.

Beldi gave her a shocked look and stopped talking.

Summer came in early with a rush, and the moon grew fat and fatter in the starry sky. Two days before the full, Arry went up to the sheep hut with an armful of blankets, and slept on the bed of planks. She slept not well, but long enough to dream. She dreamed of the cruel sisters in the stories Mally and Sune had given her: the ones who cut off bits of their feet to make their stepsister's glass slipper fit and so steal the prince who

sought her; the one who drowned her sister and married her sister's betrothed, only to be betrayed by the
harp the minstrels had made of her sister's breastbone.
Nobody came to wake her, wolf or person. When school
was over the next day, she went to find Zia.

Zia told her that Lina and Con had already invited
Halver to take tea on the bank of the stream, in the late
afternoon of the following day. It had fitted neatly into
their lessons, she said, because Halver was teaching
them the history of hot drinks. Mally, who seemed to
think the entire matter was very funny, had agreed to
supply honeycake and even perhaps gingerbread; since
she had also said something about asking Halver to dinner to make up for his ordeal, Zia seemed a little put out
by the offer, though she had accepted it.

"Con does say," she added, her brow clearing, "that
the last thing Halver eats ought to be pleasant."

Arry went home feeling she could never eat anything again. After she had fed Con and Beldi she left
them struggling to invent a new game using the chess
pieces, and walked in the kindly golden evening to
Oonan's house. He was sitting on the stone wall with his
cats, cutting splints. "No, Physici," he said when he saw
her, "I have not thought of anything else we may do to
repel Halver when the moon rises tomorrow."

"I wanted to ask you," said Arry sitting down on the
other side of the cats, "what you thought of everybody's
rejoinder to all this. Because if I don't look closely, I receive the distinct impression that they are mightily en-
joying themselves."

"Oh, they are," said Oonan, not looking up from
his work. "We enjoy drinking May wine also, but the
damage it does is done all the same."

"What will the morning after be of all this?"

"Much worse than any quantity of May wine could produce," said Oonan. "We can, I think, prevent Halver's in fact killing anybody who chooses not to become a wolf; but we cannot prevent anybody's so choosing. And that is what will wreck us."

"Does Halver think we deserve to be wrecked, or that we'll be the better for it?"

"Of course he does," said Oonan, looking at her at last. "He told you so himself; he told all of us so."

"But is he right?"

"No," said Oonan. "There is a balance here, and when he upsets it the restoration will be beyond us."

"Do you know this?"

"I know it."

"But can you, if it's to do with Halver?"

"It's not to do with Halver, except as Halver is a force like a flood or a plague. It's to do with all of us."

"Is it too late already?"

"No, I think not," said Oonan, his eyes on his work again. "We can absorb a little upset, as the body can absorb a little May wine. But the dosage Halver prescribes for us, that is fatal."

"Oonan?"

"Fatal to the larger body," said Oonan. "And, of course, to anybody who refuses the dose and then is careless whom he drinks with."

"You're being much too metaphorical," said Arry, crossly.

Oonan shrugged. "It soothes anxiety," he said.

"If you're so anxious why don't you think what else to do?"

"You're much more anxious than I am," said

Oonan, "and it doesn't seem to be helping you to think."

"Mustn't there be something wrong with us and our workings if we can't think what to do about impending harm?"

"Mustn't there be something wrong with the oak, if it but stands on the mountain and lets lightning strike it?" said Oonan. "Or to be more precise, mustn't there be something wrong with the birds who nest there, that they cannot alter the oak to be impervious?"

"Oh, never mind," said Arry, and slid off the wall and stamped off home.

She sat in the chair with red cushions, stroking Woollycat with one hand and the pile of books she had been lent with the other. It was interesting that Oonan too sometimes thought of Halver's bargain as a dreadful storm. We can't weather it, thought Arry, we can't outrun it; we must turn it back. Patrick Spens lacked a good wizard. She put Con and Beldi to bed and sat back down in the chair. This is the last night, she thought. No matter what happens, there will be change.

"Are you ever coming to school again?" said Con the next morning.

"No," said Arry.

"Shall I tell Halver?"

"I'll tell him," said Arry, "when he comes to tea."

The afternoon was sunny, kind, and tender. Summer was its most perfect green. The wild roses were blooming early. Arry went down a little early to the stream, and found Zia already there. She had brought one of Mally's finest linen cloths, but Mally or someone had prevailed on her to bring wooden cups and platters. She had laid a fire but not yet lit it. Arry gave her the oatcake and cheese she had brought, so the children, who would be far too excited to eat any dinner, would have something vaguely resembling nutrition.

Zia was sparkling and glittering with excitement. She began talking the moment she saw Arry and did not stop until Con and Tany arrived. Tany bore the food Mally had promised; Con had a large jug almost too large for her to carry.

"What's that?" said Arry.

"It's the blushful Hippocrene," panted Con, thumping it down in a patch of chickweed. "Jony says it makes all the sleepy herbs work better, and Mally says it's entirely proper to serve at afternoon tea."

"How nice for Halver," said Arry, a little hollowly.

They all looked at her. "Will it hurt him?" said Zia.

"No," said Arry.

"Lina's bringing him," said Tany. "It's her turn to help clear up, so she's bringing him."

After this there seemed nothing else to say. Tany lay on his back in the grass and stared up into the new leaves of the oak trees. Con and Zia amused themselves by throwing stones into the stream. Zia had found a good place. The bank was flat and grassy and sloped a little towards the water; the pool beneath it was wide and deep. The stream made small chuckling and splashing noises going through the narrow spot before the pool, but it was not so loud as to impede conversation.

What in the world are we going to talk about, thought Arry, while the blushful Hippocrene and the valerian work themselves on Halver? I can't do this. It's treachery, the most hurtful thing there is. Well, so is what Halver wants to do treachery. It's worse than treachery. He's using force. Is that worse than guile?

"Here he comes," said Zia.

Arry looked around. Lina was leading Halver by the hand through the stand of oaks. He looked perfectly serene. Lina brought him over and sat him on a flat stone. He thanked her, and then looked at the rest of them. "This is very good of you," he said.

"Mally says it's good of you," said Zia, "to have tea with children after spending all day with children."

"The obligations are different," said Halver. "In school, I'm obliged to teach; but now, you are obliged to entertain me. Which you seem to be doing very well. What's this?" And he took from Con a wooden cup brimming with red bubbly Hippocrene.

"It's the blushful Hippocrene," said Con.

"Ah," said Halver. "A beaker full of the warm South. Where did you get this, Con?"

"I made it," said Con.

"Truly?" said Halver. "We'll hope you can help Rine with the beer when you come into more knowledge, then." He sniffed his cup, and looked thoughtful. "Have you drunk any of this?" he asked Con.

"No," said Con. "I made pancakes of it."

"You had perhaps better not drink much of it."

"Beldi says it tastes bad," said Con, accepting a cup from Zia and regarding it suspiciously.

"To the fresh palate, it probably does," said Halver. "Mix it with water, Zia; that will give us enough for a toast."

Zia had a jug of water already, for making the tea; she did as Halver told her, and handed out the cups. Arry got the cupful Zia had originally given to Con, being, she supposed, old enough to no longer have a

fresh palate. Halver held his cup up in a shaft of sunlight. "To transformation," he said, and drank.

They all drank, including Arry. I'll show you transformation, she thought. Halver looked at her over the
rim of his cup, exactly as if she had spoken. "What have
you all decided?" he said.

Arry opened her mouth, but she was forestalled by
Zia. "Mally says," said Zia, "that asking personal questions at tea is very rude."

Arry shut her mouth in time to turn her laugh into a
snort, probably as rude in its way as a personal question.

"Mally has the right of it," said Halver, agreeably.
"But it's rude to correct your guests, as well. You must
make it up to me with more Hippocrene."

Zia poured him another cup full. Halver drank it
fairly rapidly. Arry sipped her own and wondered about
him. Either he was in fact finding the continued pres-
ence of small children wearing, or he was in some anxiety about what might happen when the moon rose.

"What isn't rude to talk about at tea?" said Con.

"Why tea?" said Arry, suffering and giving in to an
impulse of mischief. "Why is tea more polite than supper?"

"Because it's superfluous," said Zia, coming out
with the entire word in one triumphant breath. "Mally
says so."

"But surely," said Arry, "the necessary ought to be
more palatable than the optional?"

The children looked at her resignedly, but Halver
said, "Palatable is one thing, decorated another. We
decorate tea with amiable nothings."

Arry grinned into her Hippocrene.

"What *is* the blushful Hippocrene?" asked Lina, prompting Halver to quote the entire spell. While he was doing so, Con and Zia made the fire and boiled the water and made the tea, and Arry observed Halver. He was certainly rather flushed and cheerful. She hoped Jony was right about the combined effect of sleepy tea and wine.

Tany then asked how one could have a beaker full of the south, or any other direction, and in the very confused conversation that followed, the tea got brewed very strong indeed. Zia finally tore her attention away from Tany's adamant refusal to admit the value of metaphor, and poured out a greeny-yellow decoction that looked more like a medicine than a drink. Arry supposed it was. She gestured at Zia and then at the honey pot, and Zia shot a huge spoonful of honey into the cup she meant for Halver.

When Arry got her own tea, she decided that it was just as well. The tea was very bitter. She almost asked for honey herself, and then realized that the rest of them had better not drink much tea. They were all smaller than Halver and would be snoring well before him. Which would be not only disastrous to the plan, but very rude. Arry found herself chortling, and stopped hastily. Halver gave her a knowing look, and drank his tea. Arry saw that the Hippocrene had made him thirsty. This might work after all.

It did work, with an almost terrifying rapidity. Halver ate some honeycake, declined cheese and oatcake, drank another cup of tea, leaned back against his rock saying something about which bird was singing in the oak tree, and was suddenly asleep.

Lina grinned. "I put valerian in the honeycake, too," she said. "And I got a spell from Niss to say over it."

Zia began clearing cups and cakes off the cloth, which she then folded tidily. Arry sat and watched as she made an easy path for rolling Halver into the water. She watched as the four of them pulled him down off the rock and tried to roll him so he was, as he had taught them the concept, parallel to the stream. The loose gray robe he wore caught on the rough rock. He was too heavy for them. They stopped and looked at her.

"We can't do this," said Arry. "Truly, we can't."

They went on looking at her.

"You could teach us when he's gone, I think," said Lina. "We listen to you. Even Tany listens to you."

"You sound like me," said Tany. He flashed her a delighted and charming grin.

Oh, wonderful, thought Arry. "I'm glad you do," she said, "because I'm going to have to disappoint you. It was the talk of courtesy that made me realize. You can't murder your guest, you really can't. He trusted us; we can't kill him."

"Does this mean we lose the game?" said Zia.

"No, it's just a different game than we thought."

They went on looking at her, three pairs of brown eyes and one of blue, sweet little faces, a trifle flushed with their watered wine and smeared a bit here and there with honey or crumbs.

"Oh, well," said Zia suddenly, "now we know it works. This was—what does Vand call it—a dry run. We can always do it later."

"But if it's rude?" said Lina.

"*We* could be *his* guests," said Zia. "We'll think of something."

"But what do we do now?" said Lina, looking at Halver.

"You go home with your cloth and dishes," said Arry. "I'll stay with him until he wakes up."

"I'm staying too," said Con.

"All right, but go find Beldi first and let him know where we are." She looked again at Mally's children. "Thank you," she said, "for having such lovely manners."

They packed up their tea things and went off chattering. Con said, "But is he still going to hurt us, Arry?"

"Yes," said Arry, "but we needn't hurt ourselves even more."

Con went off silently to find Beldi. Arry sat looking at the ashes of the fire. Was that stupid? she thought. For he is dangerous, and something must be done, because he's hurting us all, he's hurting whatever we are together, he's ruining something bigger than all of us, whereby we live. But it would have hurt those children to let them roll his helpless body into the water.

She looked at Halver's helpless body. Nobody had been much concerned with how long their concoctions would make him sleep.

He slept for a long time. The sun went down. Con came back with Beldi and a basket of food, for which Arry was very grateful. The blushful Hippocrene had made her hungry. Con and Beldi sat down and stared at Halver while she ate everything they had brought.

"Is he ever going to wake up?" said Con.

"He's going to wake up a wolf if he sleeps very much longer," said Beldi, practically.

"Isn't a man easier to kill than a wolf?" said Con.

"Much," said Arry. She sat up straight. "Unless—"

"What?"

"Never you mind. You and Beldi had better go home, I think."

"You said you wouldn't leave us," said Beldi.

"Halver isn't going to eat me."

"How do you know?"

"Because Niss gave me a spell."

"To kill wolves?"

"To keep them off, at least." But that, of course, was not enough.

"So we'll be safe with you," said Beldi, and sat down with great firmness.

"Con," said Arry.

"Oh, no," said Con, sitting next to Beldi. "If Beldi stays I get to stay too."

"Well," said Arry grimly, "I hope the spell's a good one."

Con and Beldi had both fallen asleep by the time the moon rose. Arry got up and stood between them and Halver. This put her closer to Halver than she might have liked, but there was nothing to be done about it. The sky over the far hills grew silver, and pale yellow, lighter and lighter. Arry stared steadfastly at Halver, who had turned on his side and was snoring lightly. The ground moved sideways, also lightly, but Arry blinked, and when she looked again the wolf was lifting its head from its paws and looking at her with eyes as yellow as the moon. The loose gray robe lay puddled around it.

Silently, and with her own voice, it said, "Did you misjudge your dosage?"

"No," said Arry, softly, so as not to awaken her brother and sister. She held Niss's spell in her head like a page not yet turned to in a book.

"What do you want, then?" he said to her, as if she were talking to herself.

"I want you to go and never come back," said Arry fiercely, which was entirely true, if useless.

"No," said Halver. "I have a job to do also; this is my province."

"You're hurting us!" she said, in her levelest and most knowledgeable voice.

"For your good," he replied, with a terrifying sincerity.

"All right, then," said Arry; her voice came out loud but wavery. She steadied it and took a good breath.

"Mastiff, greyhound, mongrel grim, hound or spaniel, brach or lym, or bobtail tyke or trundle-tail, I will make you weep and wail, for, with throwing this my head, dogs leaped the hatch, and all are fled."

Halver jumped up. Tail between his legs, he went cringing to the very edge of the bank where they had meant to roll him into the water. Then he turned and faced her, ears down, the picture of canine abjection.

"She's mad," he said to Arry in her own voice, "that trusts the tameness of a wolf. You have frightened all the dogs about this night into the darkest corners they may find. You have kept me off you, too. But from those you would protect, *you have not kept me.*"

Arry picked up one of the rocks the children had put in a circle to hedge the fire with. As she lifted it, her mind presented her with a precise picture of what Halver would look and feel like if she hit him in the head with it.

"You know you can't," her voice told her.

She flung the rock. It bruised Halver's shoulder and fell splashing into the water. Arry moved forward, holding her own shoulder. One of them was not leaving here; probably, she thought, herself.

"Fear no more the heat o' the sun," said somebody behind her.

"Beldi, go home," she said.

"Nor the furious winter's rages," said Beldi. "Thou thy worldly task hath done, home art gone, and ta'en thy wages."

"I am not gone," said Halver, or Arry.

"Fear no more the frown o' the great," said Con. She did not sound as if anybody had just awakened her. "Thou art past the tyrant's stroke. Care no more to clothe and eat; to thee the reed is as the oak."

Beldi said, "Fear no more the lightning-flash, nor the all-dreaded thunder-stone, fear not slander, censure rash; thou hast finished joy and moan."

"No," said Arry, or Halver.

"No exorciser harm thee!" said Con and Beldi together, as precisely as if they were singing. "Nor no witchcraft charm thee! Ghost unlaid forbear thee! Nothing ill come near thee! Quiet consummation have, *and renowned be thy grave.*"

There was a moment of piercing silence.

Arry felt as if her bones were falling to powder, her blood evaporating, all of her raining down into the earth. The wolf that was Halver slipped backwards off the bank of the stream, and fell with a shockingly loud splash into the water where they had meant to put him.

"Killed with kindness," Arry said softly, and she sat down hard. Con ran over and hugged her around the neck, which was not at all like Con. Beldi walked, not very steadily or eagerly, to the bank of the stream, and knelt, and looked down.

"It's Halver down there," he said. "Not the wolf."

"Is he dead?" called Con.

"He's gone," said Arry, aloud, in a shaking and sandy voice that was nonetheless hers and only hers. "He's altogether away. I'm surprised there's a body in the water."

"But it didn't hurt you, did it?" said Con.

"Or him either?" said Beldi.

"No," said Arry. "No." Her eyes stung and filled and ran over. "I wouldn't say it hurt him. Or me. Only you."

"But we don't know," said Beldi.

Arry looked at the slight tousled outline of him against the moonlit sky; she started to say, "But I do," and stopped.

Nothing was there. She knew nothing. What Halver had wished to do to all of them, he had done to her. Or had she done it? She had meant to kill him; that Niss's spell was not strong enough did not, perhaps, change that. She had thrown her head at him, whatever had been in it. He had left his robe on the bank, after all his care with clothing what the wolf left naked. He would never see the summer night they had talked in, up in the high meadow.

Arry swallowed hard. He would never bring the cruel mothers, she thought, the cruel sisters, the brothers whose swords dripped with blood, the drowned maiden from whose breastbone the minstrels must make a harp.

Beldi walked back to where she sat with Con, and knelt down in front of them. "We thought," he said, in a voice almost as shaky as hers had been, "that if you could have plans, and Zia could have plans, and you and I could have plans, that Con and I could have a plan too."

His voice pleaded with her. "It was well done," said Arry. "It was very well done." Her voice cracked. "But we can't stay here. Do you feel differently, either of you?"

"I used up all my magic," said Con. "I thought I might."

"Beldi?"

"No," said Beldi, a little wistfully.

"We're outside now, I think."

"I think I always was," said Beldi.

"We have to go tonight."

"What about the cats?" said Con.

"Oonan will take them. We'll have to tell Oonan, I think; he'll need to know, whatever we did it's his to mend."

"Where are we going?" said Con.

"Home," said Arry. "Home to the Hidden Land."

They went back to their house first, and packed what they could carry. Neither Con nor Beldi gave her any trouble about anything she refused to let them take, which was alarming. And she kept looking around wildly, as if they had disappeared. They were always in the house, sometimes in the room, sometimes just beside her, but she did not know, if you could even then call it knowing, until she had them under her eye. They seemed like pictures of themselves, moving dolls made to look like her brother and sister.

While the two of them were down cellar making sure that nothing vital to their future lives had somehow lodged there, Arry found baskets for the cats and put the cats into them, which was easy with Woollycat, who promptly went to sleep, and almost impossible with Sheepnose. At least the cats were the same.

She tidied the house: somebody else would come to live here, maybe Jony, who probably felt crowded with her own family and was old enough to be by herself. The house, like the cats, seemed the same as ever, except that it felt empty even with Con and Beldi making strange hollow thumpings underneath it.

They had piled everything in the front room and were beginning to think who could carry how much when Arry realized that Oonan's house was not in the direction they were going. It would be easier to take him the cats, come back for their baggage, and then set off for the ford at Waterpale.

She explained this to Con and Beldi, who only looked at her blankly. She picked up the baskets of cats and herded the children out the front door. They went as they always had, down the hill their house sat on, and along the dry rocky path between their hill and Niss's; and then around the side of Niss's hill and up and down and up and down again and up once more to Oonan's door.

It was open. His cats were sitting on the wall. Sheepnose made a brief welcoming noise and popped her head over the edge of the basket. Arry put a hand on her neck, hustled everybody into Oonan's front room without knocking, and shut the door. Sheepnose climbed out of the basket and began to prowl the room, grumbling under her breath. Con and Beldi stood in the middle of the floor.

Arry drew in her breath to call Oonan, and he walked in from the kitchen, wiping his hands on one of the yellow towels Bec had brought back the year Con was born. He smiled around at them, and said, "Who's been hitting whom now?" He was looking at Arry, and although she had said nothing, he dropped the towel and his face flattened out like that of a shaped cookie after you bake it.

"What happened?" he said. He shut his eyes. "You've chosen."

Arry had been thinking of how to tell him carefully, but this was too much. "We killed Halver," she said.

"But you're just like him," said Oonan; he had not opened his eyes. He closed his hand over them until his finger and thumb met at the bridge of his nose. Arry thought he must have a headache, but she did not know it.

For a moment, when he first came in, he had looked like himself, but now he too seemed flat as a figure in a tapestry, moving only because air had rippled the cloth. He opened his eyes suddenly. "You killed him?"

"We all did," said Con.

Oonan sat down in one of the red chairs. He looked at Con. He looked at Beldi. He looked at Arry, and she could hardly keep from flinching: she felt like a window the sun was shining through, showing up every finger- and nose-print, every mote of dust and every spatter left behind by the rain.

"Not just like Halver," said Oonan; he himself

sounded very like Halver correcting somebody's arithmetic.

"Thank you a thousand times," said Arry, in a tone she recognized as one her mother had used.

"Tell me what happened," said Oonan. "And sit down, do." He got up himself, looking jittery. "Do you want some tea?"

"I do," said Con, sitting down on the floor.

Oonan picked up his towel and went back into the kitchen.

Arry sat in the other red chair; she felt curiously comforted. She supposed it was the tea. Oonan wouldn't give them tea if he had already judged them broken. Then she thought of the party she had just been at with Halver, and was uncomforted again at once. She looked at her brother and sister. Con was yawning and rubbing her eyes, which was hardly surprising. Beldi had a very somber face.

"Beldi," said Arry, "have you got a headache?"

He stared at her. "Don't you—" he said, and shut his mouth.

"Have you?"

"A bit of one."

"I thought so."

"But you didn't know?"

"Not since Halver." She thought about it. "Is that when you started knowing?"

"I think so," said Beldi, dubiously.

"Will I know when I hurt now, too?" said Con.

"Probably," said Arry.

"Can I try it?"

"*No,*" said Arry. Con scowled at her, and Arry added,

"It'll happen soon enough, Con, and you won't like it a bit."

Oonan came back in with a whole willow tray, with a blue cloth on it, and the big black teapot, and four black mugs, and his blue honey pot and a little green milk jug that Sune had made when she was ten, and a plate of cold griddle cakes. He put the tray down on the footstool. He looked more somber than Con. He sat on the edge of the other red chair, rubbing his forehead, and said nothing while they waited for the tea to steep. Arry kept an eye on Con, who was looking at the hot pot as if she might try burning her fingers on it.

When Oonan poured the tea, it was not the pale green or yellow of herbal tea, but the rich red-brown of black tea from the Outer Isles. Sune and Jony said the leaves came from bushes that grew high in the mountains. Wim said it cost a great deal. Oonan was very stingy with his, as a rule, Mally said.

Oonan handed the cups around, having put milk and honey into Con's and Arry's first. Then he said, "Tell me what happened."

"Well," said Arry, "Zia had a plan."

Oonan rolled his eyes and made a small groan. She told him the story, with frequent additions from Con and a little actual help from Beldi. Oonan looked at her with great intentness the whole time, even when Con was speaking. When they finished, he went on looking.

"I couldn't let them do it," said Arry. "But it had to be done."

"Bec and Frances didn't come to help you?"

"No."

"Frances always liked you to do things for yourself," said Oonan. "Even when you could hardly walk without staggering, she would say, 'Don't help her, let her find out how to do it.' "

"What did I find out how to do, Oonan?"

"You *saved* us," said Con, in astonished tones. She added, "We helped a lot, though."

"Did I save us, Oonan, or did I break us?"

"Sometimes," said Oonan, "one can't know the difference."

"Oonan."

"I'm still finding out. All things are deeply altered."

"Did we keep out the cruel mothers?"

Oonan looked puzzled and irritated; then his brow cleared. "Ah. The ones with poisoned apples; the ones who drive their sons to kill their other sons; all the cruel ones. I think so. I told you, I am still finding out what has happened. I think knowledge is altered."

"So now you can throw a child away like a batch of bad yoghurt?"

"No, not so much as that. It's not the certain knowledge, the right knowledge, that did us harm, if harm was being done to us. It was refusing to step outside it."

"We should leave soon."

"Yes, long before dawn. And I should go take Halver from the stream; it would frighten Sune to find him there. Where are you going, Arry?"

"To the Hidden Land."

Oonan frowned. "That will do you harm," he said. "Go to Heathwill Library, where they understand breaking the bounds of knowledge."

"We have to go through the Hidden Land to get there. Can we look at it a bit?"

"Travel along the borders," said Oonan. "I think you may meet someone there, or some two."

"The cruel mother I kept out?" said Arry bitterly.

"If you are looking for a cruel mother," said Oonan, "look in the stream there below Sune's house. Don't look at Frances. I think she may well have done what Halver said he always did."

Arry was too tired to think. "Will you take the cats?" she said.

"No," said Oonan. "They need to go with you."

"Oonan, who will teach the children?"

"I will, no doubt," said Oonan. "Mally thinks Elec may be a teacher. In two years, or three, she'll know. I can't do much harm in that time."

"You'll have to be Physici, too."

"As best I may."

"Will you miss Halver?"

"Don't pick at the scab," said Oonan.

They crossed the river at the Waterpale ferry just at dawn. The ferrywoman was sleepy but amiable. Arry gave her one of Frances's coins, which she took as if there were nothing unusual about it.

"You'll want to be careful," she said as they got out of her boat, hoisting the sacks and pouches and the basket with the sleeping Woollycat in it; Sheepnose jumped out by herself. "You'll want to have an eye of those cats. There are wolves about."

"Yes, we know," said Arry.

# MORE CONTEMPORARY
# FANTASY FROM TOR

| | | | | |
|---|---|---|---|---|
| ☐ | 53353-4 | SEVENTH SON<br>*Orson Scott Card* | Canada | $3.95<br>$4.95 |
| ☐ | 53359-3 | RED PROPHET<br>*Orson Scott Card* | Canada | $3.95<br>$4.95 |
| ☐ | 50212-4 | PRENTICE ALVIN<br>*Orson Scott Card* | Canada | $4.95<br>$5.95 |
| ☐ | 51620-6 | SPIRITWALK<br>*Charles de Lint* | Canada | $4.99<br>$5.99 |
| ☐ | 50912-9 | SADAR'S KEEP<br>*Midori Snyder* | Canada | $3.95<br>$4.95 |
| ☐ | 50913-7 | BELDAN'S FIRE<br>*Midori Snyder* | Canada | $3.99<br>$4.99 |
| ☐ | 54550-1 | TAM LIN<br>*Pamela Dean* | Canada | $4.99<br>$5.99 |
| ☐ | 53079-9 | A MIDSUMMER TEMPEST<br>*Poul Anderson* | Canada | $2.95<br>$3.95 |
| ☐ | 55815-4 | SOLDIER OF THE MIST<br>*Gene Wolfe* | Canada | $3.95<br>$4.95 |
| ☐ | 50625-1 | SOLDIER OF ARETE<br>*Gene Wolfe* | Canada | $3.95<br>$4.95 |
| ☐ | 55825-1 | SNOW WHITE AND ROSE RED<br>*Patricia Wrede* | Canada | $3.95<br>$4.95 |

Buy them at your local bookstore or use this handy coupon:
Clip and mail this page with your order.

Publishers Book and Audio Mailing Service
P.O. Box 120159, Staten Island, NY 10312-0004

Please send me the book(s) I have checked above. I am enclosing $ _____
(please add $1.25 for the first book, and $.25 for each additional book to cover
postage and handling. Send check or money order only—no CODs).

Names _____
Address _____
City _____ State/Zip _____
Please allow six weeks for delivery. Prices subject to change without notice.

# MORE BESTSELLING
# FANTASY FROM TOR

| | | | |
|---|---|---|---|
| ☐ | 50392-9 | DRAGON SEASON<br>*Michael Cassutt* | $4.99<br>Canada $5.99 |
| ☐ | 51716-4 | THE FOREVER KING<br>*Warren Murphy and Ellen Kushner* | $5.99<br>Canada $6.99 |
| ☐ | 50360-0 | GRYPHON'S EYRIE<br>*Andre Norton & A.C. Crispin* | $3.95<br>Canada $4.95 |
| ☐ | 52248-6 | THE LITTLE COUNTRY<br>*Charles de Lint* | $5.99<br>Canada $6.99 |
| ☐ | 50518-2 | THE MAGIC OF RECLUCE<br>*L.E. Modesitt, Jr.* | $4.99<br>Canada $5.99 |
| ☐ | 50249-3 | SISTER LIGHT, SISTER DARK<br>*Jane Yolen* | $3.95<br>Canada $4.95 |
| ☐ | 55815-4 | SOLDIER OF THE MIST<br>*Gene Wolfe* | $3.95<br>Canada $4.95 |
| ☐ | 51112-3 | STREET MAGIC<br>*Michael Reaves* | $3.99<br>Canada $4.99 |
| ☐ | 51445-9 | THOMAS THE RHYMER<br>*Ellen Kushner* | $3.99<br>Canada $4.99 |

Buy them at your local bookstore or use this handy coupon:
Clip and mail this page with your order.

Publishers Book and Audio Mailing Service
P.O. Box 120159, Staten Island, NY 10312-0004

Please send me the book(s) I have checked above. I am enclosing $ _____
(Please add $1.25 for the first book, and $.25 for each additional book to cover postage and handling.
Send check or money order only—no CODs.)

Name _____

Address _____

City _____ State/Zip _____

Please allow six weeks for delivery.  Prices subject to change without notice.